A HEARTH
in
CANDLEWOOD

A HEARTH
in
CANDLEWOOD

A NOVEL

Delia Parr

BETHANY HOUSE PUBLISHERS
Minneapolis, Minnesota

A Hearth in Candlewood
Copyright © 2006
Delia Parr

Cover illustration by Rick Johnson/Hankins & Tegenborg
Cover design by Paul Higdon

Unless otherwise identified, Scripture quotations are from the King James Version of the Bible.

Published by Bethany House Publishers
11400 Hampshire Avenue South
Bloomington, Minnesota 55438

Bethany House Publishers is a division of
Baker Publishing Group, Grand Rapids, Michigan.

Printed in the United States of America

Paperback: ISBN-13: 978-0-7642-0086-1   ISBN-10: 0-7642-0086-0
Large Print: ISBN-13: 978-0-7642-0257-5   ISBN-10: 0-7642-0257-X

Library of Congress Cataloging-in-Publication Data

Parr, Delia.
    A hearth in candlewood / Delia Parr.
        p.   cm. — (Candlewood trilogy ; 1)
    ISBN 0-7642-0086-0 (pbk.) — ISBN 0-7642-0257-X (large-print pbk.)
    1. Boardinghouses—New York (State)—Fiction. I. Title. II. Series: Parr, Delia. Candlewood trilogy ; 1.
    PS3566.A7527H43   2006
    813'.54—dc22   2006013797

Dedicated in loving memory of

Aunt Dot
(Dorothy Schiemer Giberson)

For all the love, for all the laughter,
for all the lessons, and for all the blessings
she brought to us all.

1

THE LAST THING WIDOW EMMA GARRETT needed was another guest at Hill House.

Not at ten o'clock at night. Not with guests already occupying every one of the seven bedrooms upstairs, as well as the two front parlors on the first floor.

The dim light of the oil lamp near the front door illuminated the center hall. The carpet runner muffled her steps as she hurried past the parlors on either side of the hallway, where closed pocket doors provided the sleeping guests with privacy. Exhausted to the bone and yearning for the comfort of her own bed, she took a few final steps to get to the door, pulled back the lace curtain on one of the glass panels on either side of it, and peered outside. She had not bothered to light the lantern in the overthrow above the gateway, so the world beyond Hill House remained cloaked by darkness. The relentless downpour—which had canceled the fireworks display and sent hundreds of visitors in Candlewood for the week-long Founders' Day celebrations scurrying back to their lodgings—continued to pelt the roof on the wraparound porch. Judging by the sound of the wind and the rain lashing at the house, it would probably be morning before the storm finally abated.

No one, however, was standing on the porch seeking shelter for the night.

Emma smiled and locked the door. She must have been mistaken; no one had been knocking on the door after all. She let the curtain drop back into place, turned around, and paused in front of the massive black oak hat rack where the oil lamp rested on a small center shelf below a mirror. Bending down, she checked the linens that had been placed on the floor to catch water dripping from the hats and bonnets hanging from pegs. The linens were barely damp. The umbrellas, by contrast, were bone dry, since no one had thought to take an umbrella to the fireworks display. Pleased, she straightened up again and hoped that by morning the hats and bonnets might be dry, too.

Anxious for bed, she doused the oil lamp and continued taking one last turn about the boardinghouse to make sure it was secure. She was just as ready to put Founders' Day behind her, since none of her children or grandchildren had been able to come home to see her or to participate in the ceremonies marking the fiftieth anniversary of the town her grandparents had helped to found.

She paused at the entrance to the dining room, which had been hastily converted for the night into a drying room, and wrinkled her nose. The musty odor was nearly as distressing as the sight of the wet garments hanging on the clotheslines crisscrossing the room. There was nothing to be done about the smell until the rain stopped and the windows could be opened again, and she could only hope the clothing would be close to dry by morning.

Sighing, she carefully made her way to the sideboard. Once she doused the oil lamp sitting on top, she continued through the room to the kitchen. Mercy Garrett, her mother-in-law, claimed that room at Hill House as her domain, just as she had done since coming to live with Emma many years ago when she had owned and operated the General Store.

As usual, all was in order. The new cookstove was clean again after Mother Garrett had made the guests some goodies to warm them, although the subtle aroma of coffee and cocoa yet lingered. The fire they had lit in the fireplace to chase away the dampness was almost out. The dishes had all been washed and put away, and the pitchers were lined up and ready for hot water so guests could wash up in the morning.

Almost as importantly, the snack Mother Garrett had made for Emma, buttered bread and a pot of tea, was sitting on the kitchen table waiting for her. She sat down, took a bite of bread, and savored the sweet taste of butter coating the dense, chewy bread. Instinctively, she reached into her apron pocket to finger her keepsakes and let the memories they inspired fill the aching void in her heart.

To anyone else, the tiny scraps of cloth she had sewn together at one corner would be just that—scraps of cloth. But to Emma, they were her keepsakes, each piece of cloth a tangible link to each of her three sons and seven grandchildren, as well as mementos of her married life, of her late husband, Jonas.

A piece of heavy, stiff denim. A square of smooth chintz. A bit of cozy, soft flannel. She knew them by touch, each one of her keepsakes marking a special event in her life or the lives of her loved ones. She found one of the keepsakes that belonged to Jonas, a swatch of heavy canvas from one of his work aprons, and held it tight. Her deep, wrenching grief at losing him had softened in the eight years since his passing to become tender memories of the sweet and gentle man who had been her helpmate and companion. With all her sons now married and living far away, that deep sense of loneliness—so vivid in the early years of her widowhood—had returned to haunt her. Despite the endless work at Hill House, when the day was spent and the household quiet, she missed the companionship and comfort of a loving spouse.

A sharp rap at the outside kitchen door startled her, however, and set her heart racing.

Another rap sent her scrambling to her feet.

There was no mistake this time. Someone was definitely knocking at her door, but except for deliveries, no one ever came to the back kitchen door. Arriving guests usually used the side door to her office or, occasionally, the front door.

But never the kitchen door.

More curious than afraid, she was on her way to the door when the caller rapped again. "Just a moment," she cried and quickly unlocked the door. Before she unlatched it, however, she glanced around and grabbed a rolling pin. There was a time when she would have answered the door in the middle of the night without a second thought, but that was long before the Candlewood Canal had brought so many strangers to the area.

She held the rolling pin firmly with one hand and tucked it within the folds of her skirt. With her other hand, she opened the door. Shivering against the damp night air, she took one look at the tiny slip of a woman standing ramrod straight on the threshold beneath a small overhang and blinked hard. The woman's cape was plastered against what little flesh she carried on her bones, and the brim of her soggy bonnet sagged low and nearly obscured her face. Water dripped in a steady stream from the small travel bag she gripped with both hands.

Although Emma had not seen this woman for a good number of years, she thought she recognized her. "W-widow Leonard?" she managed, completely flustered and unable to fathom why this eighty-something widow, a lifelong resident who lived some miles from town, would be at her door at this hour in such a state.

"Yes, it's me. I need your help, Emma dear. May I come in?"

"Come in? Of course. Please excuse me. Come in, come in," Emma urged and quickly stepped out of the way to give the woman entry into the kitchen. Once she had stepped inside, Emma secured the door again and slipped the rolling pin onto a nearby table.

"I hope I'm not disturbing you overly much. I tried knocking at the front door, but no one answered, even though the light was still on in the hallway. I was going to sit on the porch until morning, but then I decided to walk around and see if anyone was in the kitchen. If not, I was going to wait under the overhang instead of walking all the way back to the front porch in this rain. I can't tell you how relieved I am that you're still up," the elderly woman said as she stood with her back to the door.

Emma furrowed her brow. "I'm so sorry. I thought I heard someone knocking at the front door, but there wasn't anyone there by the time I got there. Heavens, you're soaked!"

"I got pretty wet just getting here. Are you sure I'm not troubling you?"

"Not at all," Emma insisted. "I was just hoping to have a bit of a snack before bed. Is there something wrong? How can I help you?"

"I . . . I know how crowded you must be, but I need a place to—"

"I'll make room," she quickly reassured her, struck by the memory of several years ago when not one woman but two had sought shelter here on a rainy night just like this one. Although she had yet to open Hill House at the time, she had offered them both a place to stay. Tonight, even though the only bed she had to offer was her own, Emma would take this woman in, as well.

"Please don't worry. I have a place for you for the night."

"Actually, I don't need a room just for the night," Widow Leonard countered, squaring her narrow shoulders. "I need a place to live, Emma. I've run away from home."

2

YOU'VE RUN AWAY FROM HOME?" Emma repeated.

"I'm sorry to say I have," the woman admitted and straightened her back to stretch to her full height of five feet.

Emma clapped her hand to her heart and fought back a smile of surprise and disbelief. Elderly women like Widow Leonard simply did not run away from home. Occasionally a child might run away; her oldest son, Warren, had run away from home once, although he had not gotten farther than a mile or so before the night sounds sent him scampering back. She had even seen an advertisement or two in a newspaper for runaway wives.

But not an elderly woman.

Especially not this elderly woman.

By all accounts, Frances Leonard had two devoted sons and daughters-in-law who took turns providing a home for her on their adjoining farms some seven or eight miles from Candlewood. Her sons also shared ownership of a strip of land containing a section of the toll road that had fallen into disrepair now that farmers in outlying areas relied on the canal's freight barges instead of wagons to carry their produce to market.

Emma could not recall a single bit of gossip associated with any of them. In all truth, they did not frequent town on a regular basis. In recent years, given her advanced age, Widow Leonard never came with them the few times they had come to town for supplies. As a result, Emma did not know any of the Leonard family all that well, although she had done business with them at the General Store over the years.

The look of pure determination in Widow Leonard's gaze, along with her bedraggled appearance, however, reinforced her words, prompting Emma to take the woman very seriously indeed. Later, she could deal with the matters that had sent the woman away from home and out into this storm, if indeed the woman felt inclined to explain them to Emma. Right now she needed to get her guest dry and warm.

"First things first," she insisted. She helped remove the woman's sodden cloak and draped the cold, heavy garment across the back of a chair at the kitchen table. Surprisingly, the woman's dove gray gown was nearly dry, save for the hem. Emma didn't bother taking the limp bonnet up to the hat rack in the front hall; instead, she hung it as best she could on the back of another chair.

Widow Leonard smiled as she lifted one foot out from beneath the muddy hem of her skirts. "I feel much better already, but I'd sorely love to get out of these shoes, too."

After setting the travel bag on the floor close to the door, Emma carried a kitchen chair over to the fireplace and helped her late-night guest to the chair. Once she was settled, Emma stirred the last of the dying embers back to life and quickly added a few pieces of kindling from the woodbox.

"We'll get a bit of a fire going to warm you up," she explained and retrieved the afghan Mother Garrett kept in the kitchen for when she felt a draft on her legs. She wrapped the afghan around the elderly woman's shoulders before kneeling down in front of the rocking chair to help remove her guest's shoes and stockings.

Once she was done, Emma leaned over to put the pair of shoes and stockings closer to the fire to dry before taking one of Widow Leonard's feet and warming it between the palms of her hands.

"You're a blessing this night, Emma," the widow crooned as she snuggled beneath the afghan.

Memories brought a smile to Emma's heart. "When I was a little girl, I used to rub my grandmother's feet for her when they were cold or achy. Feel better?"

"Ten times over. I'm curious, though. You haven't asked me why."

Emma looked up and cocked her head.

"Don't you want to know why I've run away?"

Emma dropped her gaze and continued to rub warmth into the woman's foot as the fire bathed her back with welcome heat. "Well, I . . . I suppose I do. But I didn't want to pry into matters that might be difficult for you to discuss."

"At least you took me in without laughing at me, and for that I'm grateful," Widow Leonard said quietly. "Imagine living long enough to see your eighty-first year, looking ahead, and seeing nothing but heartache."

Emma swallowed hard. Whatever had inspired this woman to run away from home was certainly no laughing matter, but she could not imagine how Widow Leonard might expect to hide herself at Hill House—not in a town the size of Candlewood. Despite the influx of newcomers the building of the Candlewood Canal had brought into their midst, gossip still spread pretty quickly here, especially within the town's limits. Both of her sons would be frantic to find her once they realized she was missing, and they would not overlook Hill House as a place she might be.

Reluctant to cause the woman's family undue worry, Emma smiled. "What about your sons? Aren't they going to be worried about you?" she prompted.

Widow Leonard stared into the small fire and shook her head. "James and Andrew are so busy being angry with each other, they probably won't even notice I'm gone."

Emma switched to the woman's other foot, found it alarmingly cold, and started rubbing it warm again. "Truly, I doubt that. They were both here in Candlewood with their families today, weren't they?"

A shrug. Nothing more.

"When the thunderstorm hit and everyone went into a panic, they must have started looking for you."

Another shrug. "I came to town with Andrew this morning, but I was supposed to go home with James. I change every six months, you know. It's what Enoch wanted," she explained, referring to her late husband, who had gone home to glory some eight or nine years back.

"Then James, at least, must be looking for you."

A bit of a smile. "I told him I thought I wanted to stay with Andrew a bit longer. I've done it before. Stayed a few extra weeks, that is."

Emma set Widow Leonard's foot down, leaned back on her haunches, and eased a kink from the base of her spine. Apparently, the woman had not acted on impulse. She had thought through her escape very carefully. "Andrew thinks you went home with his brother, and James assumes you went home with Andrew. Is that it?"

"And neither is the wiser. At least not for a few weeks," the widow admitted.

"What about next Sunday at services?"

"Only if they bother to come, and I'm well enough to attend," she said with a wink and a smile that quickly faded. "As cross and disappointed as I am with both of them, I'd feel guilty if I caused them to worry about me," she explained and rearranged the afghan across her shoulders. "They're good sons, each in his own way. Just stubborn, like their father, and a bit ornery at times."

Emma grinned. "Like their mother?"

Widow Leonard grinned back. "Perhaps."

"You do realize they'll find out you're here, don't you?"

"Eventually," Widow Leonard admitted, and her gaze grew serious. "I must be frank, Emma dear. I sorely need a place to live, but I'm afraid I haven't any coin to pay you."

When Emma opened her mouth to object, the elderly woman held up her hand. "Just hear me out, dear. I don't know you all that well. In my younger days, though, I did know your mother and your grandmother, rest their souls. From all I've heard, you're as generous as they both were, maybe more, but I don't expect you to take me in like you did your mother-in-law when she landed on your doorstep all those years ago. I'm not privy to all the circumstances, but I do know you did what was right by welcoming her into your home and having her stay long after your husband died. And I don't expect you to take me in on charity like you did Reverend Glenn, either. That was a very kind gesture, you know."

"Reverend Glenn is a man of God. He . . . he married my husband and me, he baptized each of our three sons, and he buried my Jonas when he died. I could hardly look the other way when he needed a place to live with folks who could care for him after his stroke," Emma countered, flushed by the praise she felt was ill-deserved.

"Yes, you could have," her guest argued, "but you didn't.

That's because you're a good woman. A kind woman. And I know you'd probably take me in on charity, too, but I won't have it any other way than my way—which is to say, I'll earn my keep here."

She held out her hands and smiled. "These old hands might look pretty awful, what with all the thick veins and swollen joints, but they're not useless, even if the cold weather does slow them down a bit. In truth, come winter, my knees aren't too good, either, but my eyesight is still sharp enough to see the dimples on the moon at night. I can still sew a stitch better than most younger women, too, so I was hoping perhaps I might work out an arrangement with you, like I used to do with your mother occasionally when she had the General Store."

Emma arched her back, stood up, and stretched her legs to bring them back to life again. "What kind of arrangement?"

Widow Leonard looked up at the ceiling. "How many bedrooms do you have here at Hill House? Five? Six?"

"Upstairs? Seven large guest bedrooms, two smaller ones, plus one for me and one for Mother Garrett. Oh, and there's one downstairs for Reverend Glenn. We converted the storage room behind the kitchen into a bedroom for him so he wouldn't have to attempt the stairs."

"That's a lot of bed linens that might need mending or replacing, what with all the guests you have."

Emma let out a long sigh and managed to stifle a yawn. "Only until November, when they close the Candlewood Canal for the winter. Then we don't usually have many guests until spring when they reopen the canal."

"Precisely my point," the widow continued. "During the next two months, you'll be pretty busy with guests, so you could use my help keeping all the bed linens in fine order. I wouldn't mind doing some embroidery, either. Come November, when business slows, I could start to embroider the linens you do have and make them extra special, something guests would really appreciate. Here, let me show you," she insisted and looked over her shoulder toward the back door. "Bring me my travel bag, will you, dear?"

Once Emma fetched the damp bag and set it on the floor alongside her guest's chair, Widow Leonard easily reached down to open it. After taking out two balls of white cotton fabric, she unrolled them, one at a time, to reveal three-inch strips of cloth, each heavily embroidered.

She handed the end of the first one to Emma so that it stretched between them. "I wasn't sure if you'd prefer color or not, but this one has lots of color. I could make the design any combination of colors you'd like, or I could do the same design in white or a single solid color," she explained. She held up the second strip of cloth with an identical embroidered design that featured an intricate band of white intertwined flowers.

Emma fingered the elaborate yet delicate design on the soft fabric. Although the woman had a garish sense of color, Emma easily envisioned the same design coordinated to match each of the colors of the different guest bedrooms. "Your work is exquisite," she murmured with all the admiration of a woman barely able to make more than a few standard stitches. She was also convinced, yet again, that Widow Leonard's plans to run away had been made well before tonight, since she had obviously made these samples expressly to show Emma.

"In return, all I would really need is a cot somewhere, perhaps in the garret? I don't eat much. Not anymore, and I'd stay out of your way for sure," the widow promised. She dropped her gaze and stared at her lap. "I've learned to be good at many things. I can learn to keep out of the way."

Emma's heart skipped a beat. As a woman of substantial means in her own right, she had escaped the plight of most widows, who depended on their husbands to provide for them in their wills. Those widows also depended on the willingness of their children to adhere to the conditions attached to their inheritances— conditions that often spelled out exactly how the new widows, their mothers, should be provided for and treated.

Apparently Widow Leonard's husband must have stipulated in his will that each of their two sons would provide for their mother equally, perhaps even dictating the six-month ritual that had her moving back and forth from her original home, which she suspected the eldest son, James, had inherited, to Andrew's home, built on the land he had inherited.

After confirming her suspicions with the elderly widow, Emma nodded. "It must be difficult for you to be a guest in the home you once shared with your husband."

A long sigh. "It's a widow's lot in life, I suppose," she replied. "I've had a good life, and I've been more blessed than most. Or at least until recently. Now . . . the situation is just unbearable. Since I can't talk any sense into either James or Andrew, I decided that the best thing to do was to leave. Maybe if I'm not there . . ."

As the woman drifted off into her private thoughts, Emma tried to sort out her concerns. Taking in Widow Leonard meant being brought into the middle of a family dispute. Once the owner of the General Store, as well as being in charge of the post office, Emma had been embroiled in such cases before. In some instances, people who had moved away would write and ask her to make arrangements for elderly relatives who had been left behind. In other cases related to her business, she had had to have her lawyer track down debtors to force them to be responsible for what they owed her. As a result, she knew more than a few families whose members turned against one another, or her, in the process.

Her position now, as the proprietress of Hill House, was very different, but guests often turned to her for advice concerning family matters. Still, she relied even more on His guidance now to know how to best use the fortune she had accumulated through her inheritances from her mother and grandmother, as well as the canal-building frenzy, which had made many of the parcels of land she owned far more valuable than she could ever have imagined. Growing interest from investors made deciding if and when to sell off more of the land a challenge, although there were a few parcels she would never sell.

Whether or not she should help Widow Leonard was not a difficult decision. She could not turn away this elderly, vulnerable widow any more than she could have ignored Reverend Glenn's plight. She had the means to provide a home for her and most certainly would agree to the woman's proposal, but she would need to rely on the good Lord to guide her in helping to bring an end to the dissension within the Leonard family itself.

She quickly dismissed the idea that if the trend of taking in permanent residents continued, she would have more staff than visitors, and instead whispered a prayer of gratitude for the family-of-sorts that God had sent to her in lieu of having her own children and grandchildren nearby.

Placing her hand on the elderly woman's shoulder, Emma answered the questions in her troubled gaze with a smile. "Before we take to our beds, why don't you tell me your ideas about the embroidering you'd like to do over a cup of tea and some buttered bread."

3

A FTER THREE SOLID DAYS of rain, Emma squinted her eyes at the bright sunlight. Finally! A break in the miserable weather. Maybe now her overflow of guests would begin to leave. She might even be able to sleep in her own bed tonight.

Humming softly, she eased from the massive leather chair in the corner of her office, ignored the pinch in her back, and stored away the blanket and pillow she had been using in her makeshift bed. She washed up and dressed quickly, slipping out of her nightgown into one of her usual long-sleeved gowns with a single petticoat she had laid out the night before.

She smoothed her full skirts and made sure the collar on the high-necked bodice lay flat. While the deep blue shade she wore today accented her pale blue eyes, the gown would show little dirt or even ink stains, which was much more important. Emma was a woman with classic and very practical taste, and she found herself gravitating toward earth tones and dark colors, as well as durable cottons, which made for easy laundering.

Once she finished dressing, she braided her blond hair. Instead of wrapping the braid into a knot at the back of her neck, however, she let it fall free down her back.

She opened the door connecting her office to the library, walked straight through to the center hall, and entered the dining room, where a platter of sliced bread and a tin of doughnuts rested on the sideboard. The smell of frying breakfast meats led her into the kitchen, where she found Mother Garrett at the cookstove, alternating her efforts between frying pans filled with links of sausage and thick slices of scrapple she would add to the platters of cooked meats on the kitchen table.

Liesel Schneider, a sixteen-year-old from town who had been hired several months ago, primarily to help Mother Garrett in the kitchen, was sitting at the far end of the table shelling boiled eggs. There was no sign of Ditty Morgan, the other young woman she had hired at the same time, although she assumed Ditty was busy upstairs changing bed linens.

Grinning, Emma snatched a sausage from the platter, took a nibble of the spicy link, kissed her mother-in-law's cheek, and waved her fingers at Liesel. "Good morning, good morning!"

Mother Garrett chuckled. "Feeling a bit touched by the sun, are you?"

Emma nibbled away the rest of the sausage, wiped the grease from her hands, and donned a heavy muslin apron, much like the ones she wore when tending the store. "I'm touched by pure joy. I think if the rain hadn't stopped and the sun hadn't come out today, I really would have started to build an ark," she teased and started filling a tray with crocks of butter, jams, and preserves. "As it is, I'd venture our guests will be just as pleased, and they'll guarantee that the packet boat will have a full complement of passengers today."

"They'll leave with full bellies," Mother Garrett noted as she lifted crisp slices of scrapple from the pan to the platter.

"They'll take lots of memories with them, too," Liesel noted and paused to scratch an itch on the tip of her freckled nose with the crook of her elbow. "Aunt Frances said she wouldn't be surprised if the stories about the storm and the ruined fireworks survived to be told at the centennial in 1891. Not that she'd be alive then, of course, but I'll be there. I told her I'd remember to tell everyone about the storm and being cooped up inside for three whole days because of the rain, too."

Emma cocked a brow. "Aunt Frances?"

Liesel's full round face blushed pink, and her eyes grew wide. "Widow Leonard said to call her Aunt Frances. She claims adding another widow to the two widows already living here, along with Reverend Glenn who's a widower, might make guests uneasy, although I'm not sure why anyone would really care. She thought Ditty and I might want to call her Aunt Frances since there's no limit to the number of aunts we can have."

"Really? Just when did you all discuss this?" Emma asked.

"Last night. She came up to the garret and brought me and Ditty the last of the sugar cookies and some milk to thank us for being so nice to her." She shrugged her shoulders as she plopped another peeled egg into the bowl. "I think she's easy to be nice to. So does Ditty. She's even offered to teach us to embroider like she does."

Mother Garrett cleared her throat, no doubt covering the same chuckle threatening to erupt in Emma's throat. Liesel was so sweet and unaffected, the idea she might be guilty of gossiping or telling tales out of turn was simply not in her nature.

Emma caught the sparkle in her mother-in-law's eyes. "I don't believe I've given the matter of having so many widows living together much thought before now. As long as she suggested it, I suppose both of you may call her Aunt Frances," she murmured and mulled the idea over in her mind.

Perhaps it took an outsider like Widow Leonard to notice that the permanent residents at Hill House had all outlived their respective spouses. Despite the deep friendship they all shared with one another, Emma could not help but wonder if any of the others ever ached for the companionship of a spouse from time to time like she did. Except for Liesel and Ditty, of course. The two young women were too young to be married, but they were not really permanent residents. They only lived at Hill House during the week and returned to their families for most of each weekend.

"I must admit, it does get confusing at times for me and Ditty, having two Widow Garretts," Liesel said while peeling another egg. "Even though I mostly work here in the kitchen with Widow Garrett, and Ditty usually helps you with the cleaning and such, since you're Widow Garrett, too . . . We tried not referring to you as Old Widow Garrett and Young Widow Garrett, at least not in front of anyone else, but Aunt Frances overheard us and told us not to worry overmuch about it. She said she'd overheard some of the guests talking about it, and they do the same thing. She'd have the same problem, except she's older than either one of you and she gets to call you both by your given names." With a sigh, she added yet another egg to the bowl and wiped her hands on a cloth.

"She's older than I am by five years, that's true enough," Mother Garrett noted as she stirred the pan of sizzling sausages.

Caught off guard by the notion her guests found it necessary to differentiate between her and her mother-in-law by referring to their age, Emma pursed her lips and tapped the tips of her fingertips against the edge of the tray while she thought about the dilemma. Mother Garrett had first come to live with Emma and her husband when they lived and worked at the General Store.

There had been no confict. Since Jonas was alive, there was only one Widow Garrett—his mother.

As a rule back then, Mother Garrett did not venture downstairs from the living quarters they shared to tend to matters in the store. Her contact with the customers remained limited even after Jonas's death, so although she and Emma continued to live together, there had been no conflict with customers getting confused about dealing with two Widow Garretts.

Ever since Emma had opened Hill House to guests two years ago, however, she and Mother Garrett had interacted with guests on an equal basis, save for Emma's role as proprietress.

Sighing, Emma picked up the tray, caught her mother-in-law's gaze, and held it. "This may be our second full season welcoming guests and only our first with hired help, but we still have much to learn about making sure they're comfortable and at ease. It never occurred to me they might find our similar names confusing."

"Mother Garrett would suit me fine, although there's no one else in the world whom I'd rather call me mother than you," she murmured in reply.

"I'm honored to share you with our guests. In all ways," Emma whispered. She looked over at Liesel, who had completely stopped working to observe their conversation, and smiled. "From now on, you can call my mother-in-law Mother Garrett. I can tell Ditty, or you can—"

"Tell me what?" Ditty asked as she descended the last few steps on the back staircase. "Did I hear someone . . . oops!"

Emma turned around just in time to see the young woman miss the last step and pitch forward. The mound of soiled bed linens she carried in her arms quickly tangled with the young woman's skirts, and she only managed to keep on her feet and avoid falling into the back of Liesel's chair by taking a series of awkward steps.

Clutching the tray tightly, Emma gasped. "Careful, child! Are you all right?"

Breathing hard, her cheeks flaming, Ditty disentangled her skirts before she managed to stand up straight to her full height of nearly six feet. "No harm done," she managed. "I thought I would change the bed linens in my room and Liesel's room while I was waiting for the guests to get up. Maybe I shouldn't have tried to carry them all down at the same time, but I wanted to get downstairs to help everyone. All the guests are going to be leaving early today, I'd imagine."

Emma held her tongue. Over the past few months, she had come to learn that Ditty was as prone to accidents as she was anxious to prove how hard she could work. She was, in point of fact, the clumsiest young woman Emma had ever met. Asking her to work alongside Mother Garrett in the kitchen instead of Liesel on a regular basis would have been an invitation to disaster. Instead, the pleasant young woman, whose family lived on an outlying farm, worked with Emma cleaning the boardinghouse.

Unfortunately, with the number of guests they had had for the Founders' Day Celebration, she had had no choice but to use Ditty, as sparingly as possible, to help both Mother Garrett and Liesel. "As long as you didn't get hurt, why don't you pile the soiled bed linens in the corner for now," Emma suggested. "I think you're right. Most of the guests will be leaving early, and they'll all want breakfast earlier than usual so they can be at the landing for the packet boat at ten."

She set the tray of condiments down. "Why don't you take this tray and set out the condiments on the sideboard in the dining room and put out the dishes and silverware, too. Carefully," she cautioned before turning to Liesel. "If you're about finished, the eggs can be set out, and once the breakfast meats are ready, take those platters, as well. In the meantime, I'll fill the pitchers with warm water. You and Ditty can help me take them to the guests' rooms while Mother Garrett finishes up at the stove."

Without further prompting, Liesel got up from the table and took the condiment tray from Emma. "I'll take this. Ditty, bring the eggs and hold the door open for me, will you?" She lowered her voice. "When we finish in the dining room, I'll carry the pitchers upstairs. Let Ditty help you down here."

Emma nodded, caught another twinkle in her mother-in-law's eyes, and took several heavy cloths out of the drawer as the young women left the kitchen to carry out their tasks.

"At sixteen, Ditty's already grown taller than most men. She just needs time to grow into her own feet. She means well," Mother Garrett said as she stepped aside to give Emma access to a pot of hot water.

Emma chuckled. "I know she does," she admitted as she wrapped the cloths around the handle and hoisted up the pot of water. "I'm not sure how understanding you'd be if she worked in the kitchen every day."

Her mother-in-law sobered. "About as understanding as I'd be if a tornado took roost in my kitchen," she quipped. "Not that you'd favor the idea of burnt meals or replacing the many more dishes she'd break. Or hiring someone else to actually run the kitchen since I wouldn't have lasted past her first day. Just what were you thinking when you asked the girl to carry that tray just a moment ago?"

With a shrug, Emma ignored the question and carried the pot of water over to the pitchers lined up on a worktable. "We've all got our special gifts," she noted as she started to add the hot water to the cold water already in the pitchers. "I'd be hard-pressed to find anyone who works as hard as Ditty does."

"And Liesel suits me just fine in the kitchen, even if she does tend to eat twice at every meal—once when she's helping to prepare the food and again when she's at the table," Mother Garrett countered, although her heavy girth silently testified to the fact that she herself had the same habit, while Liesel remained uncommonly thin.

Emma looked down at her own waistline and noted that despite her love of breads of any type, she managed to keep a trim figure. She sighed, and the sounds of the young women's chatter as they worked together in the dining room, as well as her own friendly banter with Mother Garrett, only added to Emma's sense of contentment. She had never had hired help before, and she again offered a prayer of gratitude for being guided to hire both Liesel and Ditty.

With the last of the breakfast meats now added to the platters on the kitchen table, Mother Garrett added a bowl of sliced potatoes to the drippings in both frying pans. "Speaking of gifts, are you really going to have Frances live here indefinitely?"

Emma nodded, finished filling the last pitcher, and set the empty pot aside. "There's more than enough mending that needs to be done, and she does beautiful handiwork. I think having the bed linens embroidered will add a nice touch our guests will appreciate, don't you?"

"That depends," Mother Garrett said as she stirred the sizzling potatoes.

Emma cocked a brow.

"When one of her sons shows up, you're going to be hard-pressed to explain why you're harboring a . . . a runaway, as she puts it. She'll be back on the farm before she makes many of those fancy stitches of hers."

"Nonsense," Emma countered. "Widow Leonard has a right to live wherever she chooses, assuming she can provide for herself. I can see to it that she can do just that. What other choice do I have? I couldn't turn her out now any more than I could turn her away the night she came here."

Since she and Mother Garrett had had no time to discuss the matter until now, she was anxious to explain her reasoning, although it was not like her mother-in-law to oppose her on anything she set her mind to doing.

Mother Garrett, however, had not finished voicing her concerns. "I'm not sure what it is that her sons are so angry about that they haven't talked to each other for the past few months, but causing their mother such heartache by keeping her in the middle of their argument is almost unforgivable. I assume Frances will tell us the tale in her own time. That's well and good with me. In the meantime," she cautioned, waving her spatula, "I'm not resting easy, waiting for one of those boys to show up on your doorstep to challenge you. From all I've heard—which isn't much, I admit—one of those sons of hers has more temper than common sense."

Emma walked over to the cookstove and put her arm around Mother Garrett's shoulders. "Please don't be uneasy. If you recall, I've had plenty of experience protecting people from men far bigger and a whole lot more powerful than the likes of James and Andrew Leonard," she said. Not long after Jonas died, Emma had stood her ground against his brother, Allan, an influential politician in New York City. She had not hesitated to support her mother-in-law's decision to remain in Candlewood instead of returning to New York City to the home she had once shared with her oldest son, and Emma did not hesitate to do the same for Widow Leonard now.

"If Frances needs a champion, the good Lord sent her to the right woman when He sent her to you. But I can't condone keeping her whereabouts a secret from them, even though she seems certain they don't even realize she's gone."

"I'll speak to her about it later today, after all the guests leave," Emma promised. "Maybe she'll agree to send James and Andrew a brief note so they'll know where she is. That way they won't worry. If not, I'll speak to each of them at Sunday services. In any case, we have a few days before we have to worry about that," she said before the sound of an approaching wagon drew her gaze to the kitchen window.

"It's a tad early for Mr. Westcott to make deliveries," Mother Garrett remarked without looking up from the cookstove.

Emma recognized the driver at once, but he was definitely not Adam Westcott, an area farmer who supplied Hill House with milk and butter. Even though her heart dropped to her knees and back again, she gave Mother Garrett a hug and stepped back to remove her apron and smooth back her hair. "Apparently, I have less time than I thought," she explained. "That's not Adam Westcott; it's James Leonard."

Out of the corner of her eye, she saw Widow Leonard standing on the bottom step. Turning and offering her a smile, she said, "It seems you've been discovered missing. James is here."

The elderly woman paled.

"I'll have to tell him you're here," Emma continued. "Would you like to speak with him?"

Widow Leonard held tight to the railing. "Not yet. Certainly not today. I don't want to talk to James—or Andrew, either, for that matter."

"Don't worry. Just stay here in the kitchen. I'll take care of everything." Emma started for her office, where she expected to find James waiting at the door where she customarily welcomed arriving guests. She walked slowly but steadily, ready to do battle with a good dose of common sense and the sheer power of faith as her only weapons.

4

W ITH GUESTS RISING, DRESSING, and some dining already, the boardinghouse was literally coming to life while Emma waited for James Leonard in her office. She listened as he scraped his boots before turning a knob that sounded the bell above her door and announced his arrival.

She whispered yet another silent prayer all would go well, then unlatched the door that opened onto the side of the wraparound porch. Emma gratefully noted the sun had chased away the chill of the past few days.

Straw hat in hand, James nodded. "I hope I haven't disturbed you too early," he ventured, but he did not step forward. He was well over six feet tall and carried muscles heavy from years of farming. She found it hard to believe that Widow Leonard, a small slip of a woman, had given birth to this strapping man, her firstborn. A lifetime of outdoor work, however, had leathered his features, and the heavy hint of gray in the hair at his temples put his age at close to fifty, she supposed.

Surprisingly, his gaze was troubled rather than angry. "May I come in?"

Emma stepped aside and closed the door behind him.

"I've come about my mother," he explained. "She's here, isn't she?"

"Yes, she is. Please, have a seat," she insisted and pointed to the two straight-back chairs in front of her desk. While he took his seat, she moved behind the desk and took her own. Reassured by his meek demeanor, she assumed his brother was the one with the reputation for having a temper.

She relished the modicum of authority she wielded sitting behind the massive desk, as suitable for her needs operating the boardinghouse as it was for the former owner, and far superior to a dainty lady's desk. Rather than trying to justify his mother's presence here, which would definitely put her on the defensive, she held silent.

He cleared his throat. "Let me begin by apologizing to you. Taking in my mother when you already had an overflow of guests must have been incredibly inconvenient, but I'm very, very grateful that you were able to care for her."

"We can always make room at Hill House for one more. We're happy to have her with us," she said. "I'm curious, though. How did you come to look for your mother here?"

His dark eyes flashed with guilt. "I . . . I guess this is my fault. I must have misunderstood her. I thought she said she'd be going home with my brother, so when the storm hit and I lost sight of her, I just assumed she'd left with him. She'd forgotten some of her things, so I took them to my brother's home first thing this morning. That's when I found out she wasn't there like she said she'd be. I headed straight for town, and when I stopped at the General Store to make some inquiries, I was told here would be the most likely place to find her."

Emma nodded.

He let out a sigh and toyed with the rim of his hat. "I guess I'm more relieved than anything," he admitted and looked around the room before meeting her gaze. "If you'll calculate her bill, I'll just pay what she owes. I'd like to take her home with me for a few days before she—"

Another visitor rang the bell and interrupted him.

"I'm sorry. Excuse me just a moment," Emma suggested. She rose, made her way to the door again, and nearly gasped upon opening it.

Andrew Leonard, all six feet of anger and determination, stood outside and glared at her. "I've come to take my mother home."

She stiffened her back. "Good morning," she managed. "Please come in."

He eyed his brother's wagon, hesitated, then charged past her to get inside without bothering to scrape the mud still clinging to his boots. Belatedly, he removed his hat.

Before she managed to close the door again, James had gotten to his feet, turned, and faced his brother. They were only a few years apart in age, but anger created a palpable distance between them.

She sliced the tension that separated the two brothers by walking between them to return to her seat behind the desk. Heart pounding, she folded her hands and rested them on top of her desk. "Gentlemen, if you'd both be seated . . ."

James hesitated, his right cheek twitching. His hand tightened around the rim of his hat and, reluctantly, he took his seat.

Andrew, however, remained standing. "Kindly tell my mother I'm here to take her home."

James squared his shoulders. "As we were discussing, Widow Garrett, I'll happily settle my mother's bill before we leave."

"Apparently my brother is under the mistaken impression that

Mother is returning to *his* home," Andrew argued. "Regardless of what she may have told you or anyone else, our mother is coming home with me. I certainly won't begrudge paying whatever it is her lodgings have cost, but I have little time or energy to waste arguing with you," he charged, directing his words to her and away from his brother.

Emma cast them each a hard look. She had neither the patience nor the wisdom of Solomon, but she had no intention of sending Widow Leonard home with either of these two men until the elderly woman made the decision to do so. "If and when your mother decides to leave is up to her," she said and deliberately kept her voice soft but firm.

"If and when my mother leaves is *not* up to her," Andrew spat. "According to my father's will, she's to live with one of us, and she's due, no, she's past due the time when she should have come to live with me. So I'm afraid she'll be leaving now. With me."

"Since I can't afford for her to stay here any longer," James said firmly, "she'll have to come home with me today."

Emma drew several long breaths to allow for a quick prayer. "In truth, gentlemen, your mother will not be leaving at all. She'll be staying here a bit longer. You see, she's not here as a guest, as you've both presumed. She's living here now as a member of my staff."

James's eyes widened. "Your staff? You mean to say you've actually hired her to work here?"

"Don't be absurd," Andrew charged. With his face flushed and his eyes bulging, he looked like a pot about to boil over on Mother Garrett's cookstove. "In addition to the fact that she's far too old to be working, there's little of value—"

"Actually, she's quite skilled with the needle, and she's agreed to share her talent with all of us here at Hill House," Emma interjected. "Like other members of my staff," she continued, unwilling to give either man the opportunity to argue with her, "she'll receive room and board, along with a small stipend, in exchange for her valuable services."

"I want to speak with my mother. Now," Andrew demanded as he took a step forward.

James rose from his seat so fast his chair nearly toppled to the floor. He caught the chair with his free hand and set it right before he locked his gaze with Emma's. "I was here first. I'll speak to my mother first."

Emma locked her knees together to keep them from shaking and managed a smile. "I do apologize to both of you. I know you've both traveled a long way this morning, but unfortunately, I don't allow my staff to have visitors when they're working. Your mother's free time is from noon on Saturday until eight o'clock on Sunday evening. During that time, she can stay here and receive visitors or she can return home, much the same as the other members of my staff often do. Until then, I'm afraid I must ask you both to leave. I really must get back to my guests," she announced and rose from her seat.

Andrew took another step forward and effectively blocked her way. "You have no right to keep me from seeing my mother, and I will not allow gossipmongers to label me as an ogre for putting my aged mother out to work when that's most definitely not the case."

"Nor will I," James added, although he did not move from his position on the opposite side of her desk.

Emma swallowed hard. If it was indeed true that the two brothers were not speaking to each other because of some unexplained disagreement, at least they were now united against what they perceived to be a common enemy—her. Neither man, unfortunately, seemed willing to budge, which meant the standoff would continue and she might be forced to spend some time trapped behind her desk.

Unsure of exactly what to do next, Emma simply held her ground, quite certain neither one of Widow Leonard's sons would resort to violence to get his way. For several long heartbeats, she heard her pulse pounding in her ears. When she glimpsed the sampler hanging on the wall next to the window, she let out a sigh and prayed each man would be swayed by her words.

"You might do well to remember something," she began and nodded toward the sampler. Each of the men paused and then, following her direction, glanced at the sampler and back at her.

" 'Honor thy father and thy mother,' " she whispered. "I stitched that sampler many, many years ago. How I wish my dear mother were still here, that I might love her and honor her wishes, regardless of how old she had become or how old I had grown to be. My mother passed to glory long ago, but you're both blessed to have your mother still here. It's neither my place nor my intention to question why your mother has chosen to come and work here, but she's not a child. She's eighty-one years old. She has a sound mind and a right to decide her own future."

She paused and looked from one man to the other. "I pray someday she might want to return home to live with both of you from time to time. Until then, please honor her wishes to stay here at Hill House. And honor her request not to speak with either of you today. Perhaps you might like to speak to Reverend Glenn instead. As you know, he's living here at Hill House now. I'm certain he'd be willing to discuss the merits of the fifth commandment with both of you."

James was the first to relent and step back from her desk. His shoulders were stiff with annoyance, but his gaze had softened.

"I'm not sure why my mother is being so difficult, but I trust you will provide well for her here, at least temporarily. Tell her . . . tell her to send for me when she wants to come home."

When she nodded in reply, he walked past his brother and let himself out.

Andrew simply continued to glare at her. "James is a fool, and my mother is obviously becoming senile. You have until Sunday to convince her you made a mistake hiring her. I'll expect her to leave with me after services," he hissed, then turned on his heel and slammed the door shut the moment he stepped outside.

Emma briefly shut her eyes until her heartbeat slowed to a normal rhythm. With more than a little divine inspiration, she had managed to secure a few more days for Widow Leonard to think through her troubles before she had to face either of her sons. The nature of the wedge that had driven the two brothers apart still remained a mystery, but Emma had lived enough years and learned more about the variety of troubles that could drive families apart to know the root of the problem was related to either love or money.

James and Andrew had both been married for a good number of years. Money, either the lack of it or the opportunity to acquire it, was the more likely culprit. Given the change in the economy brought to the area by the building of the Candlewood Canal, the Leonard brothers were no doubt experiencing the same challenges that faced many other longtime residents: to change and grow with the times or to cling to the past.

Faith was the one anchor that would hold them steady.

Faith would strengthen the ties that bound them together as a family.

"Simply faith," she whispered and prayed James and Andrew

might rediscover the power of faith in their lives to end the bitterness between them.

Until they did, Emma would put her own faith to work, perhaps with a little assistance from Zachary Breckenwith, who was her lawyer as well as her financial advisor.

After all her guests left today.

After Hill House was restored to proper order.

But well before either James or Andrew thought better of leaving their mother at Hill House and returned to force her to leave.

5

SIX HOURS AND COUNTLESS ACHING muscles after the last
guest had left, Emma stopped cleaning long enough to take
a turn around the first floor to survey the progress they had made
setting Hill House back to rights.

She started in the center hall at the front door. Ditty had swept
the wraparound porch free of dirt and debris left by the storm and
wiped down the porch chairs after helping Emma remove the cots
and bedding from both front rooms. Emma peeked into each
room and smiled at the well-appointed parlors they had become
once again. Instead of going through the dining room into the
kitchen, which was under Mother Garrett's control, she poked her
head into the library, where the heavy scent of leather from the
two new wing chairs added to the already strong masculine flavor
of the dark-paneled room.

The sound of Ditty's footsteps overhead as she tackled one of
the smaller guest rooms reassured Emma the young woman was
still hard at work. Before she rejoined her, however, Emma wanted
to check on Widow Leonard and Reverend Glenn, who had both

been relegated to the side patio for the day to keep them from having to move from room to room while the others cleaned.

First, though, Emma stopped in the kitchen where she found Mother Garrett sitting at the kitchen table breaking up yesterday's bread. "Is that bread pudding for supper?"

"That and some beef saved from dinner. I'm keeping it simple tonight, because the way you've all been working, I doubt a single one of you will have the energy left to eat. Except for Liesel," she added. "I've set some succotash aside for her, and I just sent her upstairs to help, in case you're wondering where she is."

Mother Garrett paused to mop her brow. "I don't know how you feel about it, but I almost wish we'd get the rain back, or at least a cooler day. Why is it nature invariably makes up for a few days of rain with more sun than we need?"

Emma wrinkled her nose. "More rain? Please! Let us dry out first." She loosened her collar and rubbed away the sweat at the base of her neck. "It does feel overly warm today, but that's probably because we've all been working so hard. The sun today is really a blessing. We're able to open all the windows downstairs and air out the rooms."

"And use the patio. Liesel took out something cool to drink for Frances and Reverend Glenn a while ago. There's a pitcher of raspberry shrub sitting in the sink. Be a dear, won't you, and see if they'd care for more? Just be careful when you go out to the patio. The mongrel is out there, too. Don't trip over him. And you might think about sitting down for a few minutes to have a glass yourself. You're looking flushed," she noted and took a sip from her own glass.

Emma retrieved the pitcher filled with the refreshing drink and took a glass from the cupboard, but Mother Garrett caught her elbow for a moment as she passed by her. "We haven't had any time alone together since earlier today, but I wanted to tell you that you did right fine this morning with the Leonard boys."

Emma paused and chuckled. "They're hardly boys, Mother Garrett. They're as old as I am. But thank you."

"You only managed to get Frances a little more time. You know that, don't you?"

"I do. Today was much too hectic, but I thought I'd go to see Zachary Breckenwith tomorrow."

A cocked brow. "You're expecting enough trouble you need to see your lawyer?"

"I expect to be prepared, just in case," Emma replied before she continued on her way. She was not as confident or as prepared to meet with her lawyer as she had led Mother Garrett to believe. In truth, she had much preferred dealing with the late Alexander Breckenwith rather than his nephew, who had come to Candlewood to assist his dying uncle with his law practice some five years ago. He had remained after his uncle's death because his newly widowed aunt, Elizabeth, simply refused to move to New York City with him.

In addition to providing legal assistance, the late Alexander Breckenwith had been a trusted friend and advisor to Emma's mother and later to Emma. Unfortunately, his nephew was far more likely to challenge Emma than abide by her instructions. She had locked horns with him more than once but never quite as forcefully as when she had insisted on buying Hill House.

A gnawing fear in the pit of her stomach told her that he would not be supportive when he discovered she had planted herself square in the middle of an argument between Widow Leonard and her sons, but she would simply have to stand her ground against his advice. Again.

The moment she stepped through the double doors in the

dining room and out onto the stone patio, however, a warm but refreshing breeze still carrying the fading sweet smells of summer greeted her and blew away her concerns about meeting with her lawyer. A stone wall surrounding the patio blocked any view of the surrounding landscape, while overhead, a network of vines laced the lattice-style roof to obscure the direct glare of the sun.

By day the small outdoor room appeared to be suspended high within the trees. By night the moon and stars that shone through the lattice seemed almost close enough to touch.

The half-dozen outdoor chairs huddled in pairs about the patio, however, were empty. No Reverend Glenn. No Widow Leonard. No Butter, the mongrel dog who was the retired minister's loyal companion and a constant source of irritation to Mother Garrett. Two empty glasses sat on a small table in front of the two chairs closest to the massive fireplace in the far corner.

When Emma first purchased Hill House, she had wondered why the original owner had built a fireplace for an outdoor patio. Now she longed for the chill nights of autumn and even the occasional winter evening when she could sit outside in the moonlight, warmed by the fire at her feet and the glory of God's universe overhead. With seven grandchildren all under the age of six, she hoped she might even have the opportunity to snuggle out here in front of the fire with one or all of them one night to count the stars overhead or just share the joy of being together as a family.

She set the pitcher down on the table next to the glasses, swatted away a pair of yellow jackets, poured a drink for herself, and looked at her surroundings.

As it stood, Hill House literally sat between two worlds—the world of commerce and industry quickly overtaking the town to the south, and the patchwork of small farms to the north on the fertile land that had lured the original settlers to the area, including

Emma's grandparents. Located high on a hill on the north side of town at the end of a winding brick lane, Hill House offered a commanding view of the town itself and of the Candlewood Canal that snaked its way north, running parallel to Main Street.

But there was a lovely view from the rear of the house, as well. After taking a few sips of her drink, she set the glass down and walked over to the wall facing the back of the property, where she had a breathtaking panorama of pastoral splendor.

A gate in the stone wall provided access to the terraced steps bordered by gardens that cascaded down the hill to a small plateau. A stand of natural forest that included pines common to the area, cedar trees, and several mulberry trees planted last year provided a lush backdrop for the new gazebo she'd had built there. Above the treetops, the Candlewood Canal flowed in the distance as it continued north and east toward Bounty and beyond, connecting Candlewood, ultimately, with the Erie Canal and the eastern markets.

Warmed by the sun overhead, Emma studied the gardens where Mother Garrett's herbs, still full and green, filled the first terrace. Everblooming summer roses—in shades of red and white and every hue of pink in between—filled the other gardens and gently scented the air. The roses were a beautiful reminder of the two women who had worked so hard to bring the formerly abandoned gardens back to their full beauty and who still returned twice a year to maintain them, more friends now than guests. She inhaled deeply and savored the heavenly scent, even as her gaze traveled down the curving steps that cut through the terraces to the gazebo.

She cupped one hand at her brow to reduce the glare of the sun now hanging low in the sky and reflecting off the gazebo's bronze roof. The latticed sides of the gazebo extended only halfway between the floor and the roof and were topped with an ornate railing. Emma smiled the moment she spied the silhouettes of Reverend Glenn and Widow Leonard, as well as Butter's tail hanging out between pieces of lattice on the near side.

She thought about going back to the kitchen to get a tray to carry the pitcher and glasses down to the gazebo, but she cast the idea aside when Reverend Glenn and Widow Leonard suddenly emerged. Butter's tail promptly disappeared from view, as well, and before the retired minister attempted the single step down from the gazebo, the dog was at his side.

She watched in awe as the aged dog hedged himself close to his master's weaker left side. When the man stepped down to ground level, the dog stayed with him, ever loyal, ever patient, as the minister turned slightly and offered his hand to help Widow Leonard from the gazebo.

Emma held on to the rough stone wall with one hand and studied the trio as they made their way along the gravel path that skirted the edge of the pond. Once a solid, robust man, Reverend Glenn was now frail and weak. At seventy-one years old, he had hair that had turned lily white and thinned so that his overlarge, gnarly ears dominated his pinched features.

Having the mite-sized Widow Leonard at his side, however, made the minister appear almost tall. His gait remained slow and unsteady, but Butter ambled close enough to prevent a fall should the man truly stumble.

Emma shook her head when she eyed the dog closely. Mother Garrett was right. Butter was indeed an ungainly mongrel. Splotches of gray now blotched his short, sandy-colored hair, but age could not alter the size of the animal's massive head that nature had mismatched to his small, squat body or the long-haired tail that carried in as much dirt or mud as his four paws. Fortunately the animal's penchant for climbing up onto the cupboard to rob the entire contents of the butter crock, however, remained as nothing more than tales the minister loved to tell and retell.

Although the trio's progress was slow, Emma was more than pleased to see them together. She could not remember a time when Reverend Glenn had felt strong enough to even attempt the challenge of the steps that led down to the gazebo. Apparently Widow Leonard's presence here carried unexpected blessings, perhaps some yet to be discovered.

Inspired by the mystery of God's work in this world, Emma recommitted herself to using all of her resources to make sure Widow Leonard was able to stay at Hill House for as long as she wanted. She also prayed for patience that she might let God's plans for reconciling the problems that had brought the elderly widow here unfold according to His will.

She stood on tiptoe, ready to call out to them, but realized she might startle them and cause the minister to misstep. Instead Emma dropped back down to the soles of her feet and turned away from the wall. She had barely started back to the house when Mother Garrett came out onto the patio.

"You have a guest. I've asked him to wait for you in your office."

Emma stopped and narrowed her gaze. "A guest? I'm sorry. I guess I didn't hear the bell."

Chuckling, Mother Garrett shook her head. "You can't hear the bell out here. That's one of the reasons I suspect the patio is one of your favorite places."

Emma shrugged, removed her apron, and smoothed her hair. "I was hoping for a day or two of peace and quiet," she admitted.

"You have a guest. You. Yourself. It's not someone who wants a room at Hill House."

Emma's eyes widened. "I have a guest?" Operating the General Store, like her mother and grandmother before her, and now Hill House, had left little time for her to develop close friendships with anyone, and her personal life was invariably intertwined with her business dealings. The men and women at church were her brothers and sisters in faith, but they were more acquaintances than friends. It would be too much of a coincidence to think the caller might be Zachary Breckenwith, which left her in a state of mild confusion about who her caller might be.

"If I have a guest, why did you ask him to wait in my office instead of the parlor?"

"Don't get all huffy. And don't get as mad as a March hen at me," Mother Garrett cautioned. "Your guest is Mr. Langhorne. That's why I put him in your office and not the parlor."

Emma blew out a breath of annoyance as echoes of her last meeting with the man rang in her ears. "He's back again? I thought I made it very clear the last time he came to call that I wasn't interested. Not then. Not ever. I suppose you had no choice but to tell him I was home?"

"Don't ask me how, but he claims he spied you on the patio."

"Wonderful," Emma grumbled and quickly tied her apron back into place. What little vanity she possessed kept her from mussing up her hair a bit to make the man feel guilty for interrupting her. "Please tell the pesky Mr. Langhorne that I've a bit of cleaning to finish before I'll have time to see him," she suggested.

"I already did. He said he'd wait, poor man," Mother Garrett countered with a definite twinkle in her eyes.

"Of course he did. How that irritating man had the gall to call me stubborn . . . Well, there's no sense putting off what needs to be done, and this time I'll make myself perfectly clear, even if that means I must be far more blunt than I like to be." She sighed. "I suppose the sooner I see him, the quicker he'll leave. For good," Emma offered, walking past her mother-in-law and back into the house.

She was in such a state she did not bother to slow down to allow her eyes to adjust from the bright light outside to the dim light in the dining room. The result: she stubbed her toes on the leg of one of the dining room chairs and again on the bottom edge of the sideboard.

Tears welled and nearly overflowed before she blinked them back. Leaning against the sideboard for support, she rubbed her foot until her toes stopped stinging. "Stubborn? You want stubborn? I'm going to introduce you to stubborn, Mr. Aloysius Lancaster Langhorne III," she muttered.

When her mind latched onto a sudden inspiration, she opened the side drawer of the sideboard and rifled through the clutter of old correspondence, newspapers, and journals that she kept hidden there behind the tins of doughnuts. When she found a letter dated a year ago that she had received from one of her first guests, State Senator Tobias Green, she checked the back of the oversized paper to make sure it was blank. After storing the letter in her apron pocket, she grinned all the way back to the kitchen, where Mother Garrett was wiping down the kitchen table.

"You keep a pencil out here somewhere, don't you?" Emma asked as she started rooting through one of the cupboard drawers.

"There's no need to make a mess. Here," Mother Garrett said and retrieved a stub of a pencil from her apron pocket. "I was planning to make a list of supplies we need from the General Store."

"Thank you." Emma shut the drawer. "I'll hand this back in just a moment," she promised as she took the pencil. She hesitated for a moment and glanced at her mother-in-law. "With your permission, I'd like to try something. It means you'll be involved a bit, but . . ."

"Will it mean the end of Mr. Langhorne?"

"I hope so." Smiling, Emma flattened the letter upside down on the table. She scribbled the date, a few lines of script, and signed it before she handed the pencil to her mother-in-law. "Would you sign this for me?" she asked, pointing to a place just below her own signature.

This time, Mother Garrett hesitated. "Maybe you should slow down and think about this. I'm not exactly sure what you're about, but it's never a good idea to act in haste."

"Do you trust me?"

Mother Garrett sighed, held Emma's gaze for a moment, and signed the paper. "I don't suppose you could slow down a moment and tell me how I'm going to be involved in your scheme?"

Emma folded up the letter, stored it in her apron pocket, and pecked her mother-in-law's cheek. "When I get back I'll explain everything," she gushed and started for her office.

"Wait! You can't just leave me here without offering me a hint of what you're planning to do."

Pausing, Emma turned to face her. "If my plan works, this will be Mr. Langhorne's last visit."

"And if it doesn't?"

"I rather doubt that."

"And if it doesn't?" Mother Garrett repeated.

Emma shrugged. "I suppose if it doesn't, then he might come back . . . to see you."

6

B Y THE TIME EMMA APPROACHED her office, her mood had
changed from annoyed to determined. Depending on the
nature of the business to be conducted, she had learned there was
a time to be conciliatory, a time to be forceful, and a time to be
coy. Since Mr. Langhorne had not responded as she had wanted to
either of the former, she chose the latter as her strategy—to a
point.

She entered her office and urged her caller back into one of
the chairs facing her desk with a wave of her hand. Wearing a
polite smile, she planted herself in the chair behind her desk. "Forgive me for keeping you waiting. We're still trying to recover. We
had almost double our usual number of guests for the week of
Founders' Day celebrations. Now, how can I help you this time,
Mr. Langhorne?"

A relative newcomer to Candlewood, Langhorne was one of
several eastern investors who had come here within the past couple of years to link their fortunes with the building of the Candlewood Canal. Like many others, he underestimated the lifelong

residents and their ability to protect their own economic futures against the fast-talking, better educated, and more experienced investors who had no interest in establishing roots within the community.

Unlike the others, however, Langhorne had taken up residence at the Emerson Hotel nine months ago with the express intention of moving here permanently. Since then, he had already purchased three warehouses built along the canal and continued to seek new ventures, although he had yet to purchase a home.

He pushed his spectacles back up the long ridge of his nose and squared his shoulders. "On the contrary, Widow Garrett. I've come to offer my help to you." With a flourish, he pulled a large packet of papers from his coat pocket and laid it on top of her desk. "My final offer," he announced. "I believe you'll be quite pleased."

She furrowed her brow in mock confusion, leaned against the back of her chair, and laced her fingers together before resting them on her lap. "Offer?"

He cleared his throat as if swallowing his annoyance with her. "For the land at the intersection of Main Street and Hollaway Lane. The last time we met to discuss the matter some months back, you said you wouldn't sell the land for anything less than the 'unattainable.' Well, consider it done." He smiled broadly. "I've done it for you. The 'unattainable' is no further away than your signature."

She held a tight rein on her temper and smiled. "My dear Mr. Langhorne, I . . . I believe I said I regretted that I would not be able to sell that parcel of land to you under any circumstances. I believe that was not long after I had to decline your kind offer of marriage, which, regrettably, I was not able to accept."

Just the memory of his audacious proposal started her blood to a simmer. Even in her loneliest moments, when she truly considered the possibility of remarrying someday, she never once considered this obnoxious man. Never.

Unlike many women, she was no novice when it came to her rights or how to protect her rights under the law. As a single woman and now, later, as a widow, her rights to do business or own property were equal to any man's. During her marriage, a separate legal estate had kept her assets under her control. Without one, everything she owned would have become her husband's property once she married.

Her dear Jonas had not objected to the existence of the separate estate when they married, and he had been perfectly content with Emma in full control of their financial affairs. Mr. Langhorne, on the other hand, was quite a different type of man. He either assumed she had no knowledge of how to protect her assets if she married him or that she would have been so flattered by his proposal, since she was now fifty-one years old, she would have learned, too late, that he had acquired the parcel of land on Hollaway Lane he truly wanted and much more.

He paled. "It was presumptive and very foolish of me," he admitted in a rare display of honesty.

She nodded and lowered her lashes. "And I accepted your gracious apology. I also recall declining not one but two different sums of money you offered for the parcel of land you apparently still want."

When his spectacles slipped down his nose again, he removed them, wiped them dry with a handkerchief, and put them back on. "Quite so. Quite so. But you did suggest there might be a way I would be able to convince you to sell me the land," he countered and spread out the papers he had placed on top of her desk. He rifled through them for several moments before handing one to her. "You should be very excited about this. I have further documentation to verify that everything in the letter is true and factual."

Curious, she skimmed the letter, then read it again more slowly. When she finished, she moistened her lips and cleared a lump of disbelief from her throat. She had been wrong about this man after all. He was not merely stubborn or persistent. He was devious beyond measure and apparently willing to go to amazing measures to guarantee his own success—assuming the document he had given to her was valid.

Still determined to emerge victorious in their battle of wills, she drew a deep breath, met his gaze, and held it. When she spoke, she chose her words carefully and kept her voice gentle, if only to make sure she would learn the full extent of his efforts before ushering him out the door for the last time. "I'm afraid I'm simply overwhelmed by your offer. I'm quite certain it took a man of considerable talent and determination to make this possible."

For the first time during their conversation, he relaxed his shoulders. The glint of confidence and superiority she had detected when he first arrived returned in full force. "As you know, until recently when I relocated to this area, I conducted most of my business in New York City. Regardless of what you must think of me, I am a man not without influence, both here and abroad. I simply made a few inquiries on your behalf," he replied.

He paused to flick a bit of dirt from his trousers. "I have no interest beyond playing an important role in the fascinating development of this region, but I have no doubt that a woman of your grace and stature would find living abroad among those of similar means far more, shall we say, suitable? It would mean liquidating the rest of your holdings here, but I would be willing to assist you in any way you might allow."

She clenched her jaw and set aside the outrageous notion he had spent the past few months investigating her circumstances or that he had done anything on her behalf without her knowledge. At the same time, she remembered he was now putting himself in a position to gain control of much more than one parcel of her land.

His assumption that simply because she was one of the wealthiest residents of the county she would be vain enough to be tempted by his offer sent her pulse into a gallop. Struggling for self-control, she braced both feet flat on the floor. "Are you quite sure this is legal?"

"It's all explained in the letter. There is proper documentation, as well, in the rest of the paper work."

She cocked a brow and fingered the letter. "I wasn't aware that titles in England were for sale."

"There's little in this world that's not available, given the right price," he noted confidently.

She nodded. "I'm sure you're aware that my grandfather came to this area from England as a young man and that he spent five years of his life fighting against England in the War for Independence, are you not?"

His eyes widened. "I'm not sure that I—"

"And that I lost my eldest brother, Samuel, when he gave his life for the same cause in the second war against England?" she asked as she placed the letter back onto her desk.

His cheeks reddened.

She sighed and shook her head. "My family's dedication and loyalty to this country have always been beyond question, just as our loyalty to the people of Candlewood has been a valued tradition. If

I agree to your proposal, accept an English title, and move to England, I'm afraid I'd be turning my back on everything my family has worked so hard to achieve. I hope you understand that I must honor my family, regardless of how fervently I might wish to claim the life you've offered to me."

She folded the papers together into a neat parcel again and held them out to him. "I'm so sorry. I wish you had discussed this matter with me in advance. You see, even if I did want to accept your offer, I could not. For the truth of the matter is, the parcel of land you so desperately want to buy is no longer mine to sell."

He pitched forward so abruptly his spectacles slipped and landed on his lap. "N–not yours to sell?"

She dabbed at a tear she forced in the corner of her eye. "I'm afraid not." She left the papers on her desk, rose, walked to the door and opened it, then turned to face him again. "I'm afraid I do need to get back to work. I trust you'll find some way to change the tenor of your day, just as I must try to forget that I let the opportunity to become Lady Garrett slip through my fingers."

He snatched the papers from her desk as he got to his feet. "Might I inquire as to who the new owner might be?"

She sighed. "You might inquire, but I'm not sure divulging that information to you will do much good. You see, there was a bit of a restriction attached to the sale. Given the price I was offered, I had no choice but to agree."

"Restriction?"

This time she did not have to force a smile. "The land itself has been placed in trust for twenty years. Until then, the land cannot be sold or developed or altered in any way. It's all perfectly legal, which I'm certain your lawyer will confirm when you consult him. In the meantime, I'm sure you'll find other ventures far more interesting to occupy your energies."

Langhorne grabbed his hat from a peg on the wall, plopped it on his head, and stiffened his back. He left without saying another word.

The moment he stepped out onto the porch, she shut the door, latched it, and leaned back against the solid wood before closing her eyes and whispering a prayer of gratitude that once and for all, Mr. Langhorne was gone.

"He's left? Already?"

Emma's eyes popped open and she smiled at her mother-in-law. "Yes, he's gone."

Mother Garrett narrowed her gaze. "What's that you said about maybe he'd be back to see me?"

"If he comes back, it won't be until . . . let's see, 1861."

"I'd be ninety-six by then," Mother Garrett countered with a snort.

"And I'll be seventy-one. Don't leave quite yet—this will take just a moment." Emma returned to her desk. "If I pen a note to Mr. Breckenwith to expect the two of us tomorrow morning, Ditty can take it to him this afternoon. While she's gone, I'll explain it all to you."

"I can't see any reason for me to go with you to see your lawyer."

"You need to write a will," Emma countered, refusing to even consider how her lawyer would react when she handed him this primitive bill of sale.

"A will? Why would I need a will? I don't own much of anything."

Emma pulled the paper that Mother Garrett had signed earlier from her pocket and held it up. "You do now that you're a land-owner. Or you will once you pay what you owe me."

Mother Garrett tilted her head a bit and frowned. "You sold

me the land he wanted, didn't you? Don't bother to deny it; I had a notion you were up to something like that. While you were with Mr. Langhorne, I had a very long chat with Frances. Go on. Write your note. By the time you finish up and get to the kitchen, I'll be finished, too."

Emma cocked her head. "Finished with what?"

"I'm not sure. I'll have to decide after you explain yourself." Her eyes began to sparkle. "I might be peeling potatoes. Or I might be packing my bag. If Frances can run away from home, I suppose I can, too, assuming I don't like what you have to say," she teased.

Emma was too stunned to reply before Mother Garrett turned and left the room, convinced Widow Leonard might have brought more, perhaps, than blessings to Hill House.

7

IF EMMA HAD NOT BEEN BORN FEMALE, she would have spent her life studying and practicing law. If she had not been widowed, she would still be operating the General Store instead of Hill House. More importantly at the moment, however, if she had not been in such a rush to be on time, she would have been sitting in Zachary Breckenwith's office wearing her finest bonnet.

Instead, she was resting on the sofa in the east parlor with a poultice propped against a goose-egg bump on the back of her head under the watchful gaze of Reverend Glenn and his faithful companion. She had no idea what Mother Garrett had used to make the poultice. She was as stingy with revealing her remedies as she was with her receipts.

Emma had no control over being born female or being widowed, but she did fault herself for ruining what should have been a productive and satisfying day taking care of a few legal matters and shopping in town. Her little mishap this morning had little to do with becoming as clumsy as Ditty, as she had first feared, and everything to do with being hasty, pure and simple. Instead of taking her time to get ready, she had foolishly rushed about her room. Unfortunately, she had gotten tangled up in her petticoats, tripped, and hit her head on the corner of the chest at the foot of her bed.

Though her head still ached, her vision was clear. Offering him a weak smile, she looked at the minister, who sat in an uphol-stered chair at the far end of the sofa near her feet. "I'm truly feeling much better. You really don't have to stay and keep me company."

"Then what would I do with myself?" he teased as he mas-saged the back of his weakened left hand.

"I believe you might be keeping Widow Leonard company. Instead, she's . . ." She let out a sigh and tried not to worry about the fact that Mother Garrett had insisted on keeping the ten-o'clock appointment with Emma's lawyer on her way to ordering supplies at the General Store and taking Widow Leonard with her to get the sewing thread she needed.

"They'll be fine," he offered, as if able to read her thoughts. "It'll do them both good to be out and about for a spell."

When Emma tried to shift her position to catch more of the morning sun that was pouring through the windows, she put too much pressure on her head and gritted her teeth. "As a point of fact, I was looking forward to being out and about myself. I don't often get a full day to spend as I please, especially not a day as glorious as this one. The sun is bright and warm, there's a bit of a breeze, and yet here I sit with a lump on my head and my day ruined, all because I was in such a rush."

Reverend Glenn moved his hand up to massage his weakened forearm. "It's not easy for any of us to accept disappointments or troubles of any kind, even little ones, regardless of how strong or how weak our faith might be."

Her cheeks flushed. Whining about a minor fall to a man who had lost both his pulpit and his independence to a stroke was truly insensitive. The notion he might be struggling to accept his infirmity and his reduced circumstances was completely foreign to her perceptions of him. "I'm sorry. I don't believe I've ever told you how much it means to me—to all of us—to have you here at Hill House. I never realized how difficult it might be for you, though."

"There are days when I wonder why I've been given such a heavy cross to carry," he admitted as he leaned down and patted the sleeping Butter on the head. "Other days I'm content enough to set my disappointments aside and enjoy the blessings I do have. Like you," he said. "For all the days and months I've been living here, I can't remember the last time we had the chance to spend time with each other without distractions."

A loud crash overhead told her Ditty had apparently knocked something over or dropped something while cleaning, and she sighed. "Obviously, we're not without any distractions today. Not with Ditty around," she teased.

Chuckling, he pulled on his chin. "Even so, I can't say I'd be happier to live alone again. After Mrs. Glenn died, the parsonage was very . . . quiet."

"We don't find quiet here at Hill House very often, at least not during canal season, do we?"

"Indeed we don't. We do have a lot of good conversation, companionship, and laughter. Great blessings all," he murmured. "I'm a bit curious, though. You don't make much mention of the General Store. After operating it all those years, I assume you must miss it—at least occasionally."

She cocked her head. "I think I do. Sometimes. But the older I got, the more I realized that I wouldn't be able to operate the store forever." She chuckled. "My grandmother and my mother warned me I would feel that way one day. Working six days a week from dawn to candlelighting can wear a body down. I tried to explain that to Ralph Iverson when he bought the General Store. I only hope he fared better after he sold the store to Wayne Atkins."

She looked around the parlor and smiled. "Here at Hill House, my life has a different cadence. During the season, I'm still working as long and as hard as I always did at the General Store, even though I have a lot more help here. But come November, I can look forward to a good five or six months of slowing down a bit. I'm not sure how many days Mother Garrett has left on this earth, but I like the idea she doesn't have to work as hard as she's had to, working alongside me all these years."

He began to massage the weakened muscles in his left thigh. "Slowing down is a challenge for me. I suppose it might be for her, too. Widow Leonard doesn't lack the energy of a woman twenty years younger, either."

"Which is precisely why I'm worried about what sort of trouble the two of them might stir up in town," Emma admitted.

"I doubt either James or Andrew would be about during the week at this time of year. They're too busy finishing the last of the harvesting and such. Besides, I've known both of the Leonard boys all their lives. They wouldn't cause their mother any trouble in town."

Emma adjusted the poultice Mother Garrett had fixed for her. "I hadn't thought about either of them being about town. I'm more concerned about the gossipmongers who will find plenty to chew on when they see Widow Leonard. Once they discover she's living and working here at Hill House, they won't be satisfied until they learn every lurid detail of why she's no longer living with one of her sons."

She paused and locked her gaze with his. "You've spent a lot of time with her. I was wondering . . . that is, has she shared whatever it is that has caused such a rift between her sons? Not that I'm asking you to break any confidences," she added quickly. "If you don't want to discuss it, I certainly understand."

He blushed. "We've talked some about it, but mostly we've been talking about me, or should I say Mrs. Glenn. Letty and Frances were friends growing up, you know. Their families both left New Jersey to move here together."

Emma sat up straighter. "No, I didn't know," she said, although she did vaguely recall the gossip ignited by his marriage to a woman some twelve or thirteen years his senior.

"I'm hopeful she'll seek our advice, if she needs it. Until then, I'm very grateful you've made a place for her here. It's almost like having Letty back with me."

No sooner did the front bell ring, startling both of them, than Liesel charged down the hall past the parlor to the front door. After a brief but muffled conversation, Emma heard two sets of footsteps approaching: one light, the other heavier. To her surprise, Liesel led Zachary Breckenwith into the parlor.

An uncommonly tall man, he was impeccably dressed in a dark serge suit, as usual, and carried himself with a confidence that stopped just short of arrogance. Although they were nearly the same age, he looked a good bit younger. While her own blond hair was streaked with white, there was not a single strand of gray in his dark hair, and she suspected it was because he simply did not allow it. Not wanting to appear weak, Emma sat up straight, tucked the poultice under the cushion, and carefully avoided touching the lump on her head. She was also vain enough to quickly smooth her hair and be grateful she had chosen a winter green linen gown to wear on her outing today, rather than one of her usual cotton work dresses.

"Since you weren't able to keep your appointment this morning, Mr. Breckenwith asked to see you," Liesel announced.

"Assuming you're feeling well enough," the lawyer said, and his dark eyes shimmered with concern. "I understand you had a fall of some sort."

"I'm feeling much better. Thank you. But I didn't expect you to come all the way up here," Emma replied.

"There's important business we need to discuss," he said curtly.

"If you'll both excuse me, I think I'll just take myself to the kitchen for a cup of coffee," the minister suggested.

When he started to edge forward in his seat, the lawyer shook his head. "Please stay here. I'd prefer to meet with Widow Garrett in her office."

Irritated by how adroitly her lawyer placed himself in control, considering he was in her home, Emma got to her feet. When she did not experience a wave of dizziness, she managed a genuine smile. "Liesel, bring Reverend Glenn a cup of coffee, won't you?" She turned her attention to her lawyer, determined to be hospitable despite her annoyance with him. "Would you care for some refreshment? Coffee? Tea?"

He held up his hand. "Thank you, but no. I promised Aunt Elizabeth I'd be home in an hour for dinner, which reminds me: Since I mentioned I was coming here, Widow Garrett asked me to let you know she and Widow Leonard will be having dinner in town."

Emma's eyes widened. "They're not coming home for dinner?"

He shrugged and did not hide a grin. "Apparently not."

"Where? Where are they having dinner?"

"She didn't say, and I didn't ask. She did say that she expected they'd be home by late afternoon," he offered as he followed her to her office.

Emma walked just a little more slowly than usual so she would not slip or fall again, most especially in front of him. By the time they had taken their respective places in her office, she was grateful to be off her feet again. "I trust you had no trouble helping Mother Garrett draw up her will?"

He shrugged. "Young Jeremy has only been in Candlewood to study law with me for the past six months, but he could have done it just as easily. The woman owns little enough, though she did mention something about a parcel of land she had recently acquired from you. In any event, her will has been duly written, signed, and witnessed."

"Good," she murmured. From the middle drawer, she took the paper she and Mother Garrett had signed yesterday to transfer ownership of the property on Hollaway Lane and handed it to him. "I'm not sure if this is exact enough. You might need to rewrite it or do what you lawyers do."

He leaned forward to get the paper and sat back again to read it. When he finished, he shook his head and frowned. "I won't bother asking why you didn't have me draw this up for you, but you're right. I need to better identify the land in question by using the survey data, but a simple addendum will do for that."

He folded the paper again. "I must admit I'm rather amazed that you sold this particular parcel of land at all. The last time we discussed the matter, which was after Mr. Langhorne asked me to intervene on his behalf, you were quite adamant that the land would not be sold under any circumstances."

When she started to protest, he silenced her by raising his hand. "Am I surprised you sold the land to your mother-in-law to outwit that man? In truth, not a bit. Not with the restrictions you placed on the transfer. But I am shocked at the sum you accepted. Then again, I've been your lawyer for five years now and should know better."

"I'm quite certain you're not as shocked as Mr. Langhorne will be when he finds out once the sale becomes a matter of public record, which will do little to support my reputation as a clever businesswoman. Not when the selling price of fifty cents is recorded. Anyone with a pinch of business sense will know that land is priceless."

Mr. Breckenwith's frown deepened. "I wouldn't say priceless, exactly, but since it's the last parcel of land in Candlewood proper with direct access to the canal, I'd say the land is very, very valuable. Definitely worth a small fortune, and one you might very well need, which I would have been able to explain to you if you had consulted me first before coming up with your scheme."

Stung by his reprimand, she stiffened her back. "As you well know, I'm quite aware of my holdings, as well as my needs. I have fortune enough—"

"You have far less than you think," he insisted. He took a packet of papers from his vest pocket and laid it on top of her desk. "You can read the correspondence I received six weeks ago, along with the documents related to the subsequent work I've done on your behalf, and draw your own conclusions—or I can explain them. In either case, you have much more to worry about than how Mr. Langhorne or the general public will react to the sum paid for that particular parcel of land you sold to your mother-in-law."

A chill inexplicably raced up her spine, and Emma let the packet of papers lay untouched. "Correspondence? Why would you be receiving correspondence that concerns me? Or wait six weeks to bring something to my attention when you obviously believe it's important enough to adversely affect the extent of my fortune?"

"I have the correspondence because six weeks ago Mr. Atkins at the General Store didn't know what to do with a letter addressed to 'a lawyer in Candlewood.' Fortunately, he gave it to me when I stopped to collect my mail. I didn't bring it to your attention until I confirmed the veracity of the letter. I know you well enough by now to suspect you would not have followed my advice and fully investigated the matter but would have chosen to ignore the letter as a hoax of some sort."

Emma decided to overlook his complaint about her instead of arguing. She moistened her lips and glanced at the papers but still resisted the temptation to read them. Since Mr. Breckenwith was so self-confident, she decided to let him explain the contents of the correspondence to her. She could always read everything later for herself. "Perhaps you should simply tell me who sent the letter and how I'm involved. Succinctly," she insisted, fearing he might prolong her unease by being overly thorough.

He captured her gaze and held it. "In a nutshell, Widow Garrett, you don't own Hill House."

8

I DON'T OWN HILL HOUSE," Emma said quietly, as if repeating her lawyer's words might help her to make sense of them.

The very idea she did not own Hill House was so ludicrous she might have laughed out loud, but Mr. Breckenwith's expression was too grim and his gaze too intense. Gooseflesh dimpled her arms, and her heart began to race. "Perhaps you might explain what you mean. Less succinctly, if you please."

He nodded but held his back ramrod straight and his gaze steady. "Four years ago you barged into my office with Michael Spencer, the lawyer who represented the estate of the late Richard Hughes, who had built Hill House for his wife, then abandoned it after she died in childbirth, along with her babe."

She blinked hard. "I wouldn't say 'barged.' I simply arrived without making an appointment with you beforehand."

He ignored her protest and continued. "Against my very specific advice, and without any prior indication you were even considering the idea, you bought Hill House that very day and paid quite an extraordinary sum for a property that had been abandoned for nearly a decade."

"You reviewed the paper work," Emma countered, as frustrated by him now as she had been on that occasion four years ago when she indeed purchased the property.

"That's true. Unfortunately, as you know, I've been trying unsuccessfully to get the deed properly recorded with the courts ever since." His gaze hardened. "As you also might recall, I specifically cautioned you against buying Hill House and, more particularly, against selling the General Store, moving into the house, and starting any renovations until we had a deed in hand."

Her cheeks burned. "Go on. I suppose you're going to tell me now that Mr. Spencer was some sort of an imposter."

He let out a sigh. "On the contrary. As far as I've been able to determine, Spencer was the lawful executor for the Hughes estate. Unfortunately, he absconded with your funds, along with the rest of the proceeds of the estate, before filing anything with the courts, and he's disappeared, no doubt enjoying his ill-gotten gains at your expense, as well as several others."

Denial and disbelief overwhelmed Emma's sense of outrage, and she blinked back tears of frustration. "But I acted in good faith! And it's been four years. Four years! If . . . if what you're saying is true, why did it take so long for anyone to . . . to discover what he had done?"

He sighed again. "A combination of factors. From all I've been able to learn, the heir is a rather distant relative who was completely unaware of his relative's death, as well as the inheritance. The only reason this has come to light is because one of the other of Spencer's victims, if you will, hired a lawyer to investigate and try to track down the man, and here we are. The court has appointed a new lawyer to serve as executor, one Jonathan Meyer of Philadelphia, which is where the late Mr. Hughes had his primary residence. Here . . . let me find his letter for you."

While Mr. Breckenwith sorted through the papers, Emma struggled for control, but she was unable to keep her heart from pounding hard against the wall of her chest. Without Hill House, she had no home, no purpose in her life. She had sold her General Store to come here, certain that this was where God wanted her to be, certain that the answer to the loneliness that filled her heart lay in doing His will and serving others at Hill House.

She had lost her Jonas. One by one, each of her sons had married and moved away. First Warren. Then Benjamin. And finally Mark. When he had married four and a half years ago, she had felt so alone and so empty . . . and so anxious to find new meaning to her life. She had prayed for God to show her how to fill her life with new meaning.

When Mr. Spencer arrived in Candlewood and offered to sell Hill House to her, she was convinced this was the answer she had been praying to receive. Despite Mr. Breckenwith's advice, she had pushed ahead, only to discover now that he had been right.

"Here it is," he said as he skimmed the letter again.

Emma struggled to find her voice. "Is it possible to simply buy Hill House again? I . . . I could manage to do that if I sold off some of my land." She was all too aware that she might have to rescind the sale of that parcel of land to Mother Garrett and actually sell it to someone else, although her mouth soured at the prospect of letting Mr. Langhorne acquire it.

Her lawyer set the letter aside. "Apparently that's not an option—at least not right now."

A band of terror tightened around her chest, making it difficult for her to draw a breath. For modesty's sake, she resisted loosening the collar on her bodice and took slow, measured breaths instead. She had never before encountered a problem she could not fix with either her wits or her fortune. Never.

Losing Hill House affected more than just Emma. Mother Garrett would be forced to move out, and so would Reverend Glenn, not to mention Widow Leonard. To make matters worse— if that were possible—even if Emma did buy another home for all of them to share, everyone in town would know what had happened, destroying the reputation as a good businesswoman she had worked so hard to establish and maintain.

Imagining someone else moving into Hill House made her tremble. She laced her fingers together, laid her hands on her lap, and kept her gaze downcast to avoid seeing the smug look on her lawyer's face now that he had been proven right.

"Widow Garrett?"

When she finally looked up at him, his gaze was gentle and understanding. "I know how much Hill House means to you. Let's not give up hope. Not quite yet."

She swallowed hard and blinked back tears. "Why not? You just said buying Hill House again wasn't an option."

"I believe I said not right now," he countered. "Mr. Meyer indicated in his letter that the heir would like to see Hill House first before he decides whether or not he wants to sell it."

Her heart skipped a beat and filled with hope. "He's coming here? To Candlewood?"

"Yes, but I'm not certain when that will be. Meyer didn't offer any explanation or any specific time to expect the heir. Perhaps he's traveling or abroad. In any event, Meyer assured me you could stay at Hill House and continue to operate it until the heir arrives."

She bolted forward in her seat and braced the palms of her hands on the top of her desk. Disbelief pounded through her veins. "Just sit and wait? That's what he expects? I'm supposed to live here, literally in limbo, until the heir decides it's convenient to schedule a visit? I can't do that. I need an answer now. I deserve an answer."

Breckenwith's gaze hardened. "I'm afraid you don't have a choice in the matter. He could have had you evicted from the property," he warned. "Instead, he's graciously allowing you to stay. Between now and whenever he chooses to visit—which I presume will be no longer than a matter of months—you should be considering all of your options."

She tilted up her chin. "The only option I find acceptable is to remain at Hill House."

"As your lawyer, as well as your financial advisor, I'd strongly suggest that you carefully consider what you'll do if you can't stay at Hill House. Think about opening a business of some sort, if you like, or simply purchasing another home. You might want to think about building a home on one of the parcels of land you own. In other words, hope for the best but be prepared for the worst by having something in mind in the event you're forced to leave Hill House."

She rejected his suggestions outright. "I'd rather be more direct. What if I fight this in court?" she asked, despite her reluctance to have her situation made public, which a court battle would do.

"You'll lose."

"You're that positive?" she snapped.

"Absolutely."

She swallowed what was left of her pride and finally admitted defeat. "Fine. I'll consider other options. Soon. But no one, I mean no one, can know about this . . . this problem. I won't have Mother Garrett or Reverend Glenn upset on my account, and I won't have gossipmongers gloating over the mistake I've made."

He flinched. "I know my ethical responsibilities."

"You're right; I'm sorry. I'm just a little bit undone by your news," Emma said and handed him back the packet of papers as a show of good faith.

"Understandably so, which is why I thought it best to discuss this matter privately in your office, instead of the parlor. Despite the fact you found my suggestion to do so a bit, shall we say, arrogant?" he said with a slight twinkle in his eyes.

She felt a blush steal up her neck to warm her cheeks. Unlike Jonas, who had never questioned Emma, Zachary Breckenwith challenged most everything she said or did, forcing her to re-examine her position or her decision, which made her strive all the more to be efficient as well as precise in her dealings with him. Unfortunately, he also seemed able to know what she was thinking, no matter how hard she tried to hide it. "There's a fine distinction between arrogance and confidence, which perhaps I misjudged earlier," she admitted.

He smiled. "Understandably so."

When he rose to leave, she urged him back into his seat. "I do have another matter I need to discuss with you."

He sat back in his seat and cocked a brow.

Briefly she explained the situation with Aunt Frances and her estrangement from her sons. By the time she finished, he was frowning. Deeply. Relieved that his concern for Aunt Frances obviously matched her own, she felt for once that he might be more ally than foe. "I was hoping you might be able to reassure me that her sons won't be able to force her to leave, and I'm grateful you understand my position in offering her a place to stay."

"On the contrary," he insisted, instantly proving her perceptions of him to be wrong. "Given the circumstances that brought me to Hill House today, the worst thing you could do is embroil yourself in a family squabble, especially when you don't know what James and Andrew Leonard are arguing about to such an extent that their mother felt compelled to run off to Hill House. Any sort of scandal or dissension that involves Hill House could undoubtedly affect the owner's decision of whether or not to sell Hill House to you, assuming he decides to sell at all. As your lawyer, I'd advise against getting involved. In any way."

She narrowed her gaze. "Then what do you suggest I do? Put Widow Leonard out on the street to fend for herself? She's desperate and heartbroken, not to mention the fact that she's eighty-one years old! She needs someone to help her."

"I'm your lawyer," he countered. "It's my duty to look out for your interests and your interests alone. Assuming you're serious about holding on to Hill House, there's no other way I can suggest you proceed, except to remove yourself from this family feud as quickly and as quietly as you can."

Emma tilted up her chin and stiffened her back. "Well, I'm not going to ask her to leave. I simply can't. And I won't. And if the owner of Hill House is any kind of man, he'll understand that I can't turn my back on an elderly widow when she's come to me for help."

She locked her gaze with Breckenwith's. "I would have expected you would understand and be more supportive."

His countenance softened. "Setting my role as your lawyer aside, I do understand. You're a caring woman of deep conviction who is passionately concerned about helping others. Quite frankly, I'd be more than disappointed if you did anything less than what you've already done for the poor woman. Unfortunately, I don't have the pleasure of letting my personal opinions or feelings sway my professional judgment as a lawyer or to compromise my responsibilities to you as my client. Just be careful. Be very careful not to get overly involved."

Stunned, Emma barely had time to register his most provocative words before Liesel charged into the office without knocking. Tears glistened on her pale cheeks, and her words tumbled out in a rush that left no moment for her to draw a breath. "I'm sorry to interrupt, Widow Garrett, but you need to come to the parlor—the west parlor. Right away. Mr. Breckenwith needs to come, too. Mother Garrett won't be coming home. And Aunt Frances won't be coming home. The sheriff is here. Sheriff North is here. Oh, hurry! Please! There's trouble. Terrible trouble."

Emma bolted from her chair and ran to the girl's side. "Calm down, child. Calm down."

"I'm trying," she cried, "but he's . . . no, I mean they. They've been arrested—Mother Garrett and Aunt Frances have been arrested!"

When Emma cast a frantic look in Mr. Breckenwith's direction, he was already on his feet. "It appears I may be late for dinner with Aunt Elizabeth after all," he said and followed her out of the room.

9

A<small>N HOUR LATER THE TWO ALLEGED</small> criminals were not exactly in a jail cell, huddling together and terrified by their ordeal, as Emma had first imagined. Instead, Emma found them in the kitchen of Sheriff North's home, where he had kindly taken them out of respect for Emma, if not for the two elderly women themselves.

While Sheriff North and her lawyer waited in the parlor, Emma stood unobserved in the doorway to the kitchen. There Joy North tended to a pot on the cookstove emitting tantalizing aromas. Emma shook her head in disbelief. Mother Garrett and Widow Leonard were sitting side-by-side at the kitchen table, and each held one of the North girls. Widow Leonard held four-month-old Pamela, while Patricia, ten months older, was in Mother Garrett's arms. For a moment, Emma almost envisioned herself sitting with them, with her two-year-old granddaughter, Grace, cradled on her lap. But Grace, as well as her big sister, Deborah, was far away, living in New York City, where Emma's oldest son, Warren, operated a dry goods store with his wife, Anna.

Unlike the two alleged criminals, however, Emma had neither the time nor the inclination to relax within the womb of female domesticity that prevailed here or to dream about holding any of her grandchildren on her lap. "I see you're both quite recovered from your ordeal," she noted as she made her presence known and entered the kitchen.

Mother Garrett looked up from the baby in her arms for a brief moment to catch Emma's gaze and frowned. "Shoplifting and disturbing the peace are crimes better suited for a pair of young rascals, not two elderly widows. Anyone with a lick of sense would recognize what happened for what it was—an oversight and a bit of a display of temper," she crooned, so intent on rocking the sleeping baby in her arms she did not bother to look up at Emma again. "I told you my daughter-in-law would come and straighten out this misunderstanding, didn't I, my precious little dumpling?"

Joy caught Emma's gaze, rolled her eyes, and held up one hand, obviously content to stay out of the conversation.

Mother Garrett's compatriot, however, shifted the baby she was holding to rest upon her shoulder. While Widow Leonard patted Pamela's back, she returned Emma's gaze with a troubled one of her own. "You can't know how terrible I feel about having to ask you to get up from your sickbed to help me."

"Us. Help us," Mother Garrett corrected.

Emma crossed the room and sat down at the table with her back to Joy North, but across from Mother Garrett and Widow Leonard.

"There's no sense pretending I'm not guilty of doing some-thing wrong, but Frances is completely innocent. She did not deliberately take those two spools of thread and walk out of the General Store without paying for them," Mother Garrett insisted.

"We were so busy chatting, I plumb forgot," Widow Leonard

offered and made a clucking sound with her mouth. "I can't believe the same thing hasn't happened before to other women. Everything is so different these days. With the town growing so fast, there are new shops everywhere. Main Street has changed each time I make it to town, which I suppose isn't odd since I only come to town every few years. The shopkeepers aren't the same, either. When you owned the General Store, you'd never have had a pair of old ladies like us arrested."

Mother Garrett stopped rocking the baby for a moment and cocked her head. "In truth, I seem to recall when Emma did do just that. Jonas was still alive, remember, Emma? To all appearances, we thought the folks who had come into the store were good people heading west who had come in for supplies. Instead, they were just a passel of thieves. The whole lot of them!"

"That may well be," Widow Leonard countered before Emma could comment. "But I'm no thief and neither are you. And I don't believe what you said about being guilty of disturbing the peace, either. That young Mr. Atkins deserved every reprimand and every smack he got from you. Some shopkeeper he's turning out to be."

Emma stared at her mother-in-law and wondered if this was the same woman she had known for nearly thirty years. "You hit the man? You actually hit him?"

"On his hand. Twice. What was I supposed to do? He had such a tight hold on Frances, I was afraid he'd crush her arm." She snorted. "From the way he described it to the sheriff, you would have thought I hit him with a shovel or a hammer instead of my reticule. He wouldn't have been hit at all if he had let go of her like I told him."

A band of frustration tightened around Emma's head so hard, the front of her head actually hurt more than the lump she still carried on the back. Even if the legal owner of Hill House might find it hard to accept Emma's involvement in the Leonard feud, she doubted he would be willing to overlook the fact that not one but two residents of Hill House had been arrested for shoplifting.

She leaned an elbow on the table and rubbed her forehead with her fingertips. "Mr. Breckenwith is in the parlor. He's agreed to represent both of you if we can't get Mr. Atkins to withdraw his complaints against you."

Widow Leonard's hand stilled against the baby's back. For the first time, her gaze grew very troubled. "He was mighty angry. I doubt he'd be willing to do that," she murmured as her bottom lip began to tremble. "When my sons hear news of this, they'll be convinced I've gone simple and need a keeper. They might even let me spend a day or two in jail."

"That's nonsense. You don't need a keeper any more than I do," Mother Garrett argued.

For the moment Emma was sorely tempted to beg to differ, but her mother-in-law gave her no opportunity to voice her opinion. "Neither one of us is going to spend any time in jail, and we don't need a lawyer, either. Emma will see that everything is put right again, won't you, Emma?"

Emma pressed her fingertips against her temple to ease the pounding in her head. "I can try. I'd rather not involve Mr. Breckenwith unless it's absolutely necessary." She looked from one woman to the other. She was willing to intervene on their behalf, but she did not want to approach Mr. Atkins unless she was assured she knew the full story. "Before I go to see Mr. Atkins, is there anything else I should know about your . . . encounter? Something you may have left out or perhaps merely overlooked?"

Mother Garrett stiffened her hold on the baby in her arms. "Certainly not."

"I can't think of a thing," Widow Leonard insisted.

Emma nodded, rose, and turned her attention to the sheriff's wife. "I hate to impose on your hospitality any further, but would it be possible for me to leave and come back later to pick up my mother-in-law and Widow Leonard?"

"In truth, they've both been such a help with the babies, I was hoping they could stay awhile longer. If you like, I can hold dinner until you return," Joy suggested.

"No, thank you. You all go ahead and eat. I'll send Mr. Breckenwith home, too, so he can have dinner with his aunt. I think I'll have more of an appetite after I've resolved this matter with Mr. Atkins."

She had gotten halfway across the kitchen when Widow Leonard's voice rang out. "Wait! I have thought of one thing."

When Emma turned around, the woman had stretched out one of her arms. Two spools of white thread rested in the center of her palm. "I . . . I just reached into my pocket for my handkerchief and found these," she insisted. Her eyes misted with tears. "I . . . I suppose in all the uproar, I never did give them back to Mr. Atkins."

Emma retraced her steps, retrieved the two spools of thread, and looked from one woman to the other again. "There's nothing more, I hope."

When both women shook their heads, Emma returned to the parlor, where Mr. Breckenwith and Sheriff North were still waiting. She addressed the sheriff first, since she was in his home. "I believe your wife has dinner ready now. In the meantime, I'm off to the General Store in search of Mr. Atkins to see if I can't convince him to drop the complaints."

The sheriff shook his head. "I tried. I can only hope you might fare better than I did. I'm not taking Mr. Atkins' side, but to be fair, the man's had a rough go of it, especially this past week when he got involved in a bit of a brawl trying to protect his store. With the crowds of people here for all the Founders' Day celebrations, he's lost a fair bit of stock to shoplifters. Not that he hasn't had his hands full with the men who work on the packet boats and freight barges. Those men just hit town and leave within an hour or two, so he has little chance to recoup his losses."

Zachary Breckenwith took a step forward. "I can't see what harm it would do to try asking him to drop the charges. I'll come along," he offered, locking his gaze with hers. "The quicker we resolve the problem, the better it will be for all concerned."

Unnerved by the protective concern simmering in his dark eyes, Emma swallowed hard but held his gaze. "I'd prefer to try speaking to him alone first. I think he'd feel less threatened and more inclined to let the complaint drop. If not, I won't hesitate to have you intervene. If you hurry, you'll still be home in time to have dinner with your aunt."

She noted the look of disappointment in his gaze but turned her attention back to the sheriff. "In either case, Sheriff, will I be able to take both Mother Garrett and Widow Leonard home with me when I return?"

The sheriff held up his hands in mock surrender. "I'm running for election again next year. I'm not locking up these elderly women in my jail."

Emma let out a sigh. "Maybe not, but I'm sorely tempted to keep them both under lock and key at Hill House," she muttered under her breath, then took her leave to try to unravel today's misunderstanding.

The distance between the sheriff's home and the General Store was a matter of less than half a mile, at most, but it took her a good while to reach Main Street because she still was not feeling fully recovered from her fall. The air was laced with the scent of dinners bubbling on cookstoves in nearby homes, yet the wagon traffic was heavy and mostly headed, she noticed, for the warehouses built along the canal.

She had easy going on the planked sidewalk, for foot traffic was light. The closer she got to the General Store, however, the more she worried about whether or not her attempt to settle this misunderstanding could be resolved. Rather than dissolve into a panic, which she could ill afford, she kept calm by focusing on the changes at the southern end of Main Street, where the General Store had once stood alone. The First Bank of Candlewood, which had opened some three years back, was a solid brick building, almost as impressive as the Emerson Hotel or Town Hall. A host of new wooden storefronts lined both sides of the street now and offered a variety of eastern and foreign goods carried to the heart of Candlewood from New York City by way of the Erie Canal. She wondered how soon it would be before the town of Candlewood evolved into a city.

It had been four short years since she had sold the General Store, but she passed by shops now specializing in goods that ranged from French tableware to the finest in ladies' continental fashions, a confectionary with a sign announcing the arrival of a new shipment of Belgian chocolates, and a millinery that offered the latest rage in women's headgear imported directly from England.

Given the international flavor of the competition now facing the General Store, Mr. Langhorne's assumption she would be tempted to sell her land in exchange for an English title did not seem outlandish at all. Emma noted he would be very pleased to discover she did not actually own Hill House, but pushed away the thought to remain focused on the task at hand.

In truth, if he had bothered to study her likes and dislikes, he would not have been surprised to find her yearning for the very American, very practical staples still available within the walls of the building her grandparents had built.

When she finally reached the General Store, she stood just outside the door for a moment to gather her thoughts and her wits. She was wary about the reception she would receive, since Mr. Atkins had not been very polite to her previously, but she was quite certain her arrival would not go unnoticed by either the shoppers or the proprietor of the store. She only hoped no one would discover that her heart was racing, her legs felt as wobbly as a toddler's, and her stomach was doing flip-flops because she was still undecided about what approach she should take with him.

Based on her previous encounters with Mr. Atkins, being coy was out of the question. Whether or not she should be forceful or more conciliatory, she decided, would be entirely up to him. In either case, she prayed God would touch Mr. Atkins' heart and make him receptive to her pleas to withdraw his complaints so Mother Garrett and Widow Leonard could return to Hill House.

Emma had not been to the General Store for some time, although Mother Garrett had been here often to order supplies. More than a little anxious, she slipped one hand into her pocket, held tight to her keepsakes, and let the memories of all the years she had spent here in this store ease the tremblings within her. Faced with the realization that she might have made a terrible mistake by selling the General Store, should she ultimately lose Hill House, Emma opened the door and walked inside.

10

E MMA TOOK TWO STEPS into the store and rocked back on
her heels. While the sound of the front bell faded, she stared
wide-eyed around the store. Although the smell of old wood min-
gled with the odors coming from the barrels of pickles and salted
fish were all too familiar, the once always orderly store was now a
virtual mishmash of disorder and chaos. Wooden shelves and tables
once neatly stocked with dry goods were now cluttered and jum-
bled. Glass in most of the display cases had been removed, leaving
the fragile contents vulnerable to pilfering or damage by careless
shoppers.

Shocked—yet helpless to restore the sense of order she had
fought to maintain in this store for so many years—she managed
her way to the counter, where she anchored herself with her back
to the other shoppers. Ignoring their hushed whispers, she glanced
at the numerous trinkets that littered the top of the counter,
resisted the urge to sweep them away so the counter would be as
neat as she had once kept it, and waited for Mr. Atkins to appear.

When he emerged from behind the very same curtain she had

hung to separate the front of the store from a storage area and a staircase that led to the living quarters on the second and third floors, she nearly gasped. The young man, barely thirty and still single, could no longer boast the good looks that had inspired many a young woman in Candlewood to set her cap for the handsome newcomer. A bruise marred his right cheek. A row of black stitches held a cut on his forehead closed, and a white cotton sling held his left arm against his body. He walked with the slow gait of a man three times his age.

From what she could see, he looked like a man who bore the brunt of a nasty fight, rather than a disagreement with a pair of elderly matrons. As he approached her carrying a small box, she saw the bruises on his face had already started to yellow and the skin around the stitches was puckered to the point the stitches would have to be removed soon.

Emma then remembered what the sheriff had said about the trouble Mr. Atkins had had last week with shoplifters. She was relieved that his most troubling injuries had been inflicted long before this morning and fought hard to meet his gaze instead of focusing on his wounds or the sling he wore.

He acknowledged her presence with a curt nod and set the box he had been carrying onto the counter.

"I wonder if I might trouble you for a moment of your time?" she ventured.

He swallowed hard. "I rather expected you would come. No, that's not true. In point of fact, I expected your lawyer," he said before turning his attention to one of his customers. "I found the hairbrush you wanted, Mrs. Simmons. I'll leave it here until you finish shopping," he suggested before turning back to meet Emma's gaze.

The whispers stopped and the shop grew very still. She

moistened her lips and lowered her voice to a whisper. "I wonder if I might impose on your goodwill and suggest we meet privately, as a courtesy?"

"I'm not sure I want to tackle the stairs again to go back up to my quarters. If you wouldn't mind, I can talk with you in the barter room in the back, but only for a few moments. As you might consider, I don't like leaving the store unattended for very long." A man of average stature, he motioned with his good arm for her to join him behind the counter.

Relieved, she rounded the end of the counter and followed him down well-worn floorboards behind the counter, beyond the curtain, and past wooden crates and barrels that lined either side of the passageway that led to the barter room. Each step, each familiar sight and smell, evoked one memory after another but also stirred not a single urge to turn back time so she could reclaim the life she had once known as owner of the General Store, despite her recent troubles. She also had no regret she had had three sons but no daughter to continue the tradition of passing down the store from mother to daughter.

He stepped aside to let her enter the barter room first. As she suspected, the windowless room itself was nearly empty and smelled musty. Several worn canvas aprons hung from pegs on the wall. Shelves lining the walls held more dust and cobwebs than goods traded for store merchandise, a clear indication that the town's economy had shifted from trade to cash.

"This room used to be chock-full," she noted. "It appears you might be better served with this area converted to serve another purpose," she suggested as she turned about.

He was standing just inside and to the right of the doorway, leaving a clear path of exit for her. His gaze clouded but not with the flash of resentment she had seen the first time she had offered him suggestions about how to operate the store.

Now closer to him, she saw that lines of fatigue etched his features. His eyes, streaked red, appeared dry from lack of sleep, and his clothes hung on his frame. He pressed the edge of his hand against his brow, closed his eyes for a moment before he let his hand drop, and cleared his throat. "Should I convert the barter room before or after the four hours of sleep I manage to get every night or before or after I have the full use of my arm again?"

"I'm sorry. I'm certain it's quite difficult operating the store on your own, let alone managing as you are."

He raised his hand as if to touch the stitches on his forehead, then let his hand drop. "It's a challenge, that's true enough." He lowered his gaze for a moment. When he looked at her again, his dark eyes were troubled, as if he were reliving the brawl the sheriff had mentioned. "I assume you've come to resolve the . . . the incident that occurred here this morning?"

She held tight to the keepsakes in her pocket and fingered the rough edges of the canvas cut from Jonas's work apron. "I have."

After drawing a deep breath, he squared his shoulders. "You once offered to assist me if I needed advice about operating the General Store," he said and ran his hand through his sandy hair. "As I recall, I responded rather abruptly in the negative."

She raised a brow. "You were impudent and rude."

He flinched. "I was warned you were not a woman to waste words."

"Only on occasion," she admitted, dismissing thoughts of her encounter only yesterday with Mr. Langhorne, as well as her meeting with her lawyer earlier. Her curiosity about Mr. Atkins grew, and she wondered if he might be establishing an opening for compromise whereby he might drop his complaint in exchange for her business advice. "May I assume you've changed your mind about asking for my help with the store?"

He shook his head. "If I hadn't put every coin I owned into purchasing the General Store, I would pack a bag, leave, and let the vultures feast on the contents of the store until they picked it clean."

"You're that disappointed?"

"No," he countered. His cheeks reddened. "I've been that angry. I work as hard as a man can work. My head barely hits the pillows before the sun brings another day of endless work. I don't bother most days to stop for much of a meal because I don't have the time or the know-how to make one. I exist on so little sleep, I can barely tend to one customer while another walks out the door without paying."

He paused and drew in a long breath. "What little hold I had on my temper is gone. I suppose my mother was right. My temper has been my undoing. Nevertheless, I cannot and will not make light of the matter. What happened here today with Widow Garrett and Widow Leonard was unconscionable. I should have known better than to leap to conclusions. I do know better. It's just that I . . . I'm so frustrated and so angry. . . ."

His distress unleashed compassion that rushed from her heart and washed away her surprise at his willingness to take full responsibility for the misunderstanding, as well as her previous impression of him. "You've forgotten that sometimes people simply make mistakes," she suggested. "You've been so consumed with making a living for yourself that you forgot that it's the way you live that matters most, not how much or how little you make. You've forgotten the most important rule a shopkeeper must follow."

He looked up. "Which is?"

"To remember to treat your customers with the respect and dignity they deserve. Most customers are good, honest, hardworking folks. That's not to say there aren't others whose goal is to cheat you out of collecting your due—there are—just as there are ways a wise shopkeeper can devise to keep his losses to a minimum."

Concerned she might have let the conversation drift too far away from the purpose of her visit, she locked her gaze with his. "How are you planning to set things right? You are planning to do that, aren't you, Mr. Atkins?"

His eyes widened. "Of course. I had planned to see the sheriff to withdraw my complaint as soon as I closed up for the day. I would have gone earlier, but I had no one to mind the store. I'm not sure if it's possible, and I wouldn't blame them for being cross with me, but I'd like to do something, anything, to make amends to both Widow Garrett and Widow Leonard."

"To see to it that word spreads so you won't lose more customers to the threat of your temper?"

"No," he argued. "To do what's right. No matter what I do, I don't think I'll ever get the image of those poor women sitting in a jail cell out of my mind."

She caught a grin before it spread beyond the corners of her mouth. "Actually, at this moment I believe they're having dinner with Sheriff North and his family at his home. Regardless, I'm not certain it's for me to say what you should do. You might want to ask them directly," she suggested.

He nodded. "Of course, but—"

"I don't believe it would take you that much time. I'd be happy to tend to your customers while you're gone. Is the cashbox still on the middle shelf behind the counter?" she asked. She removed her bonnet, hung it on a peg, and donned a work apron without waiting for him to reply.

He handed her a key he retrieved from his pocket. "The account book is there, too."

She slipped the key into her apron pocket. "If there's time, I might make a few changes in the store that you might find helpful."

He nodded again. "Anything. Change anything at all. And I'd still be grateful if you could suggest something I might take with me to give Widow Garrett and Widow Leonard."

She took a step, stopped, and retrieved the key, which she handed back to him. When he furrowed his brow, she shrugged her shoulders. "Assuming you're serious about taking something with you to help make amends, I think you might want to get some coins from the cashbox before you leave."

"Are you suggesting I . . . I *pay* them? Like I was paying some sort of fine?"

She chuckled, thinking there might be more than one reason why this man was still single. "My dear Mr. Atkins, I don't believe money ever tugged the strings of forgiveness in a woman's heart. I passed by a millinery shop on my way here. I'm thinking that perhaps a new bonnet. . . ?"

He grimaced. "You want me . . . you expect me to go into the millinery and pick out a . . . a lady's bonnet?"

"Not one. Two. One for Widow Garrett and one for Widow Leonard. I'm sure the shopkeeper will be able to guide your selections."

She took his good arm and escorted him back toward the front of the store. "One sure way to guarantee that gossipmongers, as well as the rest of your customers, notice your apology is to have both women parading about in fancy new bonnets the milliner will no doubt tell everyone were purchased by you. It might even be a good idea to escort the ladies home to Hill House before you come back to the store," she suggested, fully aware that he would have to escort them the full length of Main Street to get them back to Hill House.

When he slowed his pace, she patted his shoulder. "On the other hand, you might want to see your visit to the millinery store as taking the first step toward humility."

"I'm quite certain there will be many more," he murmured.

"Indeed," she whispered and waited while he opened the cashbox. She had lived with Mother Garrett for enough years to know that her heart was a forgiving one and she would very likely accept this young man's apology—eventually. She did not know Widow Leonard very well yet but suspected she would be just as forgiving.

He closed the cashbox and handed her back the key. "Before I take my leave, do you have any further suggestions?"

"Only one," she murmured and offered him a smile. "Just be sure to tell them both I'll be home for supper."

11

Emma trudged home to Hill House just before twi-light. Her shoes pinched her feet and her bonnet rubbed against the lump on the back of her head. Her skirts were dusted with grime and grit. Since she had skipped dinner, her stomach growled when she dared to think of food. When she finally approached the gate in the wrought iron fence that enclosed the front yard, she could not decide whether to collapse on one of the porch chairs or use what little energy she had left to manage her way to the kitchen for supper.

A good whiff of Mother Garrett's vegetable soup, a favorite of her youngest son, Mark, who now lived in Albany with his wife and two little ones, tempted her past the porch chairs and into the house. When she draped her bonnet on the hat rack, she spied herself in the mirror, but she was too tired to care that her blue eyes were streaked with weariness or that her chin was smudged with dirt to do more than rub it clean with her fingers. After smoothing her hair, she followed the sound of animated conver-sation that led her to the kitchen, took one step inside, and burst into a fit of giggles that had her leaning on the doorjamb for support.

Straight ahead, Reverend Glenn sat at his customary place at the head of the table. At the end closest to her, a bowl of soup and a plate piled high with bread sat waiting for her. In between, sitting at opposite places on either side of the table, was a vision that was pure ridiculousness.

She cupped her hand to her mouth, but she could not stop the giggles.

Mother Garrett looked up at her and sniffed. "We were just about ready to start without you. Liesel and Ditty took their suppers out to the gazebo. Reverend Glenn already said grace, so you'll have to say your own. Assuming you can compose yourself."

"Y-yes. I . . . I will," Emma stammered and looked away, only to find herself staring at Widow Leonard, which inspired yet another round of giggles. "I'm . . . I'm sorry," she managed and wiped the tears of laughter from her cheeks. "I think I've worked myself a mile past pure exhaustion."

From her seat directly across from Mother Garrett, Widow Leonard smiled, reached up, and patted the pomegranate bonnet she wore. "The color suits me, don't you think?"

Emma cleared her throat and slipped into her seat. "It's delightful."

"We thought you'd like to see us in our new bonnets. That's why we didn't take them off. I suppose we should remove them now," she suggested with a frown.

"No, please, leave them on," Emma insisted, unfolding her napkin and spreading it on her lap. After lacing her fingers together, she bowed her head and said grace quickly. After adding a prayer of gratitude that Mr. Atkins' apology had truly been accepted, she glanced at Widow Leonard again. "You're right. The color does suit you. The feather on the brim adds just the right touch."

The elderly widow blushed. "It's genuine emu, all the way from Australia. Imagine!"

Emma buttered a piece of thick, crusty bread, took a bite, and almost purred before she swallowed it and turned her attention to her mother-in-law. She cocked her head and studied the bonnet she wore. "I'm not sure what color you're wearing," she prompted. "If I look at it one way, it looks yellow. If I look at it another, it's more green than yellow."

Mother Garrett sniffed again. "It's called daffodil. The color is all the rage in bonnets, if you need to know, and this particular bonnet is one of a kind."

Emma leaned forward in her seat and poked her head forward to get a closer look. "Is that a bird's nest on the bonnet?"

Mother Garrett reached up and gently patted the brim. "It is, though it's not real. Neither are the flowers sitting in the nest, of course. Forget-me-nots don't bloom this time of year."

"I see," Emma managed, sitting back and starting in on her soup. Maybe if she concentrated on eating, she might not giggle again.

"You both look rather stunning in your new bonnets, if I may say so," the minister offered. He buttered a piece of bread and nonchalantly dropped it to the floor, where Butter was waiting. "I look forward to accompanying you both to services on Sunday, where I suspect you shall make a splendid entrance. I hope the ladies in attendance won't be so distracted they forget why we're all there," he cautioned.

"The ladies on Main Street today were distracted all to pieces as we strolled home with young Mr. Atkins," Widow Leonard noted with a twinkle in her eye.

Mother Garrett added a pinch of salt to her soup. "It's been a good many years since a head turned when either of us walked by, but I'm not foolish enough to think it was just the bonnets we wore. Given the unfortunate misunderstanding at the General Store today, I'd venture it was our being escorted by Mr. Atkins that had heads spinning and tongues wagging."

She narrowed her gaze and pointed the tip of her spoon at Emma. "I'd wager that new parcel of land I own that it was your idea to buy us both a new bonnet."

Emma coughed, quickly covered her mouth with her napkin, and nodded slightly toward the minister.

Mother Garrett's cheeks blushed pink, and she quickly corrected herself. "Oh . . . I meant only if I wasn't a churchgoing woman and I was prone to wagering, which I'm not. Definitely not," she insisted. She shook her head so hard in denial that the bird's nest flew off of her bonnet and landed smack in the center of Reverend Glenn's bowl.

Startled, Reverend Glenn stiffened, and the tips of his overlarge ears turned scarlet.

Mother Garrett gasped.

Widow Leonard's mouth dropped open.

Emma stared at her companions—the nest of forget-me-nots floating in the soup, the spreading stain on the minister's shirt—and dissolved into another fit of giggles that passed from one person to the next around the table. She was still giggling when she ladled the nest of flowers from the minister's soup and carried the soppy decoration to the sink.

After repeated apologies to the minister, Mother Garrett removed her bonnet and inspected the damage. "I'm not sure the bonnet has quite the same panache without the ornamentation."

"We can probably salvage the nest, but I'm not sure about the artificial flowers," Emma suggested, although the minister appeared too flabbergasted to be concerned with anything other than his shirt.

"You'd think the milliner would have sewn the decoration more securely. Once we clean it up, I'll do that for you," Widow Leonard offered as she removed her own bonnet.

"I'll just set these aside," Emma suggested, taking first one, then the other bonnet and hanging them both on pegs near the back door. When she returned to the table, she stopped by the minister's side and made sure she did not crowd Butter in the process. "May I get you more soup?"

"No, please don't bother. I believe I was nearly finished," he replied. He tugged at his soggy shirt, removed several chunks of carrot and a pair of peas stuck to the material, and chuckled as he slid them back into his bowl. "I haven't made a mess of myself like that since I was ten years old. Maybe I was eleven. We had little in those days, and I was so intent on finishing my porridge before my older brothers so I might have more, I knocked my bowl square into my father's lap. Needless to say, I learned my lesson that day."

He rose from the table. "If you ladies would excuse me, I'll take my leave and change into something drier."

"Bring the soiled shirt to me so I can set it to soak," Mother Garrett suggested.

He nodded and held on to the edge of the table for a moment while Butter slowly got to his feet. After he left the room, Emma took her place at the table again, buttered another chunk of bread, and polished it off in several bites.

With her cheeks still pinkly, Mother Garrett absently stirred her soup. "I'm so awfully embarrassed. I never should have worn my bonnet to the table. That's one lesson I've learned well today."

"We had good intentions," Widow Leonard offered. "We just

wanted to impress you, Emma dear." She dropped her gaze for a moment and glanced over at the bonnets hanging on the wall. "In hindsight, I suppose we were both just a tad vain, too. Or I was," she quickly added.

"No, you're right. I was vain, too," Mother Garrett insisted and reached across the table to pat her friend's arm. "There's no greater fool than an old woman."

"Or a pair of them."

Emma held silent. When she finished her soup, she set down her spoon and wiped her lips with her napkin. "I think you're both being a bit overzealous condemning yourselves. What just happened was an accident. You meant no harm."

Widow Leonard brightened. "After Mr. Atkins told the sheriff he wanted to withdraw his complaint, the sheriff said the very same thing. That taking the spools of thread out of the store was just an accident." She shook her head. "He lambasted that poor young man something fierce, in my view."

"Well, no one is going to reprimand either of you now. The minister's shirt can be laundered and the bonnet can be repaired. I would pray that neither one of you would grow morose about this incident at supper, which is more than I might hope for Mr. Atkins, who has much more regret on his plate than either of you," Emma argued.

"The poor man was utterly distraught when he spoke to us. He apologized profusely," Widow Leonard said pointedly.

Mother Garrett nodded. "He duly accepted his punishment, as well." She leaned toward Emma. "I venture to say we passed a good two dozen people when he escorted us back to Hill House, but he never faltered. Just walked straight and tall between us, even though we could all hear the twitters of gossip as we strolled the length of Main Street. I felt so sorry for him, I couldn't help but apologize for striking him, a man as injured as he was."

Widow Leonard sighed. "Poor man. I suggested we might stop in at the General Store to collect you so he didn't have to endure more, but he'd hear none of it. Insisted he'd bring us all the way home, he did, even though I tried to tell him I was partly at fault for the misunderstanding."

Emma looked from one woman to another. "Can I assume, since all has been forgiven, that we might not expect any further problems with Mr. Atkins or that we might go shopping a bit more carefully in the future?"

"Certainly," they replied in unison.

"Then I'm well pleased with the way our day has ended," Emma replied. "Still, it might be better to wait awhile before venturing out to shop. Without any reminders of the incident, the gossip that remains will die out more quickly."

"I have more than enough work to keep me home for a spell," Mother Garrett announced and rose to clear the table. "As I recall, we have four guests arriving tomorrow on the morning packet boat."

Emma groaned. "I'd forgotten."

"And I have a good bit of mending that needs my attention," Widow Leonard insisted. Her eyes widened. "The spools of thread! I need the spools of thread to do the mending." She caught Emma's gaze and held it. "I do hope you remembered to pay for the thread and bring it home with you."

Emma's heart dropped to her knees and her cheeks flushed warm. "As . . . as a matter of fact, I have the thread right here." She reached into her pocket, retrieved both spools, and set them on the table.

"You did remember!" Widow Leonard gushed.

Mortified that she had completely forgotten about the spools,

Emma swallowed hard. "In truth, I didn't."

"Yes, you did. You just set them on the table."

Emma stared at the spools. "That's true, but you see, I . . . I was so intent on resolving the misunderstanding and so surprised by Mr. Atkins' reaction when I confronted him, by the time he returned, I forgot all about paying for the spools of thread."

Mother Garrett started to chuckle, then quickly coughed to cover herself. She took Emma's plate and bowl and carried them to the sink. "I don't think you'll find a bonnet waiting for you at the end when you clear this up with Mr. Atkins."

"No, I'm sure I won't," Emma gritted, more annoyed with herself than amused by the irony of the awkward situation where she had plopped herself.

"I suppose you'll just have to leave earlier than usual to meet our guests at the landing, stop at the General Store, and pay the man for the thread," Mother Garrett suggested.

Widow Leonard collected the spools of thread and stored them in her pocket. "I'm sure he'll be very understanding."

"One might pray," Emma said, not too tired at the moment to realize that by returning to the General Store, she would be taking one of many steps toward humility of her own, especially if she was forced to leave Hill House. With a sigh, she reminded herself that on the way, she would also have to pray that He might forgive her for being a little too sanctimonious . . . and she would ask Mr. Atkins to do the same.

12

DULY HUMBLED AFTER HER VISIT to Mr. Atkins at the General Store to pay for the thread, Emma arrived at the end of Canal Street and entered the landing to wait for the morning packet boat carrying her guests. The air was thick with the smell of stale water, damp wood, the lush vegetation growing along the opposite side of the canal, and the hectic sounds of commerce.

She was not waiting alone.

Half a dozen men stood chatting on either side of the landing, poised to unload the cargo from the expected freight barges the moment the passengers disembarked and the packet boat continued on its way. Drivers from three wagons lined end-to-end on Canal Street waited to load their merchandise and produce onto the barge. The wagons effectively blocked the roadway and vehicle access to and from the landing. As always, the buggy she had rented on an as-needed basis from Thomas Adams at the livery—along with a driver, Adams' oldest son, Will—sat parked just two squares away, ready to carry Emma's guests and their baggage back to Hill House.

Dressed for the occasion in one of her finer gowns fashioned from dark gray linen, Emma shared the planked landing itself with a young man she did not know. His footsteps echoed as he paced back and forth, and she gauged him to be in his middle twenties. He was about the same age as her middle child, Benjamin, who had moved west to farm in Ohio with his wife, Betsy, their three small children, and Betsy's family. This man's hazel eyes fairly sparkled with the same optimism and excitement peculiar to the young, just like Benjamin's. Sawdust clung to his work clothes, and she assumed he worked in one of the nearby factories.

He stopped pacing and acknowledged her presence by tipping his well-worn hat. "Good morning, ma'am. I'm Matthew Cross."

She offered him her gloved hand. "Yes, it is, Mr. Cross," she said. "My name is Emma Garrett. Widow Garrett. I own Hill House, and I came to meet my guests. They'll be staying with me there."

"Yes, ma'am. I know the place." He glanced over his shoulder and shrugged. "Sits high up, right over there, but I can't see it from here."

"No. There are too many warehouses and factories," she noted. She recalled a time, years back, when Hill House was visible from any given place in the center of town. "I assume you're meeting someone from the packet boat, as well?"

His smile stretched across the full breadth of his narrow face, and his chest puffed with pride. "I'm meeting my family."

She cocked a brow.

"I finally saved enough working at the piano factory to send for them." He stared nervously down the towpath that ran alongside the canal. "I hope the travel won't be too difficult."

"I've traveled on a packet boat many times. Traveling by water is a whole sight better than bumping your way overland in a carriage or a wagon."

"Faster too," he offered before he resumed pacing with his gaze locked onto the towpath.

Hopeful she might help the time to pass more quickly and prevent the young man from wearing a path of his own on the landing, she kept their conversation going. "By family, did you mean your wife and children?"

With his back to the towpath, he braced to a halt and paled. "Me? No. I'm not married. Not yet. I'm expecting my parents and younger brother. My father has been ailing for some time. He hasn't been able to work much for the past two years. I didn't have much luck finding work that paid well back home. Then I saw the advertisement in the newspaper. That's why I came out here—to get a job. I've been living at Mrs. Grealey's boardinghouse, but that's no place for my folks, even if Mrs. Grealey would let a room to anyone other than the factory workers."

"Have you found a place for them?"

"Just last week. It's not much more than a couple of rooms, but it's a good, sturdy cabin. If anyone can turn it back into a home, my mother can. You might know the place. It's just south of the town, where the road forks and the toll road begins."

"That would be the old toll collector's cabin. Miller Flynn used to live there until they abandoned the toll gate. I believe he's living with his daughter now."

"Yes, ma'am. So I understand. The cabin's walking distance to work for me, and I'm hoping my brother can work at the factory, too. If not, I heard a rumor they might be adding another shift at the boatyard and the matchbox factory soon." He paused and checked the sky and frowned. "Packet boat's late. I hope nothing bad . . ."

"The packet boat is on time less often than it's late. I wouldn't worry," she offered.

He nodded. "I'm guessing it's close to ten-thirty. I told the foreman I wouldn't be gone much longer than an hour or two, and every hour I'm not at work means that much less I earn."

She reached into her reticule, checked the pocket watch her mother carried most of her life, and smiled. "It's only five minutes past ten." When she heard the familiar sound of hooves pounding against dirt, she nodded. "If you turn around, I believe you'll see the packet boat momentarily."

Within a heartbeat, a pair of mules with a driver walking alongside appeared in the distance on the towpath. The packet boat, *The Promise,* which followed some seventy odd yards behind, was barely visible yet slowly made an approach.

She waited and watched with him in silence as the driver and mules came down the towpath, cleared the landing without tangling any of the lines attached to the packet boat, and continued. With the packet boat now in clear view, she took a few steps back for a better vantage point to observe the passengers gathered on the flat roof above the sleeping cabin in the center of the vessel.

She recognized the four figures sitting on the far side as her guests, John and Abigail Sewell and their two daughters, who had stayed at Hill House just last fall. Emma's gaze, however, was locked on the bonnet the woman was wearing. The color of the bonnet looked remarkably similar to the one Mother Garrett had gotten from Mr. Atkins, although she could not make out the details of the bonnet itself. Mother Garrett must have been right about the color being all the rage. The other passengers standing at the front railing—a man, a woman, and a younger man—she assumed to be the Cross family.

Her companion confirmed her assumption when he removed

his hat and started waving to them. She half expected him to leap
onto the packet boat to greet his loved ones, but the flurry of men
who went into action to secure the packet boat to the landing
before the walking platform could be dropped forced both Emma
and young Mr. Cross to move back out of the way.

From past experience, she knew it would take some time for
the Sewell family to disembark. They were lovely, good-natured
people who were relatively easy to please, and she was looking
forward to their stay at Hill House from now until Friday.

The Cross family was the first to emerge. Their animated
reunion tugged at her heartstrings, increasing the longing to see
her own children and grandchildren. To her surprise, young Mr.
Cross introduced them all to one another. "Welcome to Candlewood," she said. "I hope you'll be as content living here as I have
been."

His mother held a tight hold on her son's arm. "I'm content
just having us all together again."

Out of the corner of her eye, Emma caught a glimpse of her
guests preparing to walk down the platform, excused herself, and
edged closer to get a better look. John Sewell, a successful banker-
turned-investor, wore an expensive frock coat that might have fit
him well last year, and his white cambric shirt glistened in the sun.
Unfortunately, the man had added to the considerable girth he
already carried on his short frame.

When his wife, Abigail, emerged from the shadows, she
appeared to have fared better in the past year, but Emma did not
focus on the woman's gown, though it carried enough pale yellow
silk to make several gowns for Emma and at least three or four
petticoats, given the fullness of the woman's skirts. Her gaze was
glued to the bonnet the woman wore: a daffodil bonnet replete
with a birds' nest filled with silk forget-me-not flowers.

Images of what Mother Garrett's reaction would be when she saw Mrs. Sewell arrive wearing the bonnet were so alarming, Emma turned her attention to the daughters, who waddled out into the bright sunlight behind their mother. If her memory served her right, the eldest daughter, Madeline, who shared her mother's fair coloring, was twelve now. Two years younger, Miriam favored her father's dark looks. Both girls, dressed in pale lemon silk like their mother, were still just as rotund as their parents, and she wondered if the rivalry between them—so apparent last year—still existed.

Emma stepped forward to greet her guests once they had all reached the permanent landing. "You're all looking as if the past year has treated you well," she offered.

Mr. Sewell patted his protruding stomach. "Despite appearances, I don't believe I've had an apple crisp worthy of the name since our visit last year. I trust your mother-in-law is still tending the kitchen?"

"I believe she's there right now preparing an apple crisp for dessert this afternoon."

He grinned. "Then let us make haste, shall we?"

Emma chuckled to herself, looked around, and quickly arranged for two of the workmen to carry the Sewells' travel bags to the buggy. By the time the five of them reached the buggy and climbed aboard, all four of her guests were sweating profusely and out of breath. Squeezed alongside the two girls, who sat opposite their parents, Emma smiled, even though the girls were wearing perfume that was cloying. "I'm so sorry for the long walk, but we'll be at Hill House soon."

"I'm just thrilled all to pieces to be out of the city and off that boat," Mrs. Sewell offered as she toyed with the ruffled flounces that trimmed the edge of her sleeves. "Once we get to Hill House and unpack, I'm not sitting inside that house for a solid week, except for meals and to sleep, of course. All I want to do is sit on the patio, smell your roses, sip some of your mother-in-law's mulberry shrub, and maybe tuck in a bit of shopping while Mr. Sewell is off on those business adventures of his."

"Did you get a piano yet?" Madeline asked as the buggy turned the corner and proceeded down Main Street.

"Not yet. Maybe next year. The gazebo I told you we were planning is finished, though. If you like, I can open one of the bookcases in the library so you can select a book to take out to the gazebo to read."

Madeline toyed with the hem of her sleeve. "Thank you, but I'd rather not."

"Me neither. There are too many steps to get there," Miriam complained.

"That's true," their mother offered, "but the gazebo will be pretty to look at. I was thinking perhaps we might have supper tonight on the patio, if it's not too burdensome."

Inclined to be accommodating, Emma felt obliged to remind them of the incident last year that nearly ruined the last few days of their vacation. "It's no trouble at all, though I am concerned about the yellow jackets this time of year."

Mrs. Sewell's eyes widened. She rubbed the forearm where she had been stung last year and shivered as if reliving the memory. "We'll dine inside. I'll have my refreshments inside, too. There's no use inviting disaster."

"No sense at all," her husband agreed, despite the fact he had appeared to be too preoccupied studying the businesses and homes they passed on Main Street to be aware of the conversation around him.

When the buggy started up the hill to their destination, Mr.

Sewell leaned back, wrapped his hands together, and rested them on his stomach before he locked his gaze with Emma's. "I must say I'm not surprised by the growth I've noted in town, even in the course of the past year."

"The Candlewood Canal continues to inspire a good deal of change." Hopeful he might be willing to share his business expertise with her again, Emma smiled. "I'm looking forward to hearing your views on the development here, as well as elsewhere, if you're so inclined."

He narrowed his gaze. "You may not be prepared for all that I have to say."

Emma frowned. When they had spoken last year, he had been very careful to guard his own interests, as well as his investors'. Rather than give her direct or specific information, he had provoked her interest with an intriguing concept or idea, and she wondered if he would do the same this year when she might very well need it. "Are you speaking about Candlewood or elsewhere?"

"Must you speak about business in front of the girls?" his wife whispered.

His cheeks reddened. "My apologies," he mumbled. "Perhaps we can talk later, one day this coming week."

Although Mrs. Sewell's rebuke had been clearly directed at her husband, it also served notice to Emma that her interest in business affairs defied conventional wisdom that relegated women to matters of home and hearth but reserved the world of commerce and business for men.

As the operator of Hill House, however temporary that might be, and a woman of substantial means, Emma stood with one foot in each of those spheres. Reminded of her more proper place, she directed the conversation to more traditional, if not practical, topics, considering they were mere minutes away from Hill House.

"I've been admiring your bonnet, Mrs. Sewell."

The woman's face glowed with pleasure. "It quite catches one's eye, doesn't it? I found it in a very exclusive boutique that just opened up in Utica. It's one of a kind. A true gem. The moment I saw this bonnet, I simply had to have it," she gushed.

Emma managed to keep her lips glued in a smile. The blue skies overhead held no promise of a thunderstorm, but she prayed something similar might occur; otherwise, there was no hope of preventing the fireworks either now, if Mother Garrett came out of her kitchen and saw that daffodil bonnet atop Mrs. Sewell's head, or tomorrow morning, when they all went to services together and the two women discovered that their one-of-a-kind bonnet was not unique at all.

13

NO FIREWORKS, at least for today.

Without encountering Mother Garrett, Emma escorted her guests along the upstairs hallway to the same two front bedrooms they had occupied during their last visit. She opened first one door and then the other before stepping aside. "As you requested, the Blue Room is ready for you, Mr. and Mrs. Sewell, and the Green Room is for your daughters. Your bags will be brought up presently."

While the girls explored their room on their own, Emma joined their parents to make sure they were as pleased by the room's accommodations as they had been last year.

"It's exactly as I remember," Abigail crooned. Still wearing her gloves and bonnet, she declined Emma's offer to store them on the hat rack downstairs where she had put her own. Instead, she helped herself to an almond cookie from the plate resting alongside a vase of white roses on top of a lady's bureau that hugged one wall.

Emma quickly scanned the room, which was simply drenched

in shades of blue. The gleaming, ornately carved headboard on the massive bed was made of solid rosewood and reached nearly from floor to ceiling. The pair of chairs upholstered in a striped fabric that complemented the pale blue coverlet sat in front of the two front windows that provided a view of the town's business district, the Candlewood Canal, and the homesteads that lay beyond.

A slight breeze rustled the sheer lace curtains and carried the unique scent of summer that would soon give way to autumn. The wide-planked floors had been swept clean. Emma did not have to check the pitcher resting in the washbowl on the marble-top table next to a massive chest-on-chest to know Ditty had filled it with fresh water or that the cloths and towels on a shelf at the bottom of the washstand were fresh.

She smiled. Ditty had done well.

"I'm sure you'd both like to rest a spell before dinner. I'll check in on the girls and make sure they're comfortable before I go downstairs," she suggested and confirmed that dinner would be served at one o'clock before leaving and going into the adjoining room.

Madeline and Miriam had planted themselves side-by-side in the chairs facing the front windows of their room, where they each had their own smaller plate with exactly the same number of cookies. Along with their gloves, their bonnets had been tossed to the floor.

Emma glanced about the room. The soft green coverlets on the two single beds matched the background of the floral carpet, as did the pale pink roses in either of the twin crystal vases sitting on the table separating the two beds. Satisfied all was in order here, too, she retrieved the now-empty plates from each of the girls. "I'll send up more cookies and see you both at dinner," she promised and slipped from the room.

She met young Will Adams at the top of the staircase, directed him to carry the travel bags to the appropriate rooms, and encountered Ditty while descending the stairs. She noted the three plates of cookies on the tray the young woman was carrying, smiled, and held up the two empty plates she had removed. "I was just taking these to the kitchen to ask you to take more cookies up to our guests. I see Mother Garrett has already thought of it."

"Yes, ma'am, she did."

Emma had descended two steps before she stopped, turned around, and called out to Ditty, who looked back over her shoulder.

"Yes, ma'am?"

"I wanted to tell you what a fine job you did getting the rooms ready for the Sewells."

Ditty grinned. "Yes, ma'am. Thank you."

"There's one more thing," Emma cautioned. "You'll no doubt notice Mrs. Sewell is wearing a daffodil bonnet identical to Mother Garrett's. It's highly unlikely our guest will be wearing her bonnet to dinner, but I wouldn't mention anything to Mother Garrett about it. Not just yet."

When Ditty's eyes sparkled, Emma realized the young woman had indeed heard the tale about the bird's nest on Mother Garrett's bonnet landing in Reverend Glenn's soup.

"It's identical, you say?"

"Down to the forget-me-nots in the nest, although I suspect Mrs. Sewell's flowers don't smell of vegetable soup. You might warn Liesel, as well."

Ditty's grin widened, but she turned and resumed her task without comment.

Emma took a deep breath, smelled the aroma of apple crisp baking in the oven, and descended the rest of the stairs. She waited by the front door for Will to come downstairs, paid him for carrying the bags, and sent him on his way before she ventured into the east parlor to steal a few moments to collect her thoughts. She simply needed to find a way to resolve the dilemma of the daffodil bonnets.

"As if there's an easy way," she grumbled while inspecting the floorboards to make sure Ditty had not overlooked any dust or dirt.

"The easy way isn't usually the right way."

She clapped her hand to her heart and looked up. "Reverend Glenn!"

He sat on the settee just ahead of her, with Butter lying alongside at his feet. He smiled. "I'm sorry. I didn't mean to startle you."

"I didn't realize anyone was in here," she admitted as her racing heartbeat gentled into a more normal rhythm. She crossed the room, dropped into the chair facing him, and rubbed her temples with her fingertips.

He leaned down and scratched the dog's head. "I've been here a spell. I saw you return with your guests, but I didn't want to interrupt."

"In truth, I'm pleased you didn't. I needed to get Mrs. Sewell up to her room as quickly as possible." When he chuckled, she dropped her hands and leaned against the back of her chair. "I take it you noticed Mrs. Sewell's bonnet?"

He chuckled again and patted the front of his shirt. "I'm not a man who usually takes notice of fashion, but I daresay I will take notice of that particular bonnet for the rest of my days."

She let out a sigh. "So I can imagine. Unfortunately, there's no easy way to resolve this problem. I don't want to upset Mrs. Sewell. She thinks the bonnet is an original, which leaves me no choice but to tell Mother Garrett that there's more than one daffodil bonnet in Candlewood these days. And I don't have much time. We'll all be going to services together in the morning, assuming, of course, Mrs. Sewell doesn't decide to wear her bonnet to dinner."

She sighed again and cast him a sorrowful gaze. "I don't suppose you could give me any advice on the matter, could you?"

He pushed himself to his feet and held on to the arm of the settee to steady himself. "I have but one thing to suggest."

She cocked a brow.

"You might want to make sure Mother Garrett doesn't serve soup this afternoon."

Dinner was the largest and most formal meal at Hill House, especially when guests like the Sewells were in residence. Mother Garrett enlisted both Liesel and Ditty's help in preparing and serving the three-course meal, which meant there had been no opportunity to speak with her mother-in-law before dinner. Widow Leonard was feeling a bit poorly and taking her dinner in her room upstairs, although Emma suspected the source of the elderly woman's distress might be the prospect of encountering one or both of her sons at services in the morning. Mother Garrett was too busy in the kitchen to join them at the table, which made Emma all the more grateful to have Reverend Glenn present.

With everyone seated around the dining room table, Emma caught the minister's gaze and smiled. All was well. Mrs. Sewell had not chosen to wear her daffodil bonnet to dinner, and Emma confidently ladled corn chowder into bowls for the guests.

Conversation around the table was spirited, and the young Sewell sisters seemed especially taken by the tales Reverend Glenn shared about his early days as a minister, when he rode circuit before settling down to a permanent ministry in Candlewood. Mother Garrett's veal roast captured rave approval, but it was the arrival of dessert that had her guests nearly in a swoon.

Ditty set substantial portions of apple crisp still warm from the oven in front of each of their guests, while Liesel followed behind her to pour generous dollops of cream on top of the dessert. To Emma's surprise, Mother Garrett left Liesel in charge of the kitchen and took a seat at the table.

Beaming, Mother Garrett accepted well-earned accolades for her efforts in preparing the meal and started in on the apple crisp Liesel had brought in for her.

"Are you sure I can't persuade you to come to work for us in Utica?" Mr. Sewell asked between bites.

"You should know better than to ask," his wife protested. "Mother Garrett wouldn't leave her daughter-in-law."

"No, I wouldn't, but I might be persuaded to send my receipt for the apple crisp home with you this year."

Emma narrowed her gaze. She had heard Mother Garrett's offer with her own ears, but she still did not trust what she had heard. Mother Garrett was as prone to share her recipes as a hen was to lay purple eggs.

"It's little enough to do," Mother Garrett insisted. "I don't believe we have had any other guests who have enjoyed my efforts more than all of you."

"I do believe you have been accorded a distinct honor, Mr. Sewell," Emma said. "I don't think I can recall Mother Garrett sharing any of her receipts before."

He grinned. "Then I'm doubly grateful."

"Have you plans for the afternoon?" Emma inquired.

Mrs. Sewell shook her head. "Not beyond the patio . . . I do hope you still have your subscriptions to *The Ladies' Repository* and

Godey's Lady's Book for your guests."

"The magazines are in the library. I'll bring them out to you on the patio, if you like."

"Don't bother yourself. When we're ready, the girls and I will pick out the issues we'd like to read. What time is supper?"

Emma covered her mouth with her napkin to cover a grin. Although her three sons had practically eaten nonstop from about the age of eleven to adulthood, few of her guests who had barely finished dinner would be concerned about the next meal.

"The days are getting shorter. Will six o'clock suit you?" Mother Garrett asked.

Abigail nodded. "Perfectly well. Reverend Glenn, would you join us on the patio? We'd enjoy hearing more of your stories, and perhaps you could remind us about the time for services tomorrow morning, too."

"I will indeed," he replied.

Emma opened the double doors to the patio for her guests and followed Mother Garrett into the kitchen, where Liesel and Ditty were just finishing washing up the dishes from the first two courses. "I'll take over here. Take the trays into the dining room and clear the rest of the dishes. Carefully," she cautioned.

Emma grabbed an apron for herself and tied it at her waist, too anxious to speak to Mother Garrett to bother changing into one of her work gowns. "Speaking of services tomorrow, I was wondering . . . Are you wearing your new bonnet?"

"Not very likely. I've gotten the stains out of the flowers, but with Frances feeling poorly today, I don't expect she's gotten to repairing it. Though, to my mind, she'd feel better if she stopped worrying about seeing her sons tomorrow. Why?" Mother Garrett asked as she started wiping down the cookstove.

Emma shrugged, though seeing Andrew and James tomorrow

at services lay heavy in the back of her mind, too. "I was just curious. I mean, what if someone else was to have a bonnet exactly like yours? Would it bother you overmuch?"

Mother Garrett laughed. "Don't be a ninny. No one else could possibly have a bonnet like mine."

Emma cleared her throat and plunged ahead. "Actually, Mrs. Sewell does. She was wearing it today."

"My bonnet? She was wearing my daffodil bonnet?"

Emma nodded. "I'm sorry. I know how much it meant to you to have a bonnet that was so unique."

Huffing, her mother-in-law shook the cleaning rag in her hand. "I have a mind to march myself right back to that millinery shop first thing Monday morning and get some of Mr. Atkins' coins back—after I have my say."

"I have visions of Mrs. Sewell swimming all the way up the Candlewood Canal to Utica, if she has to, just to confront the owner of that boutique to do much the same thing."

Mother Garrett shook her head and sighed. "She's our guest, after all; there's no need to upset her. I suppose it wouldn't do much harm not to tell her about my bonnet."

"Except that so many people saw you on Main Street wearing it," Emma argued. "I'm worried someone might say something to you or to her after services tomorrow."

"I'll think of something. I might even talk to Frances about it before I take to my bed. I have a notion she might have a solution, even if I don't."

Before Emma could reply, the sound of breaking dishes and a pair of yelps sent both of them charging into the dining room.

Surrounded by broken china, Liesel was helping Ditty back to her feet, unharmed but shaken by her mishap.

"If that young woman doesn't grow into her own feet soon,

you're going to have to replace your entire set of china," Mother Garrett whispered.

"Again," Emma groaned, heading back to the kitchen to get a broom to sweep up the mess.

14

B E NOT AFRAID. OUR LORD, the Creator of all the universe, will be your strength. Be not afraid. God, our all-knowing Father, will not desert you. Be not afraid. Entrust Him with your worst fears. Give Him your pain and suffering. And trust Him with the deepest of your heartaches. Be . . . not . . . afraid."

The echo of Reverend Austin's sermon resounded in Emma's mind as the services concluded with a hymn, and she tucked his words close to her heart to ease the fear that she might be forced to leave Hill House. When she turned to file from the pew in the front of the church, she caught a glimpse of Zachary Breckenwith. For just one quick moment, the interest simmering in the depths of his eyes when he glanced at her was undeniable. With her heart pounding, she looked away, only to find Mr. Langhorne staring hard at her. Unnerved, she stepped back in the aisle to allow first Reverend Glenn, then Mr. Sewell to proceed ahead of her, with her guest taking care that the retired minister did not stumble and fall. Mrs. Sewell, Madeline, and Miriam followed next, then Mother Garrett, and finally Widow Leonard.

As Emma's heartbeat returned to normal, she dismissed that most curious look in Zachary Breckenwith's eyes, certain she must have misunderstood his professional concern for her as interest in her on a more personal level. He was her lawyer, nothing more. Mr. Langhorne's hard glance, however, only reinforced her own fears that she was on the verge of losing Hill House and a new, more irrational fear that Mr. Langhorne might have discovered her current dilemma and that he would use that knowledge to his own advantage.

Emma hooked her arm with Widow Leonard's and patted her arm as they walked together down the aisle, anxious to distract herself from her troubles. "You did amazing work on Mother Garrett's bonnet. Thank you," she whispered.

"I'm a tad proud of it myself. There wasn't much I could do about the color, but replacing the bird's nest with those butterflies changed the look of the bonnet just enough, I think."

"Mother Garrett was happy, and Mrs. Sewell didn't seem overly bothered that the bonnets were the same color. I think you're a dear," Emma managed before whispering hello to other members of the congregation as they walked toward the rear of the church.

Once outside, they ventured across the grassy courtyard facing the church. Emma spied the other members of their party at the far corner near Mr. Henderson's outlandishly ornate carriage, where Mother Garrett and Mrs. Sewell were already holding court as ladies stopped to admire the finery they wore on their heads.

Widow Leonard slowed her steps. "Andrew is here, you know."

"No, I hadn't seen him. What about James?" Emma asked as she scanned the crowd of people congregating about the courtyard.

"He wouldn't be here now. He might have come. I can't say for sure that he didn't, but once he saw that his brother was here, he would have left. I'm certain of that. Let's join the others. If Andrew decides to seek me out, at least I won't have to see him alone."

"No, you won't," Emma reassured her, "but the longer the troubles between your sons remain, the harder it will be to resolve them." Troubled herself by the notion that any mother might be afraid to be alone with one of her children, for any reason, Emma stayed close to the newest member of her staff.

When Andrew did appear, he was not alone. His wife, Nora, was at his side. Andrew's gaze was set as hard and determined as when he had come to Hill House, but Nora looked a bit torn, perhaps. Emma sensed an ally in her, a sign that there was hope for a reconciliation; if not now, at some point in the future.

Emma took full advantage the moment Andrew and his wife approached them, smiled, and said the first thing that popped into her head. "We were hoping you'd be here. I do hope you can join us for dinner at Hill House. I'm quite certain Mother Garrett has made more than enough, haven't you?" she asked and caught her mother-in-law's gaze. She made a slight grimace of apology for not checking first, but her grimace tightened when she realized Liesel and Ditty had both gone home to spend their time off with their families.

"Unlike other people, I always prepare for the . . . unexpected," her mother-in-law replied with just the barest hint of sarcasm in her voice. "We have more than enough."

"Then do come," Emma gushed, taking hold of Widow Leonard again and stepping forward. "We have a carriage for our guests and Reverend Glenn, of course, but we usually enjoy the walk home while the weather is so pleasant. You can meet us at Hill House or walk along with us."

Andrew's glare darkened, and his wife edged closer to him. "I'd prefer to speak to my mother here and now, if you please. She is free on Sundays—or have the rules changed since we last spoke?"

"Of course I'm free to speak with you," Widow Leonard said. "After dinner would suit me fine." She looked up at Emma. "May I impose on your hospitality and ask that we have use of the library after dinner so we can speak privately?"

When Emma nodded, Widow Leonard looked back to her son but held silent.

"Please," Nora whispered. "Having dinner won't take up that much more time."

He paused and shifted his weight from foot to foot. "I know the way. We'll be along . . . presently."

———

The presence of the Sewell family made all the difference at dinner. Between the girls' good-natured banter, Mr. Sewell's tales of his business adventures, and Mrs. Sewell's detailed accounts of her shopping mishaps, there was little room for the stilted awkwardness Andrew's presence at the table might have induced or for Emma to worry about either Zachary Breckenwith or Mr. Langhorne.

Anxious about what might occur after dinner, Emma ate little, save for a buttered muffin and a serving of applesauce. As dinner concluded, she clung to the message from Reverend Austin's sermon. She rose and opened the double doors to the patio.

While her guests debated whether to spend the afternoon on the patio or brave the steps to inspect the new gazebo, Emma ushered Widow Leonard, Andrew, and Nora to the library and closed the door that led to her adjoining office. "You'll have the privacy you need here," she said, hoping the masculine flavor of the room would help put Andrew at ease. "I'll be in the kitchen helping Mother Garrett. Please let me know if there's anything you'd like to have or need."

"You might want to help in the kitchen, as well, while I speak to my mother," Andrew suggested to his wife.

"I'd like Nora to stay. She's family. And I'd like Emma to stay, too," Widow Leonard insisted.

"She's not family," Andrew argued. "I cannot and will not discuss—"

"You must," his mother countered. "We've tried discussing the matter on our own." Her eyes misted. "You can see for yourself what good that did. If not for yourself or for me, then do it out of respect for your father, God rest his soul. Emma has a good heart and she knows her way around business matters. I trust her to be able to help us, and you should, too."

In the awkward silence that ensued while Andrew made up his mind to stay or to leave, Emma opened the heavy drapes on the window before she closed the door to the center hallway. Sunlight warmed the dark paneling on the walls and danced on a pair of glass-enclosed bookcases on either side of the stone fireplace. She quickly rearranged several leather chairs to create one sitting area instead of two by placing them in a circle, chose one for herself, and sat down.

Moments later, Widow Leonard took a seat to Emma's right.

Without saying a word, Andrew escorted his wife to the chair on Emma's left before taking the last chair next to his mother.

"Thank you, Andrew," his mother said quietly.

"I want you to end this nonsense, Mother, and come home with us. Today."

Nora held silent, nodded, but worried at the edge of lace that trimmed her sleeve.

"Why?" Widow Leonard asked. "Because you're embarrassed that I've run off, or because you've come to tell me you've reconciled with your brother and I can come home to you both?"

His nostrils flared. "James has nothing to do with this."

"You're wrong, Andrew. James has everything to do with whether or not I return home to live with either one of you. Ever." She drew in several quick breaths as she held his gaze. "A woman's heart can be broken in many ways," she murmured and folded her trembling hands together. "To lose a husband is a heavy burden."

She turned and looked at Emma. "You've known that heartache, haven't you?"

Emma nodded, slipped her hand into her pocket, and felt among her keepsakes to find the piece of heavy serge cut from the suit of clothes Jonas had worn on their wedding day.

Widow Leonard's gaze grew misty. "You carried that burden, as well, Nora."

When Andrew's wife nodded, Emma recalled that Nora had been married once before but had lost her husband suddenly, only months after they had been wed.

"For a woman to bury her sweet babies is another heartache a woman carries for the rest of her days," Widow Leonard continued. She dropped her gaze. She did not look up from her lap to either Emma or Nora, and Emma did not expect the elderly woman to do so. She had been spared the grief of losing a child, but Nora carried the very different grief of being barren.

For several long moments, Widow Leonard stared at her lap. When she did meet their gazes again, she dropped her voice to a whisper. "For a woman to see her grown children estranged from one another, to stand by, helpless, unable to help them resolve the troubles between them day after day is a cross of guilt and grief I fear I can no longer carry."

Emma choked back the emotion lodged in her throat and noticed that Nora's eyes had filled with tears she hurriedly blinked away.

Andrew's cheeks colored, and he braced his feet to adjust his position in the chair. "I've tried to explain this to you before. This isn't your fault, but it's not mine, either. There's nothing I can do to make James change his mind. I've tried talking to him. He walks away. I've tried to show him facts and figures. He tears them up. I've even tried pleading with him, but he won't listen. Not even long enough to hear me out completely."

He raked his hand through his hair. "Tell me, Mother. What can I do? If James isn't willing to discuss the matter at all, what can I do? Nothing," he charged without giving her a chance to reply. "There's nothing to be done but to accept the fact that I no longer have a brother."

"Your father would be—"

"My father? My father should have divided the land into two equal parts in his will; instead, he created a . . . a living nightmare for all of us that has you putting yourself out to work as if you had no family to care for you."

"I'm sure your father had good intentions," Nora offered and looked to her mother-in-law for support.

Curious to learn more of the details surrounding the issue that had driven James and Andrew apart, Emma looked to Widow Leonard, as well.

The elderly woman looked at each of them in turn and sighed. "Enoch was a good husband and a good father. In all the years I knew him, he did not once entertain a wicked thought or deed, and he was a fair-minded man. To his credit, he wanted to be sure you would both benefit equally. Unfortunately, he could not predict the changes the future would bring, any more than he could envision the day when his two sons would be at odds with each other."

"He could have avoided any and all problems by dividing the land differently."

"And I suppose you wouldn't have felt slighted or cruelly treated if James had gotten the greater share?"

"To my eye, James always gets the bigger portion. He has the better land and four sons to help him work it. Must he now keep me from trying to secure what little I can for myself?"

When the echo of Andrew's bitter words faded, the cadence of uneven breathing was the only sound that filled the room. Nora dabbed at her silent tears, no doubt hurt by her husband's callous reference to her inability to bear a child. For his part, Andrew kept his gaze locked on his mother, who simply bowed her head and stared at her lap.

Andrew's words also sliced through Emma's first impression that a piece of land was the cause of the fallout between the brothers. She also knew enough to suspect the Candlewood Canal, built some years after Enoch Leonard's death, played a role in the dispute between James and Andrew.

Andrew, however, had just revealed, unwittingly or not, the truth: The troubles between them were rooted deep in jealousy and envy that had apparently been brewing for years.

Without knowing the land in question or the precise argument concerning it, there was little she could offer to guide this family toward reconciliation. "I wonder if I might pose a question," she murmured and directed her question to Andrew.

Still winded from his gust of words, he waved his hand to indicate he had no objection.

"I have a vague recollection of the extent of the land your father owned, but I'm not certain as to how he divided it in his will. Can you tell me about the land in dispute?"

He straightened in his chair. "The land separates my land from my brother's and runs north and south, covering a portion of the toll road that starts just south of Candlewood and runs north to Bounty. There are two acres on either side of the toll road, as well."

"What about the tolls that are collected? Do you share them equally with your brother?"

He shook his head. "The toll gate is at the midpoint, close to my home. I collect the tolls and take a larger portion. The rest goes to my brother."

She cocked a brow and wondered if he realized he had just undercut his own argument about his brother always getting more than he did. "A larger portion?"

"I earn it," he argued. "Not that there's much point to my efforts. Once the Candlewood Canal opened, road traffic dwindled, and it's only gotten worse. At this point in time, a week could pass before I collect a single toll, which means there's little sense wasting either time or money to make repairs. Some of the other landowners have abandoned their toll gates completely. James and I would be better served if we could just sell the land and divide the money between us."

Emma narrowed her gaze. Selling a strip of land four-odd acres wide might not be all that easy, but she supposed some investor might be interested. "That sounds reasonable."

He snorted. "Being reasonable is not one of my brother's finer qualities. He refused to consider the matter at all, despite the fact that we have a fair offer. But then, why should he? He already has everything he wants and more. Now, if you'll excuse me, I believe I've said more than I wanted to say."

He got to his feet and helped his wife from her chair. "Mother, if you'll collect your things, I'd like you to head home with us."

Widow Leonard looked up at her son. "I can't, Andrew. Not until you fix matters with your brother."

Emma rose, moved behind the elderly woman's chair, and placed her hands on the woman's shoulders. "Your mother has been wonderful company for Reverend Glenn, who is still troubled by the stroke he suffered. Your mother's presence here and her encouragement have made a big difference to him, and it might be more helpful if she stayed with us for a while longer."

When Andrew opened his mouth to argue, Nora silenced him by merely placing her hand on his arm.

He glanced down at her, looked over at his mother, and let out a deep sigh. "If you want matters settled, then you should speak to my brother. In the meantime, if you change your mind and want to come home, send for me," he said and escorted his wife from the library.

"There's no hope. Just no hope at all," Widow Leonard whispered after they left.

Emma was tempted to agree. But beyond Andrew's obvious affection for his wife and his mother, there was one sliver of light that shone through his bitterness. "As long as Andrew still refers to James as his brother, I believe there is hope."

15

WEDNESDAY DAWNED BRIGHT with the promise of another glorious day, although the day itself was remarkable simply because her granddaughter Deborah turned five today. With the arrival of thick cloud cover by midmorning, the promise faded, along with Emma's hopes that this might be the day she would be able to speak privately with Mr. Sewell.

Unfortunately, he had left at first light for the third day in a row to inspect yet another potential investment property and did not expect to return until well after supper. Other than a few moments here and there when she had answered his questions about some of the new businesses in town, there had been no time for them to meet privately to discuss business. His wife and daughters had decided to brave a walk along Main Street to shop, although Emma had sent Ditty to the livery with a note to arrange for a carriage to be available to bring them home with their packages when they finished.

Emma had been working downstairs in her office for several hours handling correspondence, while Widow Leonard worked at her sewing upstairs. She noted the change in the weather, set her work aside, and went directly to the kitchen, but she found only Liesel at the sink washing the cleaning cloths Ditty had used to freshen their guests' rooms.

She glanced around and frowned. There were no pots simmering on the cookstove, no aromas coming from the oven. With literally no sign of dinner in the making, Emma felt the first prickle of suspicion that the day held more surprises. "Is Mother Garrett about?"

Liesel paused and rested the cleaning cloth against the washboard. "She said she wouldn't be long and that she'd be back soon."

Liesel was not a young woman of few words, another sign of impending trouble. Emma waited for more of an explanation, but when the young woman offered nothing more, she prompted her. "Did she say where she was going?"

"She had an errand to run. On Main Street," she added when Emma narrowed her gaze.

"I see." She glanced from Liesel to the cookstove and back again. "May I assume dinner will be on time for our guests?"

Liesel's cheeks flushed pink. "Mrs. Sewell told Mother Garrett that she and her daughters wouldn't be here for dinner and they wouldn't return until late afternoon. I expect they'll be here for supper. She didn't say they wouldn't be."

Unaccustomed to being informed about her guests' plans after the fact, Emma felt her pulse quicken. "What about the rest of us? Will we have dinner today?"

Liesel's blush deepened. "Mother Garrett said we would—"

With that, Mother Garrett huffed her way into the kitchen. "I said we would have cold platters today, which we will as soon as I can make them. I'm sorry, Emma. My errand took me longer than

I expected," she said after she stopped to catch her breath.

When she did, she looked directly at Liesel. "Be a dear, won't you? Go out to the gazebo and take an umbrella with you for Reverend Glenn. The rain's not far off and might get here before he can manage his way back to the house. And if it does start raining, keep that mongrel out on the patio until you wipe down his paws and that mangy tail of his."

Liesel abandoned her work at the sink and left to carry out her new task without complaint. After donning an apron, Mother Garrett took the ham left from dinner yesterday from the larder to the table, leaving Emma standing next to the cookstove with a host of questions ready to bubble over in her mind.

Rather than question her mother-in-law directly as to her whereabouts, a tactic Emma had learned did not work, she took Liesel's place at the sink and began scrubbing the cleaning cloth. "It's Deborah's birthday today."

"I remembered. She's probably looking more like you than ever," Mother Garrett offered. "Has Warren written to say when they might be coming for a visit?"

"Not yet," Emma replied and quickly turned the topic back to her immediate concerns. "Did Mrs. Sewell say where she and the girls would be having dinner?"

"I believe she said they might try the hotel, though why anyone would prefer food at that hotel over mine is a wonder I haven't yet deciphered. She did say she was afraid they wouldn't be finished shopping by dinner and didn't want to come all the way back here and then have to venture out again to the shops. I suppose it's the coming back up the hill they dislike more than anything else."

Emma glanced out the window to find a drizzly mist had already begun to dampen the yard, which made today less than a good one to shop along Main Street. In the far distance she saw the dull bronze roof of the gazebo and hoped Liesel had Reverend Glenn well on his way back to the house. "I finished most of my correspondence while you were out. I had hoped to have my replies ready for Ditty to post at the General Store, since she had to take my note to the livery, but they took longer than I expected. The Worths will be coming back in late October, just for three days this time. Mrs. Parrish and her sister are coming about the same time, and so are the Behrs. We may be as busy next month as we were for the Founders' Day celebrations." She wondered if her days here at Hill House welcoming guests were indeed numbered and shivered when the image of Mr. Langhorne's hard stare at services on Sunday flashed through her mind.

"I might be recovered by then. I can't say I'm not looking forward to November when they close the canal and we all slow down a bit," Mother Garrett suggested.

Surprised, Emma turned and met her mother-in-law's gaze. "Are you finally admitting that buying Hill House was a good idea?" she asked, finding it ironic that Mother Garrett's change of heart came at a time when Emma might have to admit buying Hill House had been a very bad idea.

Mother Garrett blinked several times, then resumed carving the ham. "I never said it wasn't a good idea. I just said I thought you were being hasty. One day you say you're just looking at this place as an investment. The next morning you're asking me if I'd mind if you sold the General Store and if I'd move with you to Hill House, which you want to restore and open as a boarding-house."

Reminded yet again of how headstrong she had been about buying Hill House and the possibility that she had made a terrible mistake—one that Mr. Langhorne definitely could use to his advantage—Emma turned back to her task and kept her worries to herself, rather than burden her mother-in-law. "The Lord opens the path He's chosen for us in mysterious ways," she whispered. "I'm still awed by how quickly and simply I was led down the path to Hill House," Emma replied, though she realized she may have simply forged ahead to get what she wanted instead of waiting to be sure this was where He wanted her to be.

Mother Garrett chuckled. "'Down the path' might not be the way most folks, including the Sewells, would describe their walk up the hill to get here."

"Probably not, but there hasn't been a guest yet who complained about the view from Hill House, either." Emma gritted her teeth as she worked at a particularly stubborn stain, then smiled when she heard Butter bark. "Liesel must have Reverend Glenn back to the patio already, but I'm sure she's got her hands full getting him inside the dining room and keeping the dog out."

The next instant Butter charged into the kitchen, tracking in dirt and mud, with Liesel chasing him from behind. The dog's coat was wet and matted, adding a musky odor to the room. "I tried. I tried to stop him. But he wouldn't . . . stop," she cried, unable to keep the dog under her control.

Emma was not sure who was more agitated, the young woman or the dog. She was certain that something was very amiss when Butter kept barking, lunged at her, and started butting at her skirts with his massive head. "Where's Reverend Glenn?" she gasped and attempted, in vain, to nudge the dog away.

"He's gone. I was on my way to fetch him when Butter—I never saw the dog try to run before—but he kept trying to get up the steps and kept stumbling, even when I called for him to stop. I ran down past Butter and checked for Reverend Glenn in the gazebo, but he wasn't there. I don't know where he might be," she cried as she swiped at her tears with one hand and her damp skirts with the other.

Mother Garrett sat at the table, her knife in the air, staring at the dog, apparently too stunned to move or speak.

"I'm sure he isn't far," Emma insisted, although her heart was racing with the fear that he might have decided to take a bit of a walk and either fell or suffered another stroke. She patted Butter's damp head to try to calm him. "Liesel, I'm taking the dog with me. Once I do, you be sure to clean up the mess he's tracked into the house. Mother Garrett, why don't you check Reverend Glenn's room and the rest of the house? It's not likely, but it's possible he might have wandered back without our noticing and left Butter outside just for a moment while he got something he wanted from the house."

When Mother Garrett did not respond, Emma helped her to her feet. "I'll find him and I'll bring him back to the house. We may have to wait under the gazebo if the rain gets heavy, but don't worry. I'll take care of him," she promised and led Butter back through the dining room and outside without bothering to stop for an umbrella.

The stone patio was slick underfoot. Walking carefully, she stopped at the stone wall to view the gazebo area below, but she could not see much through the heavy drizzle. She opened the gate and let Butter go first. The garden steps that laced through the terraced gardens were wet, and she nearly slipped a few times.

When she finally reached bottom ground, she followed the dog's lead. Instead of heading directly for the gazebo, as she expected, he turned off to the path that cut past several mulberry trees and the dense screen of pine trees that led, ultimately, across the roadway and to the canal. Once they reached the protection of the tree cover, she stopped to catch her breath for a few moments and shake the drizzle from her skirts but quickly caught up to the dog, who continued to plow his way slowly back to his master.

With increasing anxiety, Emma followed him when he left the path yet again and proceeded directly into the woods. Immersed in total stillness, the heavy scent of pine and the barest whisper of cedar, her steps were muffled by the thick bed of needles beneath her feet. She had not traveled more than a few dozen yards before she saw Reverend Glenn lying flat on his back on the dry ground at the base of a majestic pine tree just ahead. She barely had a glimpse of him before Butter lunged forward and obscured her view.

"Please . . . please let him be all right," she prayed and rushed toward him.

She was halfway there when she heard the minister chuckle. "Don't rush so, or you'll find yourself flat on the ground like I am."

She stumbled in surprise and slowed her steps. When she reached him momentarily, she dropped down and knelt beside him on the bed of pine needles, with Butter already plopped against the length of his other, weaker side. "What happened? Are you all right? Are you hurt?" she gushed, searching for any visible sign of injury or evidence he might have suffered another stroke.

"I'm fine. Nothing's bent or broken, leastways not so anyone would notice," he managed and started chuckling again.

He was chuckling?

Concerned that he might have struck his head, she put the back of her hand to his forehead.

He sighed and took her hand. "You won't find a fever, and there's nothing hurt but a bit of my pride." When he chuckled again, his eyes were sparkling. "It's a terrible thing, getting old. One tiny misstep, and I was down on the ground. Try as I might,

I couldn't get up. Not even with Butter here trying his best to support me."

He paused to pat the dog's back. "I knew he'd go back to the house for help. I just hoped you folks wouldn't be too alarmed."

Relieved beyond measure, Emma lent her assistance when he tried to sit up. "Whatever possessed you to leave the gazebo to traipse through the woods?" she asked when he was finally able to sit up on his own.

He pointed to his right. "See that little pile of small branches over there?"

She nodded.

"That's mine. I would have had more if I hadn't fallen." He sighed. "I can't do much these days, but I've been trying to think of a way I could do a little to help earn my keep, like Frances is doing with her needlework. After talking with her about the old days, I thought of something and wanted to collect some branches. . . ."

"You don't need to worry about earning your keep," Emma insisted. "Hill House wouldn't be the same without you. Having you with us is a joy."

When he gazed up at her, his eyes were troubled. "I hardly think coming out to rescue me in this miserable weather is a joy."

"I think I'll save my arguments about that until later," she replied. "Right now we need to get back to the house before there's a downpour and Mother Garrett gets so upset she calls out the militia to find us both."

After several attempts, Emma finally managed to get him standing upright. With Butter close to his master's side, they started back toward the path. "Hold still just a moment," she said and ran to the pile of branches he had risked so much to collect. After removing her apron and laying it on the ground, she put the branches on top and wrapped the apron around them and carried them back with her.

She stashed the small bundle of wood under one arm and held on to Reverend Glenn with the other. "You can explain your collection later when you tell your tale. First, we get back to the house and get some hot tea into us."

"I don't suppose we could cook up a better tale, rather than tell everyone this old man fell down and couldn't get up, do you?" he asked as they walked toward the path leading back to the gazebo.

Surprised that he now felt uncomfortable about sharing the precise details of his mishap with the others, she shrugged. "I suppose that would depend on how long it takes us to get back to the house," she offered, wishing she had had time to bring an umbrella along.

"It was just a temptation. There's no sense trying to avoid the truth. Not at my age," he said. "Let's just get back inside the house so I can tell my tale and be done with it. If nothing else, I'll get a few folks to enjoy a good chuckle," he offered with a smile.

"At least you've gotten the branches of wood you wanted."

His smile deepened. "That's not just wood, my dear. That's candlewood."

16

G IVEN THE RETIRED MINISTER'S misadventure and Emma's
traipse through bad weather to rescue him, Mother Garrett
had abandoned her original plans for a cold dinner. With Liesel's
help, she set out a grand offering of the ham, potatoes bubbling
with a tangy sauce made from the renderings of the bacon laid on
top, hot muffins, and applesauce laced with honey and cinnamon.

Understandably, she had duly forgiven Butter for tracking mud
into her kitchen. Emma had also noted that his muzzle was unusu-
ally shiny. She suspected Mother Garrett might have put a crock
of butter low enough for him to reach without openly offering
the treat to him but wisely chose not to ask her mother-in-law
directly, just as she had chosen not to ask her about her still-
mysterious errand earlier this morning.

As Emma had expected, however, everyone had expressed
only sincere concern for Reverend Glenn's welfare and his good
fortune for not being injured. There had been no discussion about
the candlewood he was collecting, but there also had been nary a
word or expression that might have suggested he had been foolish

to wander off into the woods alone.

Though the drizzle had stopped, the day remained cool and dreary and inspired Emma to venture upstairs for her nap. She used the back staircase that led directly from her office to her bedroom, although she also had access through another door that led to the upstairs hallway. The bedroom itself was half the size of most of the guest rooms, which suited Emma just fine. She much preferred the simply furnished pale green room rather than the heavier, formal furniture in the guest rooms, almost all of which had been included in the purchase of Hill House—furniture that she would lose if the current owner decided not to sell Hill House to her.

She reached the top of the staircase just as the grandfather clock struck the hour of three. She opened the door and stood in the doorway for a moment to feel the memories waiting for her before slipping inside and shutting the door behind her.

She ran her hand along the top of the walnut wardrobe her grandmother had brought with her to Candlewood and felt the scratches and nicks that marred the surface after years of use. She walked over to the yellow pitcher and bowl resting on the wooden washstand that had belonged to her mother, smiled, and traced the raised bouquet of flowers on the pitcher with her fingertips.

The trunk hugging the foot of her single bed had once been filled with Jonas's clothes and, later, with her babies' clothing. Though tempted to sit awhile on the trunk, she fluffed her pillow, slipped her keepsakes underneath, and stretched out on the bed without bothering to pull the quilt up from the bottom. After closing her eyes, she snuggled her face against the soft, downy pillow. Surrounded by the familiar, she hoped to set her troubles aside and fall asleep thinking only of her children and grandchildren, especially little Deborah, since it was her birthday.

Instead, a soft rap intervened at the opposite door, which opened up to the upstairs hallway.

"Emma? It's me. Do you think you might spare me a moment?"

Emma had groaned out loud at the sound of the knock, and now she silently berated herself for begrudging Widow Leonard a moment of her time and quickly got up to open the door.

The woman stood there holding a set of bed linens as white as the full moon in winter. "I hope I didn't disturb you. May I come in?"

"Certainly." Emma stepped aside to let the woman into the room and shut the door behind her.

When Widow Leonard turned around, she was holding the linens out to Emma. "These are for you."

Puzzled, Emma accepted the linens and ventured just a peek at the heavy embroidery on the hem of the pillowcase on top. "I thought you were too busy mending bed linens to have time to embroider."

The elderly woman's eyes twinkled. "I've been working on these at night or in the afternoons sometimes." She sat down on the bed and patted the place next to her. "Sit. Let me show them to you."

The moment Emma sat down, Widow Leonard lifted the pillowcase from the top, unfolded it, and spread it out on her lap so the thicker, embroidered edge of the pillowcase was facing Emma. "Take a look."

Emma stared at the woman's handiwork and gasped. "How did you manage to do this?" she whispered. With her fingertips, she traced the outline of the General Store the woman had created with her stitchery and marveled at the detail in the white-on-white image.

"My memory is good enough, but I made sure of the details when I went to the General Store to get the thread."

"I had no idea . . ."

"There's more," Widow Leonard insisted and turned the pillowcase over, where another image brought Hill House to life.

"You even stitched the gardens and the gazebo," Emma said, unable to resist tracing these patterns, too.

"Reverend Glenn was kind enough to keep me company in the gazebo while I worked." She peered closer to her handiwork and wrinkled her nose. "I'm still not sure I'm happy with those roses."

Emma choked back tears, hugged the pillowcase to her heart with one hand, and gave Widow Leonard a brief hug with the other. "I love them just the way they are. I love you, too, for making this for me," she whispered. "Thank you. It's . . . it's the finest gift I've ever been given. Ever."

"After taking me in the way you did, I knew I had to make something special for you, and now . . . maybe now you could call me Aunt Frances like the young ones do. I know we're not blood related, but I feel like we are."

Emma swallowed hard. In the space of a few weeks, this tiny, elderly woman had made a deep impact on everyone at Hill House and had truly become a member of their family. Mother Garrett now had a friend close to her own age, a blessing that also invited a bit of mischief. Reverend Glenn had become more confident, spending more and more time out of his room and outside in the gazebo. Both Liesel and Ditty loved being a bit spoiled and were eagerly learning their embroidery stitches. And now Emma had been touched by her kindness. "I do, too," she said. She prayed with all her heart that Widow Leonard might be able to remain here at Hill House, surrounded by people who both loved her and needed her.

Grinning, her aunt-by-affection started to unfold the bed sheet. "Wait until you see—"

Another knock at the hallway door interrupted them.

"Emma? May I come in?"

Emma cleared her throat and looked down at Aunt Frances, but before she could ask her if she would mind, Mother Garrett opened the door and poked her head inside. "Oh! I beg your pardon. I didn't know you were here, Frances. I'll come back later."

"No, come in," the woman urged and patted the bed on her other side. "I'm sorry. I probably should have asked you to come with me in the first place. Do join us."

When Mother Garrett hesitated, Emma added her own invitation and studied the pillowcase again while Aunt Frances showed the images on each side.

"I knew you'd do a fine job, but this . . . this is far more than I expected," Mother Garrett said.

Emma blinked hard. "You knew about this?"

"Of course I did," she teased. "Contrary to what some people might think, I can keep a secret as good as the next."

When Emma chuckled, her mother-in-law huffed. "Maybe I haven't been very good at keeping secrets in the past, but I am now. I didn't tell you about this surprise any more than I told you about the trip I made this morning to the General Store to get more thread for Frances, now, did I? That's because it was a secret, and not keeping secrets is one of the few things I've managed to overcome in my later years."

Dropping her gaze, Emma fingered the embroidered image of Hill House on the border of the pillowcase and tucked her own secret about the possibility of losing Hill House deeper in her heart. She was not sure if keeping this secret from both of these two women, as well as the others who depended on her at Hill House, was fair to them or not, but she was positive that adding uncertainty to all of their lives was not right. Not when she had every hope the heir would eventually agree to sell Hill House to Emma. This was a burden she had to carry alone, at least for now.

"You've also managed to keep your memory as sharp as any woman I know, too," Aunt Frances insisted before she turned her attention to Emma. "She's been a great help to me while I was stitching, you know."

Curious to know how, Emma glanced up at her mother-in-law. "You helped to make this, too?"

"Not with the stitchery. With the designs. But not these. The ones on the bed sheet."

"Here. I'll show you," Aunt Frances offered, folded up the pillowcase, and handed it back to Emma to set aside. She smoothed the extra-large hem at the top of the sheet she had already spread on her lap, but before she could turn it around so Emma could see it, there was yet another knock at Emma's door.

This time the knock came from the door at the head of the staircase that led down to Emma's office.

"Widow Garrett?"

Emma recognized Liesel's voice and groaned. "As tiny as she is, I don't think we can fit another body in here," she whispered. "You're back early. Is anything wrong?" she said in a louder voice so Liesel could hear her through the closed door.

"No, ma'am. I came back early to meet up with Ditty. We're supposed to go visiting together, but she's not back yet. There's a caller at the front door. It's a Mr. Leonard. He came to see Aunt Frances, but I . . . I asked him to wait in the hall. I was wondering if I should show him to the parlor or to the office since he said he wanted to see you, too."

Emma took Aunt Frances's hand and realized she had never heard the front bell. "Is it Mr. Andrew Leonard or his brother, James?"

"That I wouldn't know," Liesel said. "Since I never met him, I'm not certain, and I don't think he told me his first name. He might have, but I . . . I don't think I heard him." She sounded flustered, even uncertain, which was not like the girl at all.

Emma turned to the elderly woman. "If you like, you can meet with your son in the parlor alone, or I can go with you. Or I can meet with him in my office first. It's entirely up to you."

"I'm not sure what to do. If it's Andrew, he must be coming back to tell me he's done what I asked and settled this problem with his brother, and I'd like to see him alone. If it's not, if James has come, it might be better if you were with me."

Emma squeezed her hand. "Why don't I have Liesel show him to the library. I'll be right next door in my office. If Andrew has come with good news, you can meet with him privately. If it's James, then you can simply call out and ask me to join you."

When Aunt Frances gave her assent to the plan, Emma smiled. "Liesel, show Mr. Leonard to the library; then you can wait for Ditty and go visiting like you planned."

While Liesel scampered back down the steps, Mother Garrett stood up. "I can't do much to help, I suppose, but I'll go downstairs with you anyway. There's plenty to do in the kitchen." She led Aunt Frances out the door to the hallway, while Emma quickly set the bed linens aside, disappointed she would have to wait until later to see the rest of her gift.

Emma rearranged her skirts and checked her hair in the small hand mirror she kept in the drawer of the table next to her bed.

Satisfied with her appearance, she slipped from her room and down the back staircase to her office. With one beat, her heart leaped with the joyful hope Andrew had returned with good news. With the next beat, her heart trembled with the dread of facing Aunt Frances's eldest son.

Her uncertainty increased with every step she took, and her heart was pounding hard against the wall of her chest by the time she reached the bottom of the staircase.

"Be not afraid," she whispered and stepped into her office to wait and to pray.

For Aunt Frances. For her two sons.

For peace between them all.

For the owner of Hill House, that he might agree to let Emma buy this home again.

And for this to be the last surprise of the day.

17

E MMA? WOULD YOU JOIN US, PLEASE?"
        The walk from the office to the adjoining library was a
matter of mere feet and gave Emma little time to prepare before
she stepped into the library. With one glance at the young man
standing next to Aunt Frances with his arm wrapped protectively
around her, Emma stopped abruptly.

"Come in, come in," Aunt Frances gushed. She had her arm
tucked about his waist as if he might suddenly vanish from sight.
"This is my grandson, Harry. He's James's second oldest. Harry,
this is Widow Garrett."

Emma smiled. "Oh, your grandson," she managed. Once her
brain abandoned her anticipation of seeing a much older man and
reconciled the image of this much younger man with Aunt
Frances's words, she was able to relax again. Harry was built tall
and sturdy, and he appeared to be in his early twenties, closest in
age to her youngest son, Mark. No wonder Liesel had been a little
flustered. Dressed for farm work in denim coveralls, he bore a
strong resemblance to his father, but his soft blue eyes glistened

with the same touch of orneriness as his grandmother's.

"Ma'am? I hope you don't mind me barging in like this, but me and Thomas had a load to bring in for the afternoon packet boat."

Emma approached him with a smile. "You've grown a bit. I don't think I've seen you since you were in short pants. Is Thomas coming, too?"

He grinned. "He's lined up behind the other wagons on Canal Street, so I figured I could run on up here and be back again before he unloaded." He urged his grandmother closer to him. "I had to see my renegade grandmother for myself, just to see how she was faring," he teased.

Aunt Frances looked up at him. "I'm missing you. And your brothers," she added before she frowned. "I gather you didn't tell your parents you were coming to see me. I hope you don't get into too much trouble on my account."

He chuckled. "When I offered to come with Thomas, I was hoping I'd have time to visit you. I wasn't sure I would, so I didn't bother mentioning it. I think Mother had her suspicions, though." He stepped back from her, pulled something from his coveralls, and handed it to her. "Mother slipped this to me before I left," he explained. "Take a look and see what you think."

Intrigued, Emma stepped a little closer to get a better view.

Aunt Frances had a round tin the size of a small apple resting in the palm of her hand. While she held the base with one hand, Harry lifted the lid. "Well?"

"Licorice root!" she cried, snatched the lid back from him, popped it back onto the tin, and kept a tight hold on her treasure. "Bless her, she knew," she whispered.

He hugged her closer and glanced at Emma. "Other than my grandmother, my mother is the only one at home who will touch licorice root. As soon as I saw it, I knew for sure I was coming up to Hill House. Not that I mentioned it to Thomas."

He laughed again. "Thomas would have lectured me all the way to town and back again. This way, I only have to hear the half of it."

"Your father will have more to say when he finds out. I've caused enough trouble running away as it is. You shouldn't be deceiving your father," Aunt Frances warned.

"I gotta go. Thomas will be apoplectic if I'm not back by the time he's unloaded." He planted a kiss on top of her head, set her back, and grinned down at her. "Don't worry, I'll tell Father I was here. But after supper, just in case. And don't stay away too long—we miss you, too." He looked up at Emma. "Thanks for letting me visit, Widow Garrett," he said and bounded to the doorway.

He charged out of the room and into the hallway but returned in two heartbeats to poke his head back inside. Eyes twinkling, he offered them both a wink. "I'll be back on Friday," he promised before disappearing again.

Emma pressed her lips together to keep from chuckling but gave up the effort when Aunt Frances started laughing. "That boy came into this world twenty-two years ago as quick as a tornado can fell a tree twice as old as I am. He hasn't let much stop him from doing anything he's wanted to do ever since."

"He's got your sparkle," Emma noted.

Aunt Frances shook her head. "That 'sparkle' has gotten him sent to bed without his supper so many times, it's a wonder he's grown as big as he is. I'm thinking he's taller than Thomas or Nathan or Paul, although it might be that I haven't seen my grandsons for a spell."

Longing to be with her own grandchildren, Emma slipped her hand into her pocket and quickly realized she had left her keepsakes under her pillow. The opening of the front door and the sound of female voices announced the return of her guests from their day of shopping. "I should probably go and help them. They're bound to have packages that need to be taken upstairs."

"Would you like to take a piece of licorice root first?"

Emma wrinkled her nose. "I'd hate to see you waste it on someone who doesn't appreciate it. Mother Garrett favors it, though," she offered and hurried out to the center hallway.

The front door stood wide open, but the three figures of Mrs. Sewell and her daughters blocked any view of what sort of purchases might be waiting on the porch to be brought inside.

Mrs. Sewell was the first one to notice Emma approaching. "What a day, what a day, what a day!" she gushed, wearing yet another fine gown made of lavender lawn that had more ruffles on the skirts than all of Emma's gowns combined.

Emma braced herself to hear the worst, starting with the walk to the center of town and ending with complaints about the miserable weather.

Instead, while her daughters finished storing their bonnets on the hat rack, Mrs. Sewell launched into a litany of glorious experiences they had shared on their outing, save for one disappointment she shared with Emma in a whisper. "I so wanted to expose Madeline and Miriam to some of the finer points of etiquette by dining at the hotel, but the food . . ."

When she shivered, every ruffle on her skirts shook. "I'm afraid after enjoying the meals Mother Garrett has prepared for us, we've been spoiled. We barely touched a thing. I know your two girls are off today, but I wonder if you could implore Mother Garrett on our behalf and have her make us a light snack, perhaps something sweet, to help us make do until supper?"

"In truth, I believe she'd be rather pleased to do that for you.

Would you like to take your snack on the patio or the dining room?"

"Upstairs in our room would probably be better. That way we could have something to eat while we're looking over our purchases again." She paused, looked around the hallway, and frowned. "I thought you might have added a bit of stenciling or a mural to add a bit of interest to the entrance by now. Then again, I suppose you don't often have itinerant artists travel this far, even with the canal."

Accustomed to Mrs. Sewell's unsolicited advice, Emma merely smiled. "No, we don't. Why don't I help you take up your things before I see about your snack."

"Ma'am? Mrs. Sewell?"

Emma looked up when she heard Will Adams' voice, but she could not see past everyone to get him in sight.

"He'll take care of the packages for us," Mrs. Sewell insisted.

"Then I'm off to the kitchen to find Mother Garrett," Emma replied and hurried on her way. When she got to the kitchen, the room was empty. No sign of Mother Garrett, Aunt Frances, Reverend Glenn, or even Butter, for that matter.

She checked the patio. Empty. She went to the gate in the stone wall and scanned down the garden steps to the gazebo. Empty.

She rolled her eyes, sighed, and returned to the kitchen. She stood very still for a moment and cocked an ear but heard only the muted sounds of her guests' voices as they chattered their way to their rooms. She grabbed a fresh apron, tied it into place, and tried not to panic.

Although Emma much preferred to be behind a counter or her desk, she could stand in front of a larder and pull together a mere snack if she had no other options. Since Mother Garrett had seemingly disappeared, Emma had no choice but to make it herself. She scanned the contents of the larder and sighed. Finding nearly a bare supply of foodstuffs, especially when guests were in residence, was as uncommon in Mother Garrett's larder as discovering a field of daisies poking through a winter snowdrift. To be fair, however, the Sewell family's healthy appetites did surpass most guests.

"I promised Mrs. Sewell a snack, and a snack she shall have," Emma said. Undaunted, she pulled several crocks and tins to the table and set out two trays and some utensils. After unfolding two crisply ironed napkins, she placed one on each of the trays before going into the dining room. She chose two oval china plates from the pieces left by the original owners that Ditty had not broken yet. Before she left, she grabbed the tin of doughnuts stored in the opposite side of the sideboard, nearly knocking over a vase of roses on the top in the process, and returned to the kitchen.

Rather than stand to do her chore, she took a seat at the table after removing the lid from the tin of doughnuts. Dismayed to find only two crullers sitting in a thick bed of crumbs, she quickly scanned the items she had brought to the table and did the best she could to improvise.

With scarcely any room to work, she started with the crullers. After slicing the fried dough lengthwise, she layered a thick coating of apple butter on top and cut them into bite-sized pieces she arranged in the center of each oval plate. She set the tin onto the floor to give herself more room, then lined up rows of wafer-thin crackers. She topped half of them with mulberry jam, then set the crock of jam on the seat of the chair next to her. She spread creamy butter on the other half and drizzled honey on top. Inspired, she got up to retrieve a stick of cinnamon and a scraper, dusted cinnamon on top of the butter, too, and stored the scraper in the sink for the time being.

After setting the cracker tin down next to the empty doughnut tin and the crock of butter next to the jam, she alternated each type of cracker in rows encircling the crullers.

"Pretty," she murmured and wiped the sticky residue from her fingertips. There was still room on the plate for more, but she had run clear out of ideas, if not ingredients.

Inspired yet again, she returned to the dining room and carried the vase of roses back to the kitchen. She managed to remove enough leaves from the stems to encircle the tidbits she had prepared without pricking herself on the thorns more than once or twice. After snipping off four of the smallest but fullest roses, all white, she placed two at the widest point of each oval and added a pale pink rosebud at the top.

"Beautiful!"

With a tray in each hand, she left the kitchen to take her efforts to her guests. By the time she had delivered the snacks and headed back down the center staircase to return to the kitchen, she was floating. Despite the challenge, she had outdone herself, and the Sewells' glowing compliments had lifted her from being self-satisfied to being overjoyed, even though she faced cleaning up the awful mess she had made of Mother Garrett's kitchen.

She took but a single step into the kitchen before she rocked to a halt and gasped. What mess she had made was nothing compared to the disaster in front of her.

"Butter! Butter, no!" she cried. "Scoot, dog."

He pulled his nose from the crock of mulberry jam sitting on the seat of the chair and plopped down on the floor, upending the doughnut tin, which spewed crumbs as it rolled across the room.

Sidestepping the crumbs, she picked up the now-empty butter

crock from the floor near the cupboard and carried it along with her as she approached the dog. "Mangy mongrel! Look what you've done to Mother Garrett's kitchen," she grumbled.

He belched and closed his eyes.

She glared at him. "I hope you enjoyed your snack."

He opened his eyes and struggled to his feet.

When he nudged at her skirts, he touched the one tender spot her annoyance had not reached. "Poor fella. You must have felt like a puppy again, and here I am yelling at you. I guess I'm not blameless. I left everything where you could reach it."

She glanced around the room and rolled up her sleeves. "I don't suppose there's any real harm done, provided I can clean this up before Mother Garrett gets back. I gather you're going to be mum about where she is and where Aunt Frances and Reverend Glenn might have disappeared to?"

He flopped back down on the floor.

"Good enough. Just stay there, please, until I clean this up and then you're going outside," she warned and got straight to the miserable task at hand, as well as foot.

". . . and thank you, Lord, for an evening with no new surprises. Amen."

Emma finished her evening prayers, pulled down the quilt on her bed, and climbed beneath the bed sheet. The air was still but warm. There was just a bare hint of moonlight outside, and her bedroom was bathed in darkness. Surrounded by a quiet household, she felt for her keepsakes beneath the pillow under her head and wrapped her fingers around them.

With her other hand, she tugged the sheet to her shoulders. The moment she smoothed the edge flat and felt the embroidery, she paused. "My gift!" She had forgotten all about her gift from Aunt Frances, but apparently either Mother Garrett or Aunt Frances had not forgotten and had put the new bed linens on her bed for her.

Anxious to see the design on the top hem of the bed sheet, she eased from her bed and lit the lamp on the table next to it. Within moments, a soft glow brought the design to life. A row of hearts stretched from one side of the sheet to the other and rested below a vine of leaves and flowers. The dates stitched within each heart drew her attention and set her heart aglow. Tears blurred her vision as she traced the dates, each a precious moment in her life. The day of her birth. The day she had become Jonas's wife. The birth dates of her children, their marriages, and the birth dates of her grandchildren.

She gave her tears free rein to fall. Amazed by Aunt Frances's work and the thoughtfulness it represented, she now knew Mother Garrett had helped by providing the dates.

"Bless you both," she whispered. She doused the lamp and climbed back into her bed of memories, all the more grateful He had saved the greatest surprise of the day for the last.

18

ARLY THE NEXT MORNING before breakfast, Emma was at her desk when Mr. Sewell appeared in the doorway between the library and her office. "I've arranged for a carriage to pick my family up at ten o'clock for an outing, but we'll be back for dinner, of course. I rose earlier than usual today to spend some time talking with Reverend Glenn again. Apparently, he overslept and is still dressing, so it appears I have a few extra moments. While I'm waiting, if it's not inconvenient, now might be the only time for us to talk privately."

"Of course. Please come in. I hadn't heard your plans for today," she offered and set aside the letter she had been writing.

Chuckling, he crossed the room and wedged himself into the chair facing her desk. "In truth, since this is our last full day here, I do believe if I hadn't planned an outing so I could spend some time with my family, they would have gone shopping again, and I might have had to hire a separate freight barge to haul all their purchases home."

She smiled. "Your wife and daughters seemed pleased with all the new shops. I hope your ventures here in Candlewood have been as successful," she prompted, anxious to learn how he had fared.

He nodded. "To a point, I believe they have, although the group of investors I represent will make the final judgment. My travels over the past few days have been most enlightening, and I daresay I would not have made nearly as much progress without your help."

"I don't know that I've been all that helpful," she admitted. She did not consider the little information she had given him this year to be much more than common knowledge.

"As uncommon as others may find it, considering your sex, your knowledge of the area and business sense have always been as solid as I could hope to find," he countered. "No one in Candlewood had the foresight to see the potential in Hill House, but you did."

"My grandmother and mother, bless their souls, would be as pleased that you're so generous with your kind words as I am," she replied, although she doubted he would have the same opinion of her if he knew about the legal troubles surrounding her ownership of Hill House.

He drummed his fingers on the arm of his chair for a few moments, as if choosing his words carefully. "You may not, however, be as informed or as aware as you should be about other . . . shall we say, developments."

Her heart skipped a beat in anticipation of hearing his viewpoints on the future of Candlewood and the surrounding area. Mr. Sewell had been very careful not to divulge the exact details surrounding his interests in the area last year, and she did not expect him to talk to her about anything in other than general terms now. Perhaps now more than ever before she needed the benefit of his considerable experience and knowledge, which was far superior to her own, especially in light of his connections to other well-established and well-heeled investors and entrepreneurs in the East.

"I fear you may be right. I am not informed as well as I'd like to be," she admitted. "You were very generous in sharing your perceptions with me last year, especially about the Candlewood Canal."

"The Erie Canal and the feeder canals, like the one in Candlewood, have been a boon to many towns and very profitable, at this point, to some investors but not all. Most towns like Candlewood have grown faster in the past five or six years than in the previous twenty-five. Some will continue to grow and prosper, while others face a much harsher future. The most difficult task, in my view, is to determine which towns offer the greatest promise of growth and how to be in a position to foster that growth to turn a profit. Not that there's ever a way to eliminate the risk when making an investment," he cautioned.

Intrigued to know his opinion about which future lay ahead for Candlewood, Emma also noted the glint of excitement in his eyes. "No, there isn't. Yet it's deciding which risk to take that separates the wise man from the foolish one," she commented, feeling very foolish indeed for not following her lawyer's advice and thinking through her rash decision to buy Hill House.

He cocked his head. "Quite a valuable observation."

She frowned. "Unfortunately, I can't lay claim to it as mine, any more than I can say I've let those words guide all of my business decisions. My grandmother deserves the merit, although to quote her accurately, I would have to say that risk-taking in business ultimately separates the wise *woman* from the foolish one."

He chuckled again. "Also true."

"To your mind, now that the Candlewood Canal is operating

well, what factors will affect the town's future most?" she asked, hoping he might be able to offer her advice she might need if she had to move from Hill House.

His expression grew serious. "The same as in the past. Geography. Geography. Geography."

When she narrowed her gaze, he laced his hands and laid them atop his stomach. "What single factor played the most significant role in determining whether or not Candlewood would grow like it has or remain simply a small anchor for area farmers?"

"The canal."

"Perhaps, but what factor led to the building of the canal on a route that led through Candlewood?"

She shrugged. "I suppose because the canal started south of here and ended in Bounty. Candlewood just happened to be in between."

"At the midpoint of the route, to be precise, where the initial investors raised a greater portion of the cost of building the canal from other investors," he corrected, reminding her that the initial investors had used naming the canal after the town as an important lure.

He paused for a moment and smiled. "Geography, then."

"Yes, but—"

"The canal era is at its peak, or nearly so. Within ten years I suspect most towns along the canal will be fortunate if they can reclaim the level of success they enjoyed before the canals were ever built."

Her concern heightened. "But the geography won't have changed."

"Essentially you're correct, but progress is not static. Progress continues as technology evolves. Interests shift from one location to another, or interest heightens in specific locations, depending on—"

"Geography," she murmured. She paused for a moment to let her brain sift through the articles she had read over the past year in various journals and newspapers, as well as gossip she had gleaned from area businessmen before she latched on to several ideas that seemed to have generated the most interest.

"Extending the Candlewood Canal is one option," she offered, choosing the one topic of most interest locally.

He shrugged. "True."

She tried again, suggesting something a bit more exotic. "Developing the silk industry seems to hold a great deal of promise for making substantial profits."

He coughed.

She proffered her final idea, although it seemed to be the riskiest of all. "The railroad?"

He rose from his seat. "The difference between a wise investor and a foolish one goes just a bit further than deciding when or how to risk one's capital. In truth, it is a wise investor who not only anticipates the future but prepares for it. The foolish one, on the other hand, sees the future only in terms of the present."

She swallowed hard. In hindsight, and in all honesty, she realized she may have foolishly rushed to buy Hill House not just as a way to create a new future for herself but more to escape the lonely reality of her life at the General Store without giving God the opportunity to show her the way He had planned for her.

"Reverend Glenn and I see eye to eye in that regard," he continued, "which is something we were going to discuss further this morning."

When she narrowed her gaze, he smiled. "Obviously I'm very interested in financial matters and being successful in this life, but the good minister reminded me only yesterday that perhaps I should be equally concerned about anticipating and preparing for eternal life." He then left her alone to ponder his final words while he went to see Reverend Glenn.

Emma sat at her desk for nearly half an hour, deep in thought about their conversation. Ultimately, she decided Mr. Sewell would not have returned to Candlewood and spent the past three days touring property in the area unless he seriously thought the area offered the opportunity to profit from wise investments, possibly related to the construction of a railroad at some point in Candlewood's future.

Given that assumption, she rifled through the clutter in her desk drawers, found a map of the area that included most of the eastern part of the state, and spread it out on top of the papers on her desk. She found Candlewood on the map easily enough, studied the area immediately surrounding the town, then put Candlewood in context with the outlying areas along the length of the Candlewood Canal.

If indeed Mr. Sewell's belief that a railroad system would one day replace the canal system was correct, Candlewood should fare well. Although the canal ran north and east, the better route for a railroad would be north.

Due north.

Directly through Bounty, like the canal.

Directly along the toll road on the Leonard property.

Still deep in thought, she refolded the map and stored it away again. Long before the canal had become a reality, a number of local businessmen had formed committees that made joint investments and reaped huge profits. She was not aware of any committees formed to do the same in anticipation of a railroad. That did not mean they did not exist; only that, as a woman, she had not been included. Again.

If indeed there might be a railroad in Candlewood's future, the value of land in and around the town of Candlewood would soar even higher, especially land suitable for business development. A wise investor would hold on to what land he or she already owned. If the legal owner of Hill House was wise, he might very well keep Hill House as an investment or raise the selling price substantially above the sum she had already paid.

Other investors, working quietly and efficiently, would acquire as much open land as possible for as little cost as possible. Land such as the parcel of land she had sold to Mother Garrett, which had disappointed one very determined investor: Mr. Langhorne.

Suddenly the man's dogged interest in Emma's land made sense. Her stipulation to protect that land from development for the next twenty years may have been prompted by her desire to hold on to a piece of Candlewood's past yet also appeared to have been very wise in light of its potential value, particularly if she had to actually ask Mother Garrett to sell her parcel of land so Emma could buy Hill House again.

Connecting Mr. Langhorne's interests to the Leonard brothers' property containing a portion of the toll road also made sense. Given Mr. Langhorne's very vocal desire to be part of Candlewood's future, it was not as much of a stretch as it might have been only yesterday to think he was pursuing a new venture or that he might actually be the buyer pushing Andrew Leonard to sell.

From experience, she knew how persistent Mr. Langhorne could be, which might explain why Andrew Leonard appeared to be so anxious to sell the land, even if it meant forfeiting his relationship with his brother. She also knew that Mr. Langhorne would let nothing stand in his way. Should he discover that Emma did not own legal title to Hill House, she should be prepared to expect him to use that as leverage, if only to force her to stop intervening in the Leonards' squabble. Buying Hill House out from under her might also be a very sweet prize of revenge.

If she was right that there was a railroad in Candlewood's future, the property at the center of the dissension within the Leonard family was potentially far more valuable than either brother assumed. Reaping a significant profit, however, was many years in the future.

If she was wrong, she might very well stir up a hornet's nest of problems—and being stung by embarrassment would be the very least of them, especially if Zachary Breckenwith had anything to say about it.

She rubbed her forehead to ease away a dull headache. Today was turning out no better than yesterday, and she had not even had breakfast yet.

19

THE SEWELLS DEPARTED FOR A RIDE in the countryside, although with the girls' bickering, Emma was not sure how pleasant the trip would be. Ditty was upstairs preparing rooms for guests arriving on tomorrow's afternoon packet. Liesel was in the kitchen helping Mother Garrett with preparations for dinner. Aunt Frances was upstairs busy finishing some sort of parting gift for the Sewell family. Reverend Glenn was on the side porch with Butter doing the same, although Emma had been given strict orders not to venture outside and spoil his surprise.

With everyone else accounted for, Emma popped into the kitchen to let Mother Garrett know her plans. To her surprise, Mother Garrett was alone at the table snapping beans. "Where's Liesel?"

"Down rooting in the cellar again. I know I have more beans, but the girl's been gone so long, either she can't find them, I've misjudged what I had, or she's planted some beans and decided to wait for them to grow."

Emma burst out laughing, but she sobered when her mother-in-law gave her a dark look. "I just wanted to let you know I'm going out to do some errands."

"Would that include a stop at the General Store?"

"Yes, I have my correspondence to post. Why? Did you need something?"

Mother Garrett stopped to wipe her hands, went to the larder, and took out a small tin and a large covered dish. "You can save me some steps and take something with you for Mr. Atkins. It's not much. Just a few pretzels." She held out the tin to Emma, who took it with the same hand holding her reticule. "We made a double batch yesterday. Even with sending some with the Sewells to enjoy for their journey home and setting some aside for the guests who are arriving tomorrow, there's more than enough left to send him a few," she explained.

"I see. What else have you got there?"

Mother Garrett handed her the covered dish. "Just a bit left from this and that. Some slices of ham. The sausages and potatoes left from breakfast. I guess I made too much. Then there's two slices of pound cake from yesterday, some apple butter . . ."

"You're in charge of the kitchen. You don't have to account for every morsel," Emma insisted. Suddenly she realized why the larder had recently been so bare and where Mother Garrett's recent errands had taken her. She also suspected her mother-in-law would be sending foodstuffs to each of her three grandsons if they lived nearby. "I'm just surprised you've taken such an interest in Mr. Atkins."

Blushing, her mother-in-law shrugged. "Somebody needs to look out for him. He's mended just fine, but the poor man still can't cook for himself and operate the store. I've been stopping in every now and then to take him what's been left behind at meals after our guests have had their fill. He's very grateful for all the help you gave him," she said, then turned to retrieve the canvas bag she used when she went shopping.

"I didn't do all that much," Emma countered.

Mother Garrett took the items Emma was holding, stored them in the bag, and handed it to Emma. "There. I think you'll find it easier going if you borrow my bag."

"That's much better. Thank you," Emma said, adding her correspondence, as well. She pecked the older woman's cheek. "Just limit yourself to feeding the man. I'm certain he's quite capable of finding a wife on his own."

This time, Mother Garrett's cheeks flamed scarlet. "I'm certain I have not the slightest inkling—"

"Yes, you do, and I wouldn't doubt for a moment that you've recruited Aunt Frances to help you. Not that I'm suggesting you shouldn't help him, even if your last attempt at matchmaking was a disaster," she teased and held up one hand to silence her mother-in-law's objections. "I'm not going to remind you about what happened when you tried to match Mark up with the Olsen girl when Catherine was much more suitable, which she's proven ten times over since they married."

"Good. A woman's entitled to an honest mistake now and then. How was I supposed to know the girl was sensitive to strawberries? Silly twit. She should have said something or turned down eating my dessert instead. She was covered with hives before she even left the table. Catherine has better sense all around."

Emma grinned. "Yes, she does. And as far as Mr. Atkins is concerned, right now I'm only asking for you and Aunt Frances to keep one thing in mind, and I'll not interfere. Agreed?"

"I suppose that depends on what it is."

Emma cocked a brow.

"Well then, agreed. What is it you want?"

"Liesel and Ditty are not, I repeat, not to be part of your plans. Aside from the fact that they're only sixteen and far too young, Liesel is irreplaceable—"

"Agreed."

Emma paused and looked around to make sure they were still alone, then lowered her voice to guarantee she was not overheard. "And until Ditty 'grows into her feet,' as you put it, even thinking about having her work alongside Mr. Atkins in the store would be like . . . like not storing your foodstuffs in the larder—"

"And not expecting trouble? Even I know Butter better than to do that," Mother Garrett teased.

Reminded of her blunder yesterday, Emma bristled. "H-how did you know?"

"I was watching Ditty sort the laundry earlier this morning. I'm not surprised to see most anything staining our aprons, but I couldn't imagine how mulberry jam stained your skirts. Once I recalled the way the Sewells raved over the snack you'd prepared for them while I was out taking Mr. Atkins a bit to eat, and remembered seeing the empty butter crock Liesel had filled just that morning, I knew something had happened."

She smiled, sat back down, and started snapping beans again. "I'd give you back that land you sold me, just to hear the real tale."

"Land you haven't paid for," Emma countered. "You still owe me fifty cents."

"I put that amount on your account at the General Store just the other day. My offer stands," Mother Garrett teased.

"I'm still not interested," Emma huffed and left by the back door. She rounded the house with the very uncomfortable notion she might indeed need that parcel of land back and quickened her steps. The thought of entertaining Mother Garrett with the details of that disastrous experience was one step toward humility Emma would seek to avoid at all costs. If the heir decided to keep Hill House for himself and she was forced to leave here, however, she would very well be humbled beyond all measure.

———

Emma sat across from Zachary Breckenwith and gazed about his office, which ran front to back along the side of the house he shared with his widowed Aunt Elizabeth. Though spacious, it was nevertheless cramped with hundreds of books left by his predecessor. Journals, newspapers, and legal papers sat in piles that zigzagged the floor and littered the top of his desk; it offered visible evidence of the differences between the two lawyers, since Alexander Breckenwith had been neat and organized to a fault.

Though surrounded by the clutter Zachary Breckenwith called "the organized chaos of an overburdened attorney," Emma was focused only on the one concern she needed to address with him. "I stopped by to see if you had had time to register the sale of land to Mother Garrett, amended as we discussed," she began.

Framed by a pair of elaborate but dusty sconces on the wall behind him, he smiled and started rooting through the papers on the floor next to his chair. "For that, I needed the final signatures. Yes, here's the paper work," he murmured.

He sat back in his chair, skimmed the paper he held in his hand, and frowned. "There seems to have been a misunderstanding. I apologize. Jeremy?" he bellowed.

The young man charged into the room, skillfully avoided disturbing any of the papers on the floor, and stopped at the side of his mentor's desk. Emma was far too taken with the color of the man's bright red hair to notice any other of his features.

"Widow Garrett has come for the paper work you prepared.

As I recall, we were going to merely draw up an amendment to the original bill of sale; instead, this is an entirely new agreement."

"Yes, sir. I thought that's what you wanted."

Mr. Breckenwith's frown deepened. "Where's the original bill of sale?"

Jeremy's Adam's apple bobbed up and down. "I . . . I . . . that is, I believe I destroyed it. You've been quite adamant about not accumulating any more paper work than necessary lately. There didn't seem much sense to keep it."

Her lawyer glowered at the younger man. "Not unless one understood that by destroying the paper before a new bill of sale has yet to be executed, the ownership of the land remains in one name instead of another, thereby negating the sale entirely," he countered and tossed the paper onto his desk.

Jeremy blushed. Even the tips of his earlobes turned nearly the same color as his hair.

"Oh, please don't be upset. This is good news. At least, I think it is," Emma quickly said. "Tell me if I understood correctly. Because there is no longer an existing bill of sale, the land is still mine. In order for me to sell the land in question, I'll have to sign the new agreement."

"And so will your mother-in-law," Jeremy added. When he received another glower from his mentor, he stepped back in silent surrender.

"I'm afraid he's right," her lawyer said and promptly dismissed his nephew.

Gladdened by the news she would have the land back without having to tell Mother Garrett the details of her kitchen disaster, if not by the opportunity to witness her lawyer being less than supremely competent and efficient, she smiled. "I was right. This is good news."

"Good?" he asked, and his brows knitted together into a single line of frustration. "Does that mean you've changed your mind about selling the land?"

"Perhaps."

"It's not in your nature to equivocate, especially in your business affairs," he commented. "Nevertheless, I'm at your complete disposal. I will personally draw up the papers for whatever you decide to do, but there'll be no charge. Not after the way this matter has been bungled. If there's anything I can do to make amends . . ."

Relishing her superior position in their relationship for once, she smiled. "I was wondering if I might ask a question."

He leaned back in his chair. "Proceed."

"Once a person dies and the heirs receive their inheritances, I believe the will becomes part of the public record. Anyone interested in the will can read it."

"Correct. Although if it's Hughes's will you want to see, I can save you the trouble. I've already read it and confirmed that not only was Spencer the duly named executor, which gave him the legal right to sell Hill House to you, but also that there is indeed only one heir who now has a legal claim to Hill House."

"Actually, I have two favors to ask of you, neither of which concerns that particular will. First, I'd like you to hold on to that paper work until I decide whether or not to sell that land."

He rooted through the papers to find the one he had tossed to his desk, folded it, and stored it in a desk drawer. "Second?"

"I'd like you to find out everything you can about Enoch Leonard's will," she said firmly.

He tightened his jaw. "Despite my advice otherwise, I believe you're venturing well beyond getting overly involved."

She grinned, knowing full well he did not approve of her

request on one level yet understood on another. "Yes, I believe I am."

––––––

Emma's second errand, at the General Store, went nearly as well as her visit to her lawyer.

After posting her correspondence, she handed over the food-stuffs from Mother Garrett and folded up the canvas bag while Mr. Atkins quickly stored the two containers behind the counter. "I have something I set aside for your mother-in-law," he whispered, keeping his gaze locked on several customers milling about the store waiting for his assistance. "Would it be a great imposition to ask you to wait a few moments until I've taken care of my custom-ers?"

"Not at all. I'll just wander about a bit and see if there's any-thing I might recommend to make operating the store a bit easier."

"I shouldn't be long," he insisted and proceeded to the cus-tomer waiting at the far end of the counter.

She chose to wait for him at a table display of bolts of fabric. By standing on the side facing the counter, she could watch him interact with the customer, a middle-aged woman Emma did not recognize, and keep watch for arriving customers by checking the small, round mirror she had re-hung for him in the corner of a shelf behind the counter.

He had a demeanor that was both attentive and respectful. Now that he had recovered from his injuries, he moved with an ease that evoked a quiet confidence. Impressed, she wandered from one table to another and noted that he had stored away most of the stock to help reduce the temptation to shoplift. Overall, the store had a neater, more organized appearance, although she won-dered if he had had a chance to do anything about clearing the crates and boxes she had seen while walking back to the storage room.

In the far left corner of the store, however, he still had open barrels of coffee and tea, and he had not hung the mirrors she had suggested. She watched as a young boy standing next to a woman she assumed was his mother scooped handfuls of coffee beans and slipped them into a bag his mother had hidden beneath the cape she wore.

Emma turned just a bit and saw Mr. Atkins approach the woman, who then waved him off. "Thank you, but I've changed my mind. I'll be back for coffee next week," she murmured and ushered her son out the door.

When Mr. Atkins did not protest, she followed him back to the counter. "You do realize the boy stole coffee for his mother, don't you?"

He narrowed his gaze. "No, I . . . I was busy wrapping up a parcel. I couldn't really see what they were doing," he admitted, then held up one hand. "I know, I know. I need to rehang the rest of the mirrors, and I intend to do that, just as soon as I find a free moment."

"Would that be before or after you hire someone to help out at the store? Contrary to what Mother Garrett may have in mind, I believe you might find time to hire someone before you'd have the time to find a wife."

He blew out a long breath. "I'm so relieved to have someone take my side. I've been holding off your mother-in-law and Widow Leonard as best I can. Choosing a wife is not something I can do right now. I can't even entertain the notion until I get the General Store operating like I should. I've even been too busy to think beyond needing to hire someone, but I'm not certain I trust myself to know whom to hire. You wouldn't happen to know someone needing a job, would you? Or be willing to help me find someone? I could really use your help."

She laughed. "You can't be serious."

"I'm perfectly serious," he said. "If I trusted you enough to leave you in my store with the key to my cashbox, why wouldn't I trust you with finding someone to work for me? I don't need more than someone who is honest and willing to work hard unloading and loading shipments so I have more time for my customers."

"And have more time to sleep and to eat?"

He smiled. "That too."

She let out a sigh. "Let me think on it," she said, then suddenly remembered Mr. Cross at the boat landing and meeting his family, including a younger brother who needed work. "Actually, I may know someone. I'm not sure if he's found work yet or not—"

"He's hired!"

She laughed. "You'd make a poor bluffer," she teased.

He cocked his head. "But a good shopkeeper?"

"I believe you will," she murmured, and she meant it. "I believe I have the time right now to see if the young man I have in mind is still looking for work. Unless you have more questions."

He ushered her to the door.

Emma made it half a block down the planked sidewalk before he caught up with her and pressed a small package into her hands. "Tell your mother-in-law this is for her. She mentioned needing one. Oh, and tell Reverend Glenn that if he needs help with the vise to let me know. I can stop by after services on Sunday to lend a hand," he offered and left her standing there on Main Street with two nagging questions.

She could probably guess what was in the parcel for Mother Garrett. From the feel of it, the parcel probably contained some sort of kitchen tool or utensil, and she quickly stored it inside Mother Garrett's canvas bag. The answer to the second question was far more elusive. What possible use would Reverend Glenn have for a vise?

20

EMMA WALKED ALONG A DIRT ROADWAY on the outskirts of town past a string of small wooden structures, home to a growing number of factory workers and their families. Women were setting out clothes to dry in the sun, while children raced about. A light breeze carried the aroma of dinners simmering inside the tiny homes and the sound of workmen hammering on more new construction somewhere nearby.

In the far distance, mountaintops stretched high into the clouds huddled together across miles of gorgeous blue sky where a brilliant sun hung high, bathing the forests and farmlands with warmth.

As she left the town behind her, she considered how much the landscape of her life had changed. The General Store. Her courtship and marriage. Birthing and raising three children. All were mountains that rested securely on love and her faith in God, which washed the deep valleys of life's troubles with hope.

In all but a whisper of time, each of those mountains had disappeared into the mists of yesterday, leaving but a path she thought had led her to Hill House, a place where she still hoped she could build the mountains of her future.

With that future now in doubt, she concentrated on the present. Change had also altered the land she passed by to such an extent she had a hard time remembering exactly where Mr. Stengel's apple orchard had once stood, stretched along this roadway for miles. In her mind's eye, she could once again see the endless parade of apple trees, their branches bent low this time of year with luscious red fruit.

Whether from goodness of heart or necessity, Mr. Stengel used to tie a ribbon of burlap to the trees closest to the roadway to signal that those trees were open for passersby to plunder at will. She and Jonas used to bring their three boys here every autumn to pick apples, but the boys invariably spent more time climbing and chasing one another from tree to tree than actually picking apples. The rest of the orchard was reserved for Mr. Stengel, and he fiercely protected his bounty each fall from folks too greedy to be satisfied with what he had set aside for them.

She sighed and plodded forward. Mr. Stengel was long gone now. When he finally passed, some years after his wife, his sons had sold out and moved west, but this was well before the Candlewood Canal had been built.

When she heard an empty wagon approach from behind, she stepped back to avoid being engulfed in road dust and turned toward the wagon. With her eyes shaded by her bonnet, she studied the driver, smiled, and waved when he drew near.

A longtime customer at the General Store, Paul March was a bit older than Emma, and his trim beard was as white as the hair on his head. He had bought his farm some years ago and still lived there with his second wife and their several young children. "Mr. March! Hello!"

He slowed the wagon as he approached. "Greetings to you, as well, Widow Garrett. May I offer you a ride?"

She hesitated, thought about the time it would take to cover the mile or two to the Cross cabin and back again to return to Hill House in time for dinner, and nodded eagerly. "Thank you, yes."

Once the wagon had completely stopped, she waved for him to remain seated. After putting her reticule and the canvas bag containing the parcel for Mother Garrett on the seat, she turned just a bit for modesty's sake, hitched up her skirts with one hand, and managed to climb aboard with her dignity still intact. She got herself situated on the plank seat, braced her feet, and held on to it with both hands. "I'm ready."

He chuckled and flicked the reins. "You're as spry as you were years back."

She laughed. "Only on a good day. You're also looking well," she offered.

"Raising three boys, all under the age of ten, will do that for a person. You did the same once."

"That was also years back," she teased and held tight as he maneuvered through several deep ruts in the roadway. "How are Sally and the boys? All well, I hope."

He grinned. "The boys are growing faster than summer hay, and Sally's teeming again. Come spring, I'm hoping we'll have that girl she wants."

"And if she has a boy?"

"Then Matthew, Mark, and Luke will have a new brother, John, and we'll be finished with the Gospels," he teased. "Where are you headed?"

"Not far. You remember the old toll collector's cabin?"

"Pass it every time I come into town. It's just ahead, around the bend. There are new folks living there now," he offered.

"The Cross family. I met them a week or two back. They seem to be good people. I thought I'd stop in to see how they were faring." She shook her head. "The new factories are drawing so many workers, I don't know half the folks in Candlewood anymore."

"Makes me glad there are a good ten miles between me and the town. Any less, and I'd be tempted to sell out like Stan Oliver and move west."

She blinked hard. "Mr. Oliver sold his farm? I hadn't heard."

"He came by yesterday to see if I wanted to buy his livestock, which I did."

"Do you know who bought the farm?"

He shrugged. "I can't recall the name. According to Oliver, the buyer is one of those fancy types from back east. Claims he wants a country estate for himself." He laughed. "Can't quite say I'd describe that farm as a country estate, any more than I'd say that about my own."

She nodded, silently attempting to place the Oliver property within the context of the Leonards' properties but failing. She needed her map, but that was back in her office. When Emma turned her attention back to the roadway, they were rounding the bend. Once they did, the Cross cabin came into full view. The thought suddenly occurred to her that there might not be anyone at home, until she remembered that Mrs. Cross was probably there to care for her ailing husband.

Minutes later, she was out of the wagon and back down on the ground again. "Thank you. Please tell everyone at home I send my regards."

He tipped his hat. "And the same to everyone at Hill House."

"You're not . . . you're not thinking of selling out, are you?"

He laughed. "Not until roosters lay eggs, chickens crow, and wolves lie down in the hen house to sleep," he teased, flicked the reins, and headed for home.

Filled with the contentment that comes from seeing an old friend, Emma approached the cabin with little anxiety about meeting again with a new acquaintance. The narrow path to the front door was so overgrown with bushes and prickly vines she had to stop several times to unsnag her skirts.

The front door, like the rest of the old log cabin, was dry and battered by the elements. The one window to her right, however, glistened clean, and the once-white curtain blocking any view inside appeared yellowed with age rather than dust and grime.

Realizing she had come to call empty-handed, she quickly decided an invitation to supper or dinner at Hill House would be an appropriate substitute, even more so if they could come within the next few days, especially considering the guests arriving tomorrow afternoon.

She knocked at the door, waited, then knocked again before the door finally opened.

Mrs. Cross held Emma's gaze while she wiped her flour-dusted hands on her apron. "It's Widow Garrett, isn't it? I'm so sorry to keep you waiting. I was making bread while Mr. Cross was resting abed for a bit. I heard your first knock, but I was so surprised at the sound, I didn't recognize it for what it was until you knocked again."

"Please call me Emma. I hope I'm not intruding, but I—"

"Come in out of that sun before you ruin that fair complexion. And Diane will suit me just fine," she urged and swung the door wide open.

When Emma stepped from bright sunlight into the cabin, it took several moments before she could see the interior clearly. To her left, two side-by-side doors provided entry to rooms she assumed were bedrooms. The single room she stood in served as both kitchen and living space. The dirt-packed floor beneath her feet had been swept clean, and there was not a cobweb in sight on any of the log walls. The massive stone fireplace sat cold, waiting to be called into use when autumn chilled the air a bit more, but a fairly modern cookstove held a huge pot of simmering soup or stew of some sort that filled the interior of the cabin with delicious aromas. Save for the benches at the table littered with flour and several cloths covering dough at rest, however, there were no other chairs or furniture of any kind.

"I was out on errands and thought I might stop to see how you were faring now that you've had a chance to settle in," she offered.

"One day at a time," Diane replied. "I . . . I'm afraid I haven't a chair to offer you."

"I can't stay long. A seat on one of the benches would suit me just fine. Please don't let me keep you from your work."

"At least give me your gloves and bonnet. I don't think a dusting of flour would be considered very fashionable."

Emma chuckled as she removed her gloves and bonnet, along with her canvas bag and reticule, and handed them to her. "You might be surprised what passes for fashion these days."

Diane slipped into one of the bedrooms to store away Emma's things and quickly returned. She ushered Emma to one of the benches and brushed off the flour with the hem of her apron before she went to the opposite side of the table to resume her work. She started kneading one final lump of dough. "You had a good long walk to get here. Oh, I'm sorry. I never offered you something to drink."

"I'm not thirsty, but thank you. On my way, I met an old

friend coming from town, and he gave me a ride. He was passing right by your cabin."

"As much as I appreciate our new home, it would be easier if it were closer to town, especially for Mr. Cross," Diane gritted as she worked the dough, pressing side to middle and top to bottom in a soothing rhythm of form and motion. She paused to wipe the perspiration from her forehead. "This old place is sorry to look at now, but we're fixing to change that. Matthew promised to clear the front path, but he's badly tired at the end of his day."

"What about his brother?" Emma asked. She was curious to know if he had found work and she had come in vain, although she certainly needed to get to know the young man better before she recommended him to Mr. Atkins.

"Steven?" She frowned. "The days he finds work unloading the freight barges, he's tuckered out, too, but there won't be any work when the canal closes in November. The other days, when he's looking for steadier work, he's been coming home so restless he's got almost all of the backyard cleared so I can put in a winter garden. That's a whole lot more important than the front path."

"I thought Matthew said they were hiring workers in town."

Diane shrugged. "Gossip and rumors were more wishful thinking than anything else. There may be jobs come spring. I'm not sure what we'll do if he hasn't found work by then, but I'm certain the good Lord will provide. He always does. There!" She gave the dough one final swat and covered it with a cloth.

"I didn't bring something as a welcome gift," Emma ventured. "I thought instead you and your family might like to come to supper at Hill House."

The woman's smile was immediate but quickly disappeared. "That would be lovely and it's very kind of you to invite us, but . . . after traveling with the Sewells and seeing how fine they were dressed, I doubt we'd be . . . We're just plain people," she murmured, pausing to look down at her homespun gown that appeared very plain, even when compared to Emma's brown calico day dress.

Though similar in style, with a high neckline and full skirts, the fabric of Diane Cross's gown easily separated the two women's stations in life. Given Mrs. Sewell's preference for silks and brocades, however, Emma clearly understood Diane's reluctance to wear simple homespun to supper at Hill House.

"At Hill House, we're as formal or informal as our guests prefer," Emma countered. "In point of fact, the Sewells are leaving this afternoon. A couple of very special guests are arriving tomorrow, but I can promise you there won't be more than two ordinary homespun gowns between them. Please say you'll come. I seem to know so few people who have come to make Candlewood their home in the past few years. I'd like to change that."

"I'd have to speak to Mr. Cross first," Diane said as a smile tickled the corner of her lips. "Even if he's having a good day, I'm not sure he'd be up to walking that far. Maybe Matthew can think of—"

"I have a buggy ordered to meet my guests. They're coming in tomorrow on the afternoon packet boat. If you can come for supper tomorrow, I can have the driver stop here to pick you up, too. If the packet boat's on time, they wouldn't get here much before four-thirty. It would be later if the packet boat's late. If we don't plan to have supper until seven, that would give us time to chat, and both of your sons would be able to come after work, as well, as long as they don't mind the walk."

"I'm not sure you should go to all that bother."

Emma waved away her objection. "It's no bother at all."

Diane's smile deepened into a grin. "Matthew and Steven are

young. They can walk to Hill House together."

"Good. Then it's settled. I'll arrange for the buggy. If by chance Mr. Cross isn't having a good day, just tell the driver and we'll have supper together another time."

"Fine, but we're only coming if you'll let me bring something for supper."

Emma shook her head. "That's not necessary."

"It's a special receipt. Mr. Cross says my rye bread is fit for the president's table."

Emma's mouth began to water. "Did you say rye bread?"

"With a crust as thick as the blade of a knife and a center that melts in your mouth faster than butter."

"We'd probably need two loaves to have enough for everyone," she cautioned and moistened her lips.

Diane laughed. "I'll bring three. There might be too much soup or too much meat or too much dessert, but there's never too much bread."

Emma grinned. "Never."

21

L ATE WAS LATE.
Emma could walk, skip, hop, or run the rest of the way up the brick lane to Hill House, but she would still be late for dinner. Even if she could sprout wings and try to fly up the hill, her skirts and shoes were so heavy with caked mud and dirt, she probably would not have been able to get off the ground.

She hurried up the brick lane. She should not have been late; her visit with Diane Cross had not been any longer than she had planned, and her walk home had not taken longer than she expected. But she could hardly have anticipated the row on Main Street, the crowd of people who thronged the street as well as the planked sidewalk, or the mishap that had forced her to zigzag around them, going from one side street, back to Main Street, then on another side street just to get home.

"Simpletons!" she muttered as she made her way to the wrought iron gate and let herself into the front yard. She glanced down at her soiled skirts and rolled her eyes. There was no chance she could waltz into dinner looking as if she had fought a battle with a mud turtle and lost—which was an excuse Benjamin had tried to use once when he had come home late for dinner and caked with mud—any more than she could explain the disturbance that had delayed her.

Not at the dinner table.

She frowned. The whole affair was distasteful. Certainly not the sort of tale to share in polite company. Definitely not in front of the two Sewell girls. And decidedly not in front of Reverend Glenn.

Even if the tale was oddly humorous.

She giggled in spite of herself, then sobered at the dismal prospect of soothing Mother Garrett's ruffled feathers, even if she did have a gift from Mr. Atkins as a quasi–peace offering for being late.

"Late is late," she mumbled. She hurried up to the house and around the porch, let herself into her office, and slipped up the back staircase to her room. She heard the grandfather clock chime two o'clock and groaned. She was terribly late. But if she hurried, she might not be late at all . . . for dessert.

Emma's entrance into the dining room caused less of a stir than she expected, and she noted that all the dishes had been cleared away. She was indeed too late for dessert.

In fact, everyone was so preoccupied giving and receiving accolades about the gifts given to the Sewells, that Emma managed to slide into her seat next to Mother Garrett without much more than a stern look for a reprimand.

"I'm deeply sorry for being so late," she offered. "Main Street was blocked and I had to take another way home."

Mr. Sewell smiled and patted his vest pocket. "You missed an excellent meal, not the least of which was the amazing apple crisp we had for dessert—and I have the recipe right here."

"But you're not too late to see our gifts," Mrs. Sewell countered. Her smile quickly dropped into a frown. "Unless you've seen them already."

"No, I haven't, except for the tins of pretzels Mother Garrett made for your journey home," Emma suggested and caught a glimpse of Madeline and Miriam comparing the gifts they had been given.

Mrs. Sewell held up a dainty white handkerchief with both hands so it hung like a picture in front of her. "Widow Leonard made each of us one of these. See? There's an *HH* stitched in the top corner in white that looks exactly like the sign on the front of the house, and a long-stemmed rose in the opposite corner. My embroidery is white, but the girls have different shades of pink. The handkerchief she made for Mr. Sewell is bigger but doesn't have a rose, of course."

Emma caught Aunt Frances's gaze and held it. "What a lovely idea. Thank you."

The elderly woman beamed. "I thought it might be a nice memento for your guests so they wouldn't forget what a lovely time they had and so they'll come back to Hill House for another visit."

"Miriam and I have crosses, too," Madeline murmured and passed hers down the table to Emma. "Reverend Glenn made them for us."

Emma laid the simple wooden cross in the palm of her hand. Though no more than an inch long, the cross had clearly been whittled by hand and dried by the fire to seal the sap, and she now understood why he had been collecting the branches of wood the day he had fallen. With his weakened left arm and hand, such a task should have been impossible for him. When she looked more closely, she saw the slight indentations where the wood had been held steady, which explained his need for the vise Mr. Atkins had mentioned.

"It's made of candlewood, and Reverend Glenn told us all about it—how it burns for hours and hours and how his mother used to burn candlewood instead of candles because they were too poor to afford them," Miriam explained, clearly anxious to steal the limelight from her sister.

"And what else did Reverend Glenn tell you, Madeline?" Mrs. Sewell prompted.

Madeline smiled. "That God loves us and . . . and that God's love is like a light shining on us to show us how to be good."

"And since there's lots of candlewood here, that's why the town is called Candlewood," Miriam added, not to be outdone.

Emma passed the cross back to Madeline. When she looked at Reverend Glenn, his eyes twinkled. "I told the girls you helped me gather up the candlewood from the woods behind the gazebo."

"All I did was carry it back for you. You did the rest, although you kept what you were doing a secret. The crosses are beautiful. Thank you for making them for the girls."

"I'm just pleased to have something to offer to earn my keep a bit," he murmured, and his voice carried a note of confidence she had not heard before.

She was humbled by the gift of having this man as part of her family at Hill House. She was also awed by his ability to continue a ministry of sorts with his whittling, and her heart was deeply troubled by the thought that his time here, as well as her own, might come to an end should the legal owner refuse to sell Hill House to her.

"Do you have a gift for us, too, Widow Garrett?" Miriam asked.

"Don't be rude," Madeline scolded. "Widow Garrett's gift is Hill House and all the nice people who live here."

Mother Garrett slipped her hand over Emma's and squeezed gently. "Amen," she whispered.

Emma blinked back tears and prayed Madeline was right and that Emma might be given the chance to continue operating Hill House for many years to come.

———————

After waving one final good-bye, Emma waited until the packet boat disappeared from view before hurrying back to Hill House to keep her promise.

Not seeing Steven Cross among the workers at the landing, she did not know if that meant he had found another job or if he simply had not been hired for the day. She decided tomorrow would be soon enough to find out. Fortunately, the disturbance earlier this afternoon had long been resolved, at least to the extent that Main Street was no longer blocked, and she rushed back to Hill House without incident.

By the time she reached the patio, she was breathless and nursing a stitch in her side. She charged past Mother Garret and Aunt Frances and went directly to the north wall. "You haven't seen the packet boat pass by yet, have you?" she asked as she scanned the length of the Candlewood Canal in the distance, just above the tree line.

"Not from here," Mother Garrett replied. "Why?"

"I promised Madeline and Miriam that I'd do my best to get back and wave good-bye from Hill House."

"Standing on tiptoe like that, you're likely to lose your balance and fall over that wall," Aunt Frances warned.

Emma dropped back to the soles of her feet, even though the

wall was wide enough that standing on tiptoe did not pose any sort of risk.

"The packet's probably passed by already. Besides, you won't see much more than specks, and neither will they. It's too far," Mother Garrett added.

"No. There they are," Emma said, removing her bonnet and waving it until the forest eclipsed all view of the boat.

When she turned around, Mother Garrett patted the seat of the empty chair she had pulled between herself and Aunt Frances. "Sit and tell us about this so-called disturbance that kept you from dinner."

Emma took a deep breath, sat down, and played with the ribbons on her bonnet. "I didn't invent a tale. There really was a disturbance on Main Street."

"Then, what happened?" Aunt Frances asked.

Emma looked around the patio to make sure they were alone and kept her gaze on the door to the dining room.

"We're going to hear about it anyway," Mother Garrett prompted.

"That's true, but I don't want Reverend Glenn to appear in the middle—"

"He's napping," Aunt Frances offered.

Emma frowned. "This isn't the sort of tale I'd want Liesel or Ditty to overhear, either."

Mother Garrett urged her chair closer to Emma's. "They're off visiting. I told them they could have a bit of free time after working so hard all week."

When Emma still hesitated, Aunt Frances nudged her chair closer, too. "We're old women, Emma. There isn't much that can shock us. Do hurry, though. As old as we are, we don't have time to waste."

Emma chuckled. "All I know is what I was able to piece together. The details might be off a bit, but from all accounts, one of the workers in the piano factory went outside to use the privy. Since there were several men ahead of him, he walked up Beckett Street and . . ." She lowered her voice. "He 'made his water' against the side of a building."

"Near Main Street?" Aunt Frances asked.

Emma nodded.

"That would probably be near Mr. Schindhaus's butcher shop."

"Exactly," Emma replied. "Apparently, the factory worker wasn't paying much attention and did it right through an open basement window. Mr. Schindhaus just happened to be in that basement under that very window grinding meat for sausages. Naturally, the whole lot of sausage was ruined."

Mother Garrett and Aunt Frances started laughing at the same time. "No wonder there was a disturbance. Mr. Schindhaus has a fierce temper," her mother-in-law managed between laughs.

"That's only the half of it," Emma countered. "Word has it that Mr. Schindhaus stormed outside and grabbed the first poor soul he found on Beckett Street by the scruff of his neck. He started yelling and screaming that the riffraff working at the factories the Candlewood Canal had brought to town were not going to turn his butcher shop into a privy."

"And that drew such a crowd they blocked Main Street?" Aunt Frances asked.

"No, that happened after the man broke free from Mr. Schindhaus, charged onto Main Street without bothering to look first, and ran right in front of two wagons traveling together. Somehow, both wagons managed to avoid hitting the man. One driver was able to control his wagon, but the other driver hit a pothole or something. In any event, one wagon collided with the other. They both overturned, and out spilled their loads of crated chickens that proceeded to escape from their broken crates."

Emma fought back a bubble of laughter. "Chickens were everywhere. Shoppers went scurrying off, terrified by the frightened, squawking creatures. Shopkeepers were shooing chickens out of their stores with shovels or brooms or anything they could think to use. I heard one woman say there were so many chickens in the bank, Mr. Meyer locked himself in his own vault to escape them. If they don't catch all those chickens, I'm afraid they're going to find eggs laid from one end of Main Street to the other by this time tomorrow."

By the time Emma reached the end of her tale, Mother Garrett had lost all control of herself, laughing so hard Emma was afraid she might fall out of her chair. Aunt Frances's face was nearly purple, because she was laughing so hard she could barely draw a breath.

Unable to resist, Emma dissolved into a fit of laughter, too. They laughed until they cried and were too tired to laugh any more.

Plainly exhausted, Emma wiped the tears from her face. "Now you know why I didn't want to explain what had happened at the dinner table. I was so relieved that the Sewells' gifts provided a distraction." When she looked at Mother Garrett, her eyes widened. "Oh! I almost forgot your gift."

She hurried up to her room, got the parcel from Mr. Atkins, took it back to the patio, and handed it to Mother Garrett. "This is for you. It's from Mr. Atkins."

Mother Garrett untied the twine holding the parcel together, peeked inside the paper wrapper, and quickly closed it up again.

"Wait! I didn't get a look," Emma pleaded.

"Me either. Show us your gift," Aunt Frances urged.

"You won't believe it," Mother Garrett argued and started chuckling.

Before she had the paper half off, Emma could see what was inside and started chuckling, too. She had been right. Mr. Atkins had given Mother Garrett a kitchen utensil—one she might need soon, especially if a few of those chickens made their way to Hill House: an eggbeater!

They all dissolved in laughter again. When Emma caught the sound of the front bell, she urged her companions to remain seated and went to the front door. She paused for a moment to compose herself and opened the door, only to find Sheriff North standing there. He had Liesel on one side of him and Ditty on the other. Both girls, however, kept their heads bowed and their gazes glued to the porch floor.

"I believe these two young ladies belong here at Hill House," he stated. Though his voice was as stern as his demeanor, he had just a brief glint of amusement in his eyes, as if to remind her of the last time he had come to Hill House with news of Mother Garrett's and Aunt Frances's arrests. While he briefly detailed the reason he had escorted them home, his gaze turned serious. "I stopped by Liesel's home, but her parents weren't there, so I thought it was better to bring her here for now."

Both surprised and deeply disappointed by his tale, Emma shook her head. "I'm sorry you were troubled to bring both of them all the way to Hill House. I'll see they're both properly disciplined," she promised and held the door open until the girls shuffled inside while the sheriff took his leave.

When she shut the door, she sent both young women to their rooms, closed her eyes for a moment, drew in a deep breath, and prayed she would not find Sheriff North on her front porch again for a very, very long time . . . if ever.

22

SEVERAL HOURS AFTER SUPPER, Emma sat at her desk and wished she had just a spoonful of the laughter from this afternoon to stir into the caldron of her troubled emotions.

Whether she was more annoyed or disappointed or frustrated was irrelevant. She had a blinding headache all the same.

She folded up the area map, the font of her frustration, and stored it away again. She was not sure if she was too upset with Liesel and Ditty to concentrate, too upset by the prospect of losing Hill House, or too dulled by her headache, but locating the Oliver property on the map posed far too many questions instead of the answers she thought she would find.

In either case, at least she had learned one thing: the Oliver farm did not border the Leonard land at any point but sat some miles due west, not east between the Leonards' property and the Candlewood Canal, as she had suspected. Any notion the Oliver farm would tie in to the possible coming of the railroad was now severed.

Confounded, she set aside all of her concerns about the future to handle the more immediate problems of the present.

Liesel, the source of Emma's annoyance, was in her bedroom with orders not to talk to Ditty, the source of Emma's disappointment, who had likewise been sent upstairs to her bedroom in the garret.

Unfortunately, from the young women's perspective, both Liesel and Ditty had been caught with a number of other young men and women, all of whom had been congregated together along the canal in a secluded area that had apparently been a secret gathering place for some time, at least over the past summer.

The young people had been smart enough not to choose a spot along or near the towpath, where they would easily have been discovered. Instead, they had crossed over the canal to the berm side and gone out of sight beyond a copse of native pine trees. For some unexplained reason, they had built a campfire this afternoon. They had not been smart enough to realize the smoke would be noticed.

Although neither Liesel nor Ditty appeared to have partaken, at least this time, there was evidence at the site that the young people had been drinking. Sneaking off to a secluded place without being properly chaperoned posed many dangers to young women, the very least of which was the damage they would do to their reputations. Emma shivered just considering what more might have happened to them, but Sheriff North had assured her that from all he could learn, neither of the young women had ventured beyond engaging in the mild flirtations typical for young women just discovering a fascination with the opposite sex.

Burdened by the responsibility she carried for the welfare of these two young women and the promises she had made to each of their parents to provide their daughters with proper guidance as well as employment, Emma closed her eyes and pressed her hands to her heart. The mere thought that the girls might very well be sent back home, forced to search for new positions if she lost Hill House, only heightened her concern for them now.

She had discussed the girls' escapade with Mother Garrett, who suffered from her own guilt for giving the young women permission to go visiting this afternoon, and Aunt Frances, too. Each of the women had provided insight into what might be the proper punishment. Reverend Glenn had even offered to intervene, but Emma had asked him to wait, in hopes he would be someone Liesel and Ditty could turn to—after they had received their punishment.

Emma briefly closed her eyes and turned to the Source of all love and wisdom and prayed. For forgiveness for herself for failing in her role as the young women's guardian and employer, and for putting their futures in jeopardy should the owner of Hill House refuse to let Emma purchase it again. For Liesel and Ditty, that they might realize the mistake they had made. And for wisdom, to know how to punish the young women so they might learn from their mistakes, and to learn from the mistakes she had made, as well.

When Emma lifted her head, the pain that had wrapped around her head like a tight band was gone. Fortified with faith, she started up the back staircase. She was winded by the time she reached the garret on the third floor and paused to glance around the large storage room at the top of the stairs.

With twilight quickly approaching, the unadorned windows that faced the back of the house provided just enough light for her to walk between the still-unexplored trunks and crates left behind by the original owner. Another trunk held clothing and unclaimed personal possessions previous guests had left behind. Cobwebs decorated the cloths covering an assortment of unused furniture, and while Liesel and Ditty kept the wooden floor swept clean to avoid tracking dust down to the other floors, there was little to be done about the musty odor here.

Three smaller rooms, each with separate doors and dormer windows, stretched across the front of the house. Liesel claimed the room at one end, while Ditty's room was at the opposite corner of the house. The larger room in between had once served as a dormitory of sorts, with five or six cots wedged inside, but now served as a sitting room the young women shared for those moments at night when their chores were finished and they had time to be together to laugh and giggle the way young women do.

Tonight, however, Emma claimed the sitting room for her own purposes. After placing a chair in front of the old settee, she lit a lamp to chase away the shadows of evening that were quickly approaching. Satisfied that the stage had been set, she knocked on each of the young women's doors and summoned them to appear. Emma had no set plans or dialogue prepared, but she prayed the Lord would guide her as the drama of confession and punishment unfolded.

Emma was seated in her chair when Liesel and Ditty arrived and sat down side-by-side on the settee, but she took no joy in their distraught appearances. Liesel seemed smaller, even frail, and the freckles that sprinkled across her cheeks looked darker than usual against the pallor of her skin. Her blue eyes were swollen from crying and streaked with red, and her skirts were badly wrinkled. She sat wringing her hands together and, all in all, looked fairly pitiful.

Ditty was faring no better. Her hands trembled. Her fingers worried at a piece of her muslin skirts so hard, Emma feared the young woman would work a rather large hole in her gown. She was as limp as a wet cloth. Her lips drooped. Her brows drooped.

Her shoulders drooped. Even her eyelids drooped. When fresh tears glistened on her cheeks, she weakly wiped them away.

"I'm not certain how to begin," Emma admitted. She kept her voice firm but low. She had never been one to yell, even with her boys, and she had learned long ago that children of good conscience tended to be much more unforgiving of their own transgressions than the adults in their lives. Still, providing proper guidance for these two young women was proving much harder than it had been with her three sons. "Perhaps one of you might like to try."

Liesel's bottom lip trembled. "I'm sorry, Widow Garrett. It's all my fault. I made Ditty go with me because I was too . . . too scared to go alone. Please don't be mad at Ditty. We . . . we really didn't do much more than talk with our friends," she offered by way of explanation.

"I'm just as much at fault as Liesel," Ditty argued, keeping her tearful gaze on Emma. "I'm sorry, too. Terribly sorry."

Emma let the echo of the young women's apologies slip away before she spoke again. "You're both sorry. I could see that before either one of you said a word. But in truth, I'm not sure if you're sorry for what you've done or sorry because you've gotten yourselves caught. May I assume you'll both admit it's a bit of both?"

Liesel's eyes flashed with surprise. "Yes, ma'am."

"Me too," Ditty whispered.

Nodding, Emma steepled her fingers. "Let's start with being sorry about being caught, shall we?"

Ditty's eyes widened and filled with fresh tears that spilled down her cheeks. "I'll do anything. Anything. I don't care what my punishment will be, but please don't fire me. Please," she cried. "My parents need most of what I earn. If I'm let go and I . . . I don't have this position—"

"I have no intention of firing you. You're not going to lose your position," Emma insisted. She was only too aware that as the eldest of eight, Ditty's contribution to her family, who eked out their existence on a worn-out farm, made a great difference in their struggle to survive. "At least, not this time," she added.

More tears. More sniffles. "There won't be a next time," Ditty promised.

Liesel chewed on her bottom lip and blinked back tears.

"You're not going to be fired, either. Not this time," Emma reassured her.

"Not ever, I hope. At least, not because I did something wrong like this again. I worked at the piano factory, and I don't ever want to go back to sweeping up sawdust and choking all day long. And my father won't let me work at the match factory with him. He says it's too dangerous."

"Your family relies on you, too," Emma prompted as she struggled with guilt for how so many others might be affected once the owner of Hill House arrived in Candlewood.

"Now that you both understand that your positions here at Hill House are not at risk because of what you've done and that I'm both annoyed and disappointed in your behavior, perhaps you can focus more clearly on what you both did wrong. And I might suggest it goes far beyond simply meeting up with your friends," she insisted.

Liesel glanced at Ditty first, then drew in a deep breath. "We lied about going visiting, and we disappointed you and Mother Garrett and everyone else here at Hill House."

Ditty paled. "Our parents. We'll have to tell them what we did, won't we?"

When Emma cocked a brow, the young woman closed her eyes for a moment. "We lied to our parents, too."

Liesel nodded and sighed again. "I probably won't be allowed to walk between here and home on Saturdays and Sundays by myself for months, maybe never."

"Probably not," Emma agreed. "Once your reputation is soiled, you may never launder out the gossip, and once trust is broken, it's very difficult to earn it back," she admonished.

"W-will you go with me to tell my parents?"

"First thing tomorrow. Ditty, I'll have to wait until Saturday when your father comes for you. Let's not forget it's entirely possible your parents may decide it's not in your best interests to remain here at Hill House, even though I'll do my best to assure them that my lapse in your supervision will not happen again. Aside from your punishment at home, however, there must be punishment here, as well," she cautioned.

Both of them stiffened a bit, but Emma continued undaunted. "I need you to pack your things. Your clothes. Your knickknacks. Everything and anything that belongs to you."

"But I thought you said we didn't have to leave Hill House," Liesel cried.

"You're not leaving. One mistake I made was giving you both too much freedom in the house, so I'm making the garret off limits from now on. Both of you are moving down to the second floor and sharing the bedroom next to mine. You'll be cramped a bit, but I'm sure you'll manage. And if you want somewhere to sit and talk together or to read or sew, you'll have to join us in one of the parlors or outside on the patio. Do I hear any objections?"

"No, ma'am," they whispered in unison.

"As for venturing out of the house," Emma continued, "you're not to use the gardens or the gazebo, unless you're helping Reverend Glenn."

Another dual reply. "Yes, ma'am."

"And finally, no more doing errands for Mother Garrett or anyone else. You're to confine yourselves to Hill House, at least during the week. What your parents decide about how you spend Saturday afternoons and Sunday is entirely up to them." Emma stood up and looked down at the young women, completely satisfied she had done her best to keep the two of them from meeting up with any young men, at least for now.

"When you say your prayers tonight, you might want to ask for God's forgiveness and thank Him that you came to no harm. In the meantime, you'd best start moving your things. After you've finished, come down to the kitchen so Mother Garrett can make you something to eat," she added and left the room.

Emma was halfway across the storage room when she heard Liesel call out to her, and looked back over her shoulder. "Yes?"

"Ditty and I were wondering . . . that is, how long will our punishment last?"

Emma caught her bottom lip to keep from smiling. She had gotten much the same question from each of her own sons at one time or another, especially from Benjamin, who seemed to find himself in trouble more often than either Warren or Mark. "You mean how long am I going to keep you under my wing and away from seeing young men? At the moment, I'd plan on a good while. Until you're thirty, I should think," she replied, smiled, and continued on her way.

When she got down to the second floor, she peeked into the room where Liesel and Ditty would be sleeping. Satisfied that their new room was ready, Emma returned to the first floor, where she found Mother Garret and Aunt Frances at the kitchen table, just finishing up a pot of tea.

After accepting an invitation to join them, Emma declined Mother Garrett's offer to fix more tea for her.

"We were just talking about that nice Mr. Atkins," Aunt Frances offered.

"Along with the young women you've been considering as a potential wife for him?" Emma teased.

"I've only met two so far that I'd even consider for him," Aunt Frances admitted.

When Emma cocked a brow, Mother Garrett shrugged. "Since Frances hasn't been living in town, she wouldn't know any of the eligible young women who might be suitable, so I've started to introduce her around while we're doing our errands so she could meet them."

Aunt Frances nodded. "We're not finished yet, but I should think Liza Shipley or Marguerite Hammer might be good choices. Liza works with her father at the apothecary, you know, so she'd be accustomed to helping with customers. Marguerite's a seamstress in Mrs. Bergens' dress shop and she's—"

"I told you she's too young for him. She's only eighteen," Mother Garrett countered. "I still think you should give Cassie Young a second look. She's twenty-three and works hard every day at the confectionery."

Aunt Frances sniffed. "She's too far on the shy side. The girl doesn't even look you in the eyes when she's helping you make a selection."

Emma cleared her throat. "For now, maybe the two of you should confine yourselves to matters closer to home," she suggested before they got so wrapped up with their matchmaking efforts they forgot there were two young women here at Hill House who needed better supervision. She quickly detailed the punishment she had just rendered to Liesel and Ditty, if only to clarify the restrictions she expected the two elderly women to enforce.

Aunt Frances's eyes began to twinkle. "We'll be like mother hens watching over our chicks."

Mother Garrett pursed her lips. "I never quite thought of Hill House as a hen house before now, but . . ."

"No more reference to chickens," Emma pleaded before a bubble of laughter escaped and her thoughts wandered back to the misadventure on Main Street earlier in the day. "This is important. Maybe if we keep these young ladies at home for a while, they won't be so besotted with young men. Oh, and I told them both they can come down for something to eat after they've moved their things. Not that anyone here would entertain the thought of slipping them something, like sugar cookies, perhaps?" she teased.

"I only did that once or twice, but they weren't being punished at the time," Aunt Frances countered.

Emma chuckled. "True."

"We don't have any sugar cookies or much of anything else," Mother Garrett noted. "The larder is near empty. I'll have to get up extra early to get ready for all the guests coming tomorrow."

"I did tell you the Cross family would be coming for supper tomorrow, didn't I?"

"Yes. How many of them did you say again?"

"Four. Mr. and Mrs. Cross and their two sons, Matthew and Steven," Emma explained and quickly recapped how she had met them and about her visit with Diane Cross that morning.

Aunt Frances cocked her head. "The Cross boys. How old are they?"

Emma shrugged. "I'm not certain. One is eighteen or so. The other might be twenty or thereabouts."

Mother Garrett grinned.

Aunt Frances chuckled. "Tomorrow's Friday. Harry might be coming, too."

Emma frowned. "What's so funny?"

"Nothing. Nothing at all," Mother Garrett insisted. "It just seems odd, sort of like inviting the foxes to the hen house."

Emma blinked hard and quickly realized that tomorrow, the first full day of Liesel's and Ditty's punishment, not one but three strapping young men would be in their midst.

Her headache returned with a vengeance.

23

AFTER SPEAKING WITH LIESEL'S MOTHER, Emma returned to Hill House with her charge in tow, humbled and yet heartened that Liesel would still be permitted to remain in her employ. She hung up her bonnet, sent Liesel to the kitchen to help Mother Garrett prepare for all the guests expected for supper, and waved to Ditty, who was polishing the banister on the main staircase.

The sound of laughter drew her from the hallway to the west parlor. She stood in the doorway, but in a matter of seconds, her curiosity hit a wall of bewilderment that left her speechless, as well as immobile.

Aunt Frances was sitting on one sofa with her grandson Harry. James Leonard sat on another sofa facing them, while Reverend Glenn occupied one of the two wing chairs at the head of the sofas. Oddly, Butter was nowhere in sight.

The moment one part of her brain identified all of them, the other part of her brain struggled to reconcile the amiable atmosphere in the room with the tension she expected.

Aunt Frances waved and broke through Emma's disbelief. "Oh, there you are. Come in, Emma dear. I was just telling James and Harry about the chickens getting loose on Main Street, but don't worry. I was very proper about it."

James and Harry both rose, greeted Emma warmly, and remained standing until she sat down in the wing chair next to Reverend Glenn. She caught James's gaze, noted no sign of resentment, and chuckled. "In the same vein, while I was out on an errand, I heard that Mr. Emerson at the hotel was considering a new feature on the dinner menu. Apparently, it's some sort of chicken stuffed with sausage."

When another round of laughter faded, Reverend Glenn edged forward in his seat and smiled. "I wonder if I might impose and ask young Harry to walk along with me. It seems Butter is out of sorts today."

Harry bounded to his feet without further prompting.

Concerned, Emma turned toward the elderly minister. "Is Butter sick?"

He chuckled. "Not really. When we were out at the gazebo earlier, he tried running after something he saw in the woods. Might even have been one of those chickens. I couldn't say, but he plumb tuckered out those old bones of his. He was so exhausted I had to leave him there. If I go back to check on him now, I could take full advantage of young Harry here and get down the garden steps a little easier than when I came up by myself."

"Don't be too long, Harry. I'll meet you at the wagon in the backyard," his father suggested.

While the two of them crossed the parlor to the center hall, Emma worried how Reverend Glenn would manage day to day without his loyal companion. But she tucked that thought behind the greater concern at hand—the nature of James Leonard's visit.

"Harry mentioned he might stop by today, but I must admit I'm surprised you came, as well. Pleasantly surprised," she added.

When he smiled, the corners of his eyes crinkled the flesh at his temples. "When Thomas and Harry got home the other day, we had a long talk."

"After dinner," Aunt Frances noted.

He chuckled. "I didn't raise dumb ones, that's true enough. Some days I think maybe the boys are a whole lot smarter than I am." He raked his fingers through his hair. "The older I get, that's happening more often than not. After the boys turned in for the night, I let Sarah speak her piece and realized . . ."

He paused and looked directly at his mother. "I still want you to come home with us. We miss you. But I realize now that someday Sarah, like as not, will be in the same situation as you are, left alone with no choice but to wander from one of our sons' homes to another, getting caught in the middle of one squabble or another."

"Most widows don't keep their own home," his mother said quietly.

Emma held silent, listening and praying at the same time.

"I can't do much about that," James said, then drew a long breath and squared his shoulders. "I can do something about the squabbling between me and Andrew. I suppose it took your running off to make me realize how much we had upset you. If it means you'll be happier and you'll come home again, then I'm willing to sit down and listen to my brother to see if we can't get this matter settled."

Emma closed her eyes for a moment and lifted her heart to heaven in gratitude.

Aunt Frances dabbed at the tears in her eyes. "Thank you,

James. I know this isn't easy for you. You never did like confron-
tation, but ignoring a problem or refusing to talk it through won't
make the problem go away, especially this one."

He swallowed hard and looked at Emma. "Mother told me
how happy she's been living and working here at Hill House and
how accommodating you've been. I wonder if I could impose and
suggest that my brother and I meet here instead of at one of our
homes?"

"Hill House is neutral territory. Of course you may," she
replied.

"Thank you, Emma," Aunt Frances said. "For all their good
points, both of my sons have their faults, as well. My Andrew can
be a hothead, and he's a tad more ornery than he is stubborn. My
James is more like a rock, steady and solid and stubborn, but once
he's pushed hard enough, he can be just as ornery as his brother."

She paused to look lovingly at her son before turning her
attention back to Emma. "I'm their mother. I love them both, and
I refuse to take sides. But if anyone could keep Andrew from
steaming up and James from holding silent and help the two of
them find a way to settle their disagreement, you could, Emma."

Emma narrowed her gaze. "I'm not sure that's what James
meant. I don't think he was asking for my help—I think he just
wanted to meet his brother to talk here at Hill House. Is that
right?" Emma asked, turning to face James.

"Yes, but my mother may be right. Having a referee of sorts
to hear both sides if we can't come to some sort of agreement is
not an altogether bad idea. I'll agree to it if Andrew will."

"He'll agree," Aunt Frances said. "James, you tell him I expect
him to agree."

James's eyes widened. "Me?"

"No, my other son James. Of course I mean you," she argued.

"If you go the right way home, you'll practically pass by Andrew's front door. Stop and tell him. Unless you expect me to rent a carriage and ride all the way out there, old as I am, when you could much more easily—"

"I'll do it. I'll stop on my way home," he gritted. "When would be a good time for us to come, Widow Garrett?"

Emma hesitated and thought out loud. "I have guests coming in this afternoon and several more arriving off and on for stays lasting through this week and next. Would two weeks from tomorrow suit? I'm reluctant to ask you to wait that long."

"Two weeks from tomorrow will suit everyone just fine," Aunt Frances insisted.

James shrugged. "Agreed, then."

"I do have a few questions I'd like to ask you about the toll road property," Emma ventured. "I've already spoken with Andrew about it, but I'd be interested in hearing your view."

"There's not much I have to say," he said. "Andrew wants to sell the land, along with his own. I don't."

His mother gasped. "Andrew's selling *all* his land, not just the toll road property? He wants to move away?"

"Just to town. He's got his mind set on opening some sort of business in Candlewood."

Emma's pulse quickened. "So he wants to sell everything, the land you own jointly and his own land?"

"That's the deal he's been offered, but it's all or nothing—or so he claims. I stopped listening after I told him no for the second time."

"But why would you refuse to sell the land you own jointly with your brother? It's common knowledge the toll road is in disrepair and there's little enough acreage to be of interest. Are your

217

father's wishes that important to you?" she asked, bringing Andrew's claims to the forefront.

He frowned. "My father made his wishes very clear in his will, but they're written on paper, not stone tablets. He'd be the first to tell us to do what's smart and what's right."

"You're the oldest. You have the greater responsibility to keep peace in the family. That's what's right," his mother argued.

He squared his shoulders. "What's smart as well as right is to keep Andrew from falling victim to some smooth-talking, eastern profit-monger. I threw the man out of my house three minutes after he got there to ask me to sell my land, too."

"Why?" Emma asked.

"If the land is that valuable now, it'll be all the more valuable in a few years when all the boys are grown and I'd be tempted to think about selling out. But no. Andrew wants to sell now. He even sent that buyer of his back to see me to try to change my mind, at least on the land I own with him. There's no way I'll sell that land and risk having the new owner deny me access to the toll road that I use to take my produce to Candlewood. My brother claims the man just bought Stan Oliver's land, too. I tossed him out again just yesterday." He chuckled. "That man left in such a rush, his spectacles slipped right off his face and landed in a mud puddle, along with his hat. He won't be back to see me again."

Emma's heart skipped a beat. "Do you happen to recall the man's name?"

"Langtree. Lowhorne. No, Langhorne. That's it, Langhorne."

She swallowed hard. "I've met him. He's very persistent. He'll be back to see you."

"He won't get past the front door this time," James vowed and got to his feet. "Unfortunately, I have work waiting for me at home." He stooped to kiss his mother's cheek. "I'll see you in two weeks," he promised, stood tall again, and faced Emma.

She got to her feet. "Thank you for coming."

"I'll let myself out the front and head around back to the wagon. Harry's probably there waiting for me by now. When we first arrived, he brought in a couple of bushels of apples and some sweet potatoes and turnips we brought for your larder."

"That was very kind of you. Thank you for going to all that trouble."

"No trouble. That's part of my father's will, too."

When she cocked a brow, he shrugged. "There's more to it, but let's just say he kept my mother's well-being in mind in a number of ways," he offered and took his leave.

She took a few steps and sat down next to Aunt Frances. "If all goes well after James and Andrew talk, you'll be able to go home with your sons. It appears we can look forward to having you with us for at least two more weeks, and you won't have to worry from day to day whether one of them might come to try to get you to leave."

"If I'm not a bother."

Emma took the older woman's hand into her own and smiled. "In truth, you haven't been here but a few weeks, but it won't be easy for us to see you leave. You've become part of our family now, too, and we're going to miss you."

A muffled *thud* interrupted their conversation.

Emma hurried out to the hallway with Aunt Frances on her heels and spied a red-faced Ditty sitting at the bottom of the staircase surrounded by several cleaning rags and the furniture polish she had been using.

"I'm fine. I just missed the last step or two," she quipped, got to her feet, and started to pick up the cleaning rags. "Nothing broken, nothing harmed."

Aunt Frances nudged Emma and leaned close. "That young woman's as clumsy as a caterpillar missing most of its legs, but she'll turn into one fine butterfly someday, you'll see."

Emma sighed. "Even if Hill House survives, I'm not sure I'll live that long."

24

H ILL HOUSE WAS READY to receive her next guests, the Mitchell sisters. Whether or not Candlewood was any more prepared for this visit than for their first remained to be seen, although by now, most people accepted the ladies as darling eccentrics.

Emma slipped out to the porch, sat down on one of the chairs, and tucked her legs beneath her to wait while Mother Garrett met their guests at the landing. Hill House stood ready; the guest bedrooms were dressed with fresh linens, and in both parlors sat vases of fresh-cut roses, truly the last of the season, offering sweet allure, while the fruits of Mother Garrett's labors crowded the sideboard, ready to fill the plates already set on the dining room table.

Grateful for a bit of time to herself, Emma leaned her head back and closed her eyes. Her mind, however, would not let her rest. Even though she trusted in God's wisdom, she still remained troubled about the future of Hill House, Reverend Glenn's health, Liesel and Ditty's escapade, the ongoing feud between the Leonard brothers, and Mr. Atkins' struggles at the General Store, as well as the fear Mother Garrett and Aunt Frances might yet be match-making, though neither one had said much about it in the past few days.

With a shake of her head, she shoved all those worries aside and thought about the Mitchell sisters, who would be arriving within the hour. Adapting from the Sewells' more formal stay to the very down-to-earth days ahead with the Mitchells meant more than a shift in attitude or mood. Mother Garrett's menu changed. Ordinary crockery replaced the china at mealtimes. Emma dressed more casually, wearing gowns much like the dark gray cotton one she wore today, and let her braid hang free instead of coiling it into a bun. She also spent more time with her guests, especially outdoors.

She did need to be careful, though. When the Mitchell sisters were in residence, Emma was sorely tempted to shed her prim image, letting her urge to be spontaneous and carefree match the sisters' daring lifestyles.

For a woman like Emma, who had spent most of her life indoors working in the General Store from dawn to dusk, redis-covering the wonders of nature with her guests, however, was one of the greatest gifts she had received since coming to Hill House.

Unfortunately, between restoring and operating the boarding-house, she made little time for appreciating this gift unless the Mitchell sisters were here. Anticipating their arrival, she opened her eyes, scanned the view from the front porch, and realized sum-mer had faded. The scent of autumn was heavier now, promising the crunch of crisp apples and days when the air would be heavy with the smell of farmers making fresh cider. For the first time, she noticed some of the trees were trading bonnets of deep green for crimson, persimmon, and gold, while others remained ever-green.

Beyond the rooftops of homes and businesses clustered in the center of town, the deep blue ribbon the Candlewood Canal had worn all summer had turned murky from use, but the sky itself was crisp blue, decorated with a bouquet of white clouds stretching to reach the sun before it slipped below the horizon.

Her heart filled with wonder. Her soul trembled with the awareness of His presence in all that surrounded her—a presence that eased all of her fears about the future. "Be not afraid," she whispered, and the stirring of the trees carried her words back to her. She closed her eyes again, slipped her hand into her pocket, and dozed off with her keepsakes held tight.

"There she is, looking like a lady indeed!"

"Miss Em-ma! Yoo-hoo! Miss Em-ma!"

Startled, Emma snapped awake and blinked the sleep from her eyes. Disoriented for a moment, the instant she saw her guests approaching the gate, she bolted to her feet. She had not even heard the buggy approach or depart but spied it now heading back down the lane. "I must have really needed that catnap," she muttered, then waved to her guests as she descended from the porch.

The Misses Mitchell were leading the other guests—no surprise there. The two sisters never walked when they could ride nor stopped talking until they were asleep.

Unless they were gardening.

Indeed, they were chattering with one another as one sister unlatched the gate and stepped aside for the other to hold it open for the Cross family.

Their straw bonnets, as plain as their homespun beige gowns, and the burlap bags, which they carried instead of reticules, represented the only bow to conventional attire the spinsters allowed—and only while traveling beyond the confines of the home they still shared with their parents in New York City. Once they reached Hill House, the gowns they wore would be packed away, except for Sunday services, until they were ready to travel back home.

Only a year or two shy of turning forty years old, Opal and Garnet Mitchell were identical twins who preferred to wear their curly brown hair cropped short, just covering their ears, men's trousers, suspenders, soft flannel shirts, and boots. Since they were both built exceedingly thick through the middle, they might easily have passed for brothers, not sisters, when they were dressed like men, at least from a distance. Up close, their flawless complexions, gentle blue eyes, and outrageously long eyelashes made them decidedly female, if the dainty pins each of them wore faithfully on their collars did not give them away.

As Emma approached the group of people in the front yard, she greeted Diane Cross and her husband, who seemed to be having trouble breathing, and their son Steven. Out of concern for Mr. Cross, Emma directed them into the house before welcoming her newest resident guests. She glanced at the two women standing side-by-side, took note of the pins they wore, and gave the woman standing on the left a hug first and then the other. "Miss Opal, it's good to see you again. And you, too, Miss Garnet. Welcome back to Hill House."

Opal pouted. "You're just no fun anymore."

"She knows to look for the pins to tell us apart," Garnet quipped.

Emma grinned.

Opal's eyes twinkled. "What if we switched pins?"

"No! You promised you wouldn't! I'd never be able to tell you apart."

"We won't. My sister's just teasing, aren't you, Opal?"

"Of course I am. I had enough fun on the packet boat. Not a single passenger between New York City and here thought to tell us apart by our pins. Of course, Father did make them for us so he and Mother could tell us apart," Garnet offered, as if Emma had not heard the same tale every time the sisters came for a visit.

To hear the sisters tell it, Mr. Mitchell was a jeweler by vocation, and he had fashioned the pins for his twin daughters with his own hands within days of their birth. By avocation he was a gardener and operated a small nursery next to their home, where Opal and Garnet developed a love for gardening and honed their skills.

Each of the sisters hooked an arm with Emma and started toward the house, but Emma quickly braced to a halt and looked back over her shoulder. "Mother Garrett! I almost forgot. She should be with you."

"We let her off at the General Store," Opal offered.

Garnet patted Emma's arm. "She won't be long. We told her not to hurry on our account. We'll keep ourselves busy until supper."

"Diane Cross is lovely. Just so sweet. She loves gardening, too, so we thought we'd all take a peek at those rose gardens of yours before supper. And we want to see how the mulberry trees did over the summer this year, too," Opal said. "We've brought something special to add this time."

Her sister scanned the front porch and smiled. "The hydrangeas we planted in the spring look like they're doing well. We've brought some tulip bulbs to plant for you."

"There's no time to waste, you know," Opal added. "The almanac calls for an early frost this year."

"You know you don't have to bring something new for the

gardens every time you come, but I'm not going to complain because you've made Hill House look so beautiful. You'll want to change first, won't you?" Emma asked.

"We're like the militia," Opal noted. "Always ready."

Her sister grinned. "And always prepared."

Simultaneously, Opal and Garnet lifted the hem of their skirts and poked out a leg.

Emma laughed out loud.

The two sisters were wearing their trousers and boots under their gowns.

By five o'clock, Reverend Glenn, Mr. Cross, and both of his sons were sitting together on the patio. Butter was resting on the stone floor in between the two older men, while both Matthew and Steven Cross attempted to lure Liesel and Ditty into prolonged conversations as they served refreshments. Opal and Garnet, dressed in their trousers and shirts, along with Diane and Aunt Frances, were wandering about the terraced rose gardens. Each sister pointed or gestured occasionally to indicate which rose bushes were in need of a final pruning before the first frost or to describe how to prepare the gardens for winter.

Emma had accompanied the women for a polite period of time, then excused herself and returned to the patio, where she could keep one eye on all of her guests and the other on the door to the dining room to watch for Mother Garrett's return.

By six-thirty, Emma was frantic. The guests were all gathered back together again on the patio. Both Cross boys had been paying so much attention to Liesel and Ditty that the poor girls had pleaded with Emma for permission to retreat to the house for a spell to escape even the slightest appearance of impropriety and

Emma's strict guidelines for redeeming themselves. The light refreshments were long gone. Supper was a mere half hour away, and Mother Garret was as scarce as a rose would be in the gardens come winter.

With one heartbeat, Emma was concerned that, despite Liesel's assurances to the contrary, supper would be ruined and she would disappoint her guests. In the next heartbeat, Emma almost relished the notion of Mother Garrett being late for a meal for a change, then rejected the idea as petty. She was halfway across the patio to check the kitchen again when Mother Garrett emerged from the dining room with Mr. Atkins in tow.

"I'm sorry I'm late, but I knew Liesel could manage until I got back. I've brought a guest with me," she gushed. "I thought Mr. Atkins might enjoy the company of some younger people as much as he would a good meal."

He blushed. "Mother Garrett insisted I come to supper. I hope it's not a problem."

"Not at all. Why don't you join the menfolk while I help Mother Garrett set out supper?" Emma suggested, taking hold of her mother-in-law and ushering her into the house. "I thought you promised not to do any matchmaking," she whispered. "That's what you were doing when you invited him to supper, wasn't it?"

"Of a sort," she admitted and started for the kitchen.

Emma followed her mother-in-law but kept her voice low. "After promising me you wouldn't? And after what Liesel and Ditty both did? Are you seriously thinking that either one of them—"

Mother Garrett stopped and turned to face Emma. "Yes, I'm matchmaking, but not that kind," she insisted.

Emma rolled her eyes. "Is there any other kind?"

"Of course there is. Yes, Mr. Atkins needs a wife, but he needs help in that store of his even more. The minute I met young Steven Cross, who sorely needs a job, I knew I had to bring Mr. Atkins here to meet him. All I'm trying to do is match them up and solve two problems at once. I can always worry about finding a wife for Mr. Atkins later."

When Emma's jaw dropped, she snapped it shut. "You just met Steven this afternoon. Don't you think you should know him for more than twenty minutes before leaping to the assumption he might be suitable as Mr. Atkins' employee?"

Mother Garrett cocked a brow. "Did he or did he not clear the backyard behind that cabin of theirs for his mother so she could put in a winter garden?"

"He did, but—"

"Does he or does he not help take care of his ailing father, a man who has trouble drawing an even breath?"

"He does, but—"

"Then enough said. Any young man that devoted to his parents is good enough to introduce to Mr. Atkins. Am I right or am I not?"

As usual, Mother Garrett's insight proved far more simple and direct than Emma's. "You're right."

Mother Garrett grinned. "I know, but it's sweet to hear you say it. Now if you'll excuse me, I have supper to set out."

And set out supper she did.

Hearty servings of cornbread and gravy, baked beans thick with molasses and chunks of tender pork, along with an assortment of pickled cucumbers, red cabbage, and corn relish left little room for dessert. The guests, however, finished every single one of the apple fritters dusted with sugar and nutmeg, while Emma polished off two more pieces of Diane's amazing rye bread.

Including Liesel and Ditty, who joined them at the table at

Opal and Garnet's insistence, there were eleven all told around the dining room table, twelve if you counted Butter. The Mitchell sisters had everyone so enthralled, there had not been a single lapse in conversation. After supper, Steven left with Mr. Atkins to go to the General Store, where the young man would be starting work on Monday. Soon after, the buggy returned as Emma had requested to take the rest of the Cross family home. Reverend Glenn and Aunt Frances, tuckered from a long day, retired to their rooms. While Mother Garrett supervised the cleanup, Emma escorted Opal and Garnet out to the front porch so they could sit awhile before taking to their beds.

The air was cooler now, and few lights from Main Street filtered through the trees to disturb the darkness. Soft light filtered from the windows behind them, however, providing just enough light to be able to distinguish one another's features.

"It's so good to have you both back," Emma murmured. "I wish you could stay longer than a few days. By the time you finish with the rose gardens doing whatever it is you do to prepare them for winter, there won't be any time left to spend visiting together."

Opal nudged her sister's chair. "We were hoping you'd say that, weren't we?"

"We'd like to·stay a full week this time, providing you have the room," Garnet suggested. "We were hoping we might visit with Mr. Breckenwith while we are here, too."

"I'm delighted! Yes, I do have the room."

"Provided you let us pay for our rooms for the extra days," Opal added.

Garnet nodded. "We insist."

Emma shook her head. "There's positively no way I can allow you to pay for your rooms. Without both of you, there wouldn't have been a rose garden in the first place, and you'd both be daft to argue the point because what I know about gardening in general and roses in particular would fit through the eye of a needle."

"But—"

"In the second place, you visit twice a year but spend all your days working in the garden, except for the time you go riding in the morning. I think it's time you stayed for a few days just to enjoy yourselves."

"But we love taking care of the gardens for you," Opal countered.

Garnet nodded. "It's little enough to do for you, considering all you did for us." Her voice dropped to a whisper. "You were like an angel. If you hadn't helped us, I don't know what would have become of us."

Memories of their first meeting surfaced, along with the memory of Aunt Frances's arrival here, and brought a smile to Emma's heart. Three years ago, both Opal and Garnet had appeared at her kitchen door late at night, drenched to the skin by a day-long downpour and badly shaken. Stranded some miles from town when one of their horses pulled up lame, they had lost all but the clothes on their backs to the same pair of bandits who had been responsible for a rash of robberies in the area.

Dressed as men, without a coin between them, the two sisters had been turned away at the tavern, as well as the hotel. Alerted by Mr. Emerson at the hotel, the sheriff at the time, Robert Lindlow, had detained the sisters for questioning. Once he realized the two women were indeed victims and not the bandits, he had released them and suggested they might find shelter at Hill House, although he had not had the decency to take them there. He had not been reelected, either, and Emma was quite certain Sheriff North would never have turned Opal and Garnet out the way his predecessor had done.

She smiled at the two sisters. "I hardly think offering you shelter here when Hill House was nothing more than a shadow of what it is today qualifies as angelic. Be that as it may, if you hadn't come here, I would never have discovered two wonderful new friends. Please allow me to invite you to stay for a few days as my friends," she insisted.

Garnet sighed. "At least let us do something for you in return."

Emma grinned. "I was hoping you'd say that. Take me riding with you."

"Riding?" they cried in unison.

"Yes, riding. You do intend to get horses from the livery and go riding for several hours each morning, don't you?"

Opal's eyes widened. "Would you really want to come with us?"

Emma chuckled. "I really would. I haven't been on a horse in years, but I'm sure the livery can provide me with a sweet, gentle mount who won't mind a rider who's a bit rusty."

"We're serious riders," Garnet cautioned. "If you want to ride with us, you'll need to wear trousers and a sensible straw hat instead of a bonnet."

Emma swallowed hard, then dismissed concerns about appearing in public dressed in trousers. Just this once. "I'm sure if I sort through some of the clothing guests have left behind, I'll find something suitable."

Opal grinned. "We like to leave early, at first light."

Emma groaned. "I don't suppose we could compromise and leave at eight?"

"Seven."

Emma cleared her throat. "Seven-thirty, and Mother Garrett packs a picnic so we can ride most of the day."

Opal and Garnet clapped their hands and took turns describing where they would like to go with Emma. The more she listened, the more excited she became about exploring some of the land she had been studying on her map.

And the less she worried that the gossip surrounding the runaway chickens might quickly pale once the very prim and proper Widow Garrett, proprietress of Hill House, paraded down Main Street on horseback wearing men's trousers.

25

O VER THE NEXT FEW DAYS, Hill House was a flurry of activity. Once Liesel and Ditty left to return home for the weekend, work for nearly everyone was nonstop, from predawn to well past twilight. Sleep was little more than a few hours of rest at night, leaving not a moment for Emma to think about resolving the dispute between James and Andrew Leonard. She did, however, make time to pick out a gift and send it to Warren and Anna, along with a note, so it would arrive in time for their sixth wedding anniversary, which was in but a few weeks.

Four unexpected guests arrived—two at a time, but several hours apart—on Saturday morning while the Mitchell sisters trudged back and forth from the terraced gardens to the house. Emma spoke with Ditty's father when he came to pick up his daughter and had reassured him of closer supervision when he agreed to let the young woman return to work on Sunday evening.

Sunday itself was a blur. Mother Garrett, who was on her own in the kitchen, needed help serving breakfast. Tidying guests' rooms rather than stopping to eat kept Emma busy until Sunday services, where she nodded off twice during Reverend Austin's sermon. Then back to Hill House to more work.

By the time Liesel and Ditty reappeared Sunday night and Emma took to her bed, she fell asleep listening to the young women in the room next door comparing punishments they had each received from their parents.

Monday morning, Emma woke up shivering. Overnight, autumn had arrived to chill the air as well as the floorboards, promising an early frost. "Exactly as Opal and Garnet claimed," she muttered, donning her robe and hurrying across the cold wooden floor to the trunk at the foot of her bed to find her slippers.

Once she had her slippers on her feet, she knelt, said her morning prayers, and went to the window. She pulled the curtain aside and glanced down at the gardens. The terraced display of roses that had been a glorious feast of color all summer was gone and would not return until late next spring. The bronze roof on the gazebo did not glare under the gentler autumn sun.

In the seasons ahead, however, nature had other gifts in store for her when she glanced out her bedroom window. A delicate etching of frost on the terraced hill would quickly give way to winter ruffles of snow, and later, a patchwork of budding spring greenery. The gazebo would soon wear a lace cap of frost until winter arrived, covering the roof with a bonnet of snow and adding a necklace of glistening icicles that would last until warm spring breezes melted it all away.

A knock at her door pulled her from her reverie. Emma tightened the sash on her robe and answered the door that opened into the upstairs hallway. "Yes, Liesel?"

"Aunt Frances sent me to tell you she's on her way to the

garret and to meet her there so you can find something for her to alter."

"Already? Oh dear." She paused. It might be easier to try on the trousers without being fully dressed. At this hour, her guests should still be abed and she could slip up to the garret and back again without being noticed. "Tell her I'll be there as soon as I wash up and re-braid my hair."

The young woman's blue eyes twinkled. "Yes, ma'am." She looked about, as if making sure they were alone, and leaned closer. "Is it true? Are you really going to wear men's trousers like Miss Opal and Miss Garnet?"

Emma's eyes widened. "Who told you that?"

Liesel grinned. "Aunt Frances did. She came down early and had breakfast with Ditty and me."

Emma chewed the inside of her cheek. Defying convention might not be the best way to prove she was offering proper guidance to Liesel and Ditty, and she did not dare consider what might happen if the legal owner of Hill House arrived unexpectedly and caught a glimpse of her. "You must have misunderstood. Aunt Frances is going to help me go through some of the apparel our guests have left behind, but . . ."

"I wouldn't tell a single soul if you did. Ditty wouldn't, either," she promised and scampered back down the hallway.

"You'd be the only two in all of Candlewood who wouldn't relish telling that tale," Emma grumbled. Mindful of her lawyer's admonition to avoid scandal and gossip of any kind, she set aside her urge to challenge convention and wondered how she might tell the Mitchell sisters she had changed her mind about wearing trousers.

With nothing suitable of her own to wear riding, however, she washed up, dressed her hair, and hurried up to the garret. As anxious as she was about getting something appropriate to wear riding, she was just as pleased to have some time alone with Aunt Frances. With all the commotion of the past few days, they had not really discussed James's visit or the plan that both James and Andrew would be coming to Hill House in two weeks to try to resolve their problem.

When she reached the garret, Emma saw that the trunk containing the former guests' possessions lay open. Aunt Frances sat on a crate in front of the trunk and pointed to a wooden box resting along the narrower side, swinging her sewing bag in the process. "I thought if we had an early start, I'd be sure to have enough time to alter the trousers to fit you, but don't worry. I waited. I didn't want to go through the trunk without you."

Emma sat down and rubbed her arms. "It's chillier up here than I'd hoped. Maybe we'll just find something quickly and take it back down to my room where it's a little warmer. And feel free to take anything that suits your fancy. No one's ever written to me asking for something they've left behind," she added and lifted the old sheet protecting the contents of the trunk.

Working in tandem, Emma would lift one item from the trunk after another, from women's and men's nightclothes to an assortment of mismatched slippers, a lady's broken hair comb, and several hat pins, and pass it to Aunt Frances to set aside. Half the trunk was empty before Emma lifted out a dark brown cotton gown, unfolded it, and laid it across her lap. The bodice was badly stained, but the skirts were relatively unscathed. "It's a bit large for me, but this might do."

Aunt Frances frowned. "There's more than enough fabric, but it's awfully dark, like most of what you wear. Don't you want to look through the trunk some more to find something else a bit prettier for your trousers?"

Emma shook her head. "I'm happy with the color, but instead of trousers, I was thinking a split skirt might be more appropriate. I've seen several women wearing one to ride, including the midwife, Mrs. Sherman, and she's still held in high regard," she suggested. She explained her concerns about having a proper influence on Liesel and Ditty keeping to herself her worries about what the legal owner of Hill House might think—and waited to hear her companion's opinion.

"They'll be disappointed, you know."

"Who? Liesel and Ditty?"

Aunt Frances chuckled. "Them too, but I was thinking of Opal and Garnet. They're both quite excited you'll be wearing trousers like they do."

Emma pursed her lips and hid her own disappointment. "Maybe we should compromise and make the skirt not so slim as trousers, but not so full as regular skirts. Can you do that?"

Aunt Frances smacked her knees with her palms and stood up. "The sooner we get you fitted, the sooner I can get started."

"Did you see anything you liked?" Emma asked as she handed over the gown.

Aunt Frances eyed the pile of left-behinds, shook her head, and grabbed her sewing bag. "Not a thing for me."

Once Emma had shoved everything back into the trunk, she shut the lid and followed Aunt Frances back down the steps. Once they were both in Emma's room, Aunt Frances went straight to task. Though gnarled and sprinkled with age spots, her fingers were sure. With a few quick snips of her scissors, she had the bodice separated from the skirts and set it aside. With more than a few careful snips, she had opened one of the side hems on the skirts. "Slip off that robe and let me fit this to you," she suggested.

Emma removed her robe and laid it on the bed next to where Aunt Frances was sitting.

"Stand right in front of me. That's it," she crooned and worked one end of the fabric around Emma's hips to the other side and handed both ends to Emma. "Just hold on to that for a moment," she offered and reached into her sewing bag for a pincushion that looked older than the woman herself.

"I'm so pleased you've a gift for sewing," Emma murmured. "If it were up to me, I wouldn't have the job done before next summer."

Aunt Frances chuckled and set pins in a row at Emma's still-trim waist. "My mother used to say I was born with a silver needle in my fingers rather than a silver spoon in my mouth. In my much younger days, I was hoping to have a daughter so I could make her pretty things to wear, even teach her to sew and embroider." She paused and patted Emma's thigh. "Turn a bit. Perfect. Naturally, I had boys. First James, and then Andrew," she continued. "Later, in my younger days, I was hoping to have a granddaughter. It's a pity Andrew and Nora haven't been blessed with children, but James and Sarah have given me four good grandsons. Now at least I've got Liesel and Ditty to teach to embroider."

Emma tried not to think about all she was missing by having her grandchildren live so far away, looked down at the skirt pinned in place, and wrinkled her nose. "It looks awfully full."

"I'm not close to being finished," Aunt Frances argued and removed several pins to let the fabric fall to the floor.

Emma managed to step out of the fabric without pricking herself on a pin and slipped back into her robe. "We haven't really spoken together privately since James's visit. He seemed willing enough to settle the problem," she ventured before picking up the fabric and handing it very carefully to Aunt Frances.

"James said he was willing to sit down and listen," the older woman cautioned. "I'm not holding out much hope beyond that, assuming Andrew even agrees to come here."

Emma sat down on the bed next to Aunt Frances. "James said he might consider selling out in a few years. If that's true, and if Andrew can make his case, why wouldn't James sell out now, especially if it means that much to Andrew and keeping peace? Or if James can make his case about holding on to the land or convinces Andrew not to sell the land they own together, why wouldn't Andrew simply try to find another buyer for just his land?"

"Because James and Andrew . . ." She paused and looked up at Emma. "You have three sons, don't you?"

Emma nodded.

"All alike, are they?"

Emma snorted. "Hardly."

"If you had to describe each of them in, say, three or four words, the way I described James and Andrew to you the other day, could you?"

"I suppose."

Aunt Frances nudged Emma with her elbow. "Try. Just to satisfy an old lady's curiosity. Try, starting with the oldest and ending with the youngest."

Emma moistened her lips. "Warren is steady and reliable, like his father. Benjamin is, too, but he needs adventure and constant challenges to keep him happy. Mark . . . Mark is a quiet, reflective young man who prefers the books he sells in his store to most anything else, other than his family, of course."

"I'd say that took you all of a minute. Maybe less."

"They're my sons!" Emma argued.

"Exactly my point. You know them better than anyone in this world, don't you? Their good qualities as well as their faults."

"Yes."

Aunt Frances smiled. "I know my boys, too. Andrew will come here and plead his case—hard. James will listen, if only to please me, but he won't change his mind. James and Andrew have been playing tug-of-war all their lives. As the oldest, James has always had the advantage, and Andrew has spent his whole life trying to catch up to his brother, which in turn makes James try all the harder to do even better."

She sighed and shook her head. "If James helped his father put up twenty feet of fence, Andrew had to help put up thirty. If James brought home a deer from hunting, Andrew would stay out until he either had a bigger deer or two of them. And on and on. I couldn't stop them while they were growing up any more than I seem to be able to stop them now. If James plants four acres of corn, Andrew plants six and hires men to help him. If James buys a pair of mules, Andrew buys horses.

"At this point in time, James has three times the rope his brother has in their foolish game, and Andrew's yanking hard on the little he has left. It's not just about the land. Not anymore. It's about settling their ridiculous battle over which one of them is the better man, the smarter man, the more successful man, once and for all. I've talked about it at length with Opal and Garnet. Maybe because they're twins, they understand what I mean better than most people."

She folded her hands together. "I keep praying those two boys will make peace, but I'm also praying for the grace to accept that they maybe never will, even if you try to help. In the end, I truly believe God will do what's best for all of us."

Surprised by the acceptance evident in the elderly widow's words, Emma laid one hand atop the other woman's. "If there's one thing that might encourage James not just to listen but to actually consider doing what Andrew wants and sell the land, what would that be?" she asked, desperate for some hint to guide her as the referee.

"Winning. Being right and winning the argument."

"And what about Andrew?"

"The same. Being right and winning."

"Then if they don't settle their differences on their own, I'll try to find a way for that to happen," Emma promised and prayed that she might do just that long before the owner of Hill House arrived, putting all of their futures in jeopardy.

26

A S MOST ADULTS COME TO REALIZE later rather than
sooner, life can have a perverse notion of justice and a
quirky sense of humor, especially when it comes to doing what is
right.

With Liesel and Ditty confined to Hill House indefinitely, the
easy way to get errands done on Monday would have been to
rescind that part of their punishment. Turning Mother Garrett and
Aunt Frances loose on Main Street together was not an option,
any more than asking Reverend Glenn to attempt such a long
walk. Instead, while Opal and Garnet finished the last of their gardening, Emma hiked to town to do the errands, something she
could have done after seeing her guests off on the morning packet
if she had thought of it. Since she was alone, however, she bought
some small gifts as a surprise for everyone back at Hill House and
finished the errands at the same time.

Emma trudged down Main Street on her way back to Hill
House in late afternoon. Thoroughly convinced she had punished
herself along with Liesel and Ditty—not an uncommon feeling she

had while raising her boys—she tried to keep Reverend Glenn's advice in mind: the easy way was not usually the right way.

When she reached the end of the planked sidewalk in front of the businesses, she descended the steps and stopped at the bottom to shift the bags she carried from one hand to the other. As she did, Sheriff North crossed from the other side of the roadway, and he headed straight toward her.

Her heart leaped against the wall of her chest and pounded with fear that yet another disaster had taken place. She tightened her hold on her bags.

When he approached her, he tipped his hat. "I'm heading your way. Let me carry those bags for you."

"My way? You were coming to see me?" she managed.

He chuckled and eased the bags from her hands. "Don't get all flustered. I'm only heading up Main Street a ways; then I'm afraid you'll have to manage these on your own. There was a bit of a problem at Mr. Henderson's yesterday, and I promised him I'd stop back today."

She sighed with relief. "You weren't going to Hill House?"

"Not this time," he noted with a decided twinkle in his eyes before they started walking along the side of the roadway.

"I'm sorry. It's just that . . ."

"There's no need to apologize. When most folks see me coming, unless they've sent for me, they usually think I'm about to deliver bad news. I've gotten accustomed to it over the past few years, but I must admit I never thought much about it before I got elected."

"I don't suppose I would have, either," she admitted and increased her pace a bit to keep up with him. "I hope the problem at the Hendersons' isn't serious." Although anxious to change the topic of their conversation away from her erroneous assumption, she was just a tad curious as to what type of problem Mr. Henderson would be having that required the sheriff's attention this time.

A pompous, fussy man by nature, Mr. Henderson's duties as the local tax collector did little to make him the most beloved man in town any more than the ridiculously ornate carriage he used every Sunday—to travel less than a mile from his home on Palmer Avenue to attend services, no less—created envy in anyone who noticed.

When the sheriff glanced down at her, he was smiling and his dark eyes were twinkling again. "You heard about the chicken episode the other day?"

She caught a grin. "Actually, I got to Main Street right after the wagon overturned."

He tried to assume a serious expression but failed to extinguish the humor in his eyes. "Apparently, some of the chickens that escaped decided to roost in Mr. Henderson's shed."

Her eyes widened so much her lashes touched her brows. "Not the shed where he keeps his carriage!"

He laughed. "As far as I could see, he's only got one shed, and that carriage of his with the pale blue velvet seats is what the chickens claimed as home. Between the droppings and the feathers and the eggs, the upholstery is ruined."

She clapped her hand to her mouth to hold in bubbles of laughter but lost the battle. "I'm sorry. I know it's not funny. . . ."

He laughed with her. "The poor man is threatening to sue everyone involved: Mr. Schindhaus, the worker at the piano factory, Mr. Caulfield—he's the man who was shipping the chickens—the drivers of both wagons . . . Fortunately, Mr. Breckenwith is up to the county seat on some legal business."

"So I heard. I stopped to see him just a bit ago, hoping to invite him to dinner with some of my guests," she said but did not share her hope that the lawyer was gone to research Enoch Leonard's will on her behalf. "Maybe by the time Mr. Breckenwith gets back, Mr. Henderson might have a change of heart."

"I doubt it, but there's always hope," he replied. When he stopped, she realized they had reached the intersection of Main Street and Palmer Avenue, and he handed her back her bags. "I'm afraid here's where we part company. I have to make sure we rounded up all those chickens and see if Mr. Henderson is any calmer. I'd ask you to wait until I'm finished so I can carry these the rest of the way for you, but I half suspect my visit will last the better part of an hour or so."

She smiled and shifted the weight in the bags. "I appreciate your help, but I can manage the rest of the way. Thank you."

He tipped his hat. "Next time we meet, maybe I'll get a smile, especially if I'm not standing on your doorstep," he suggested and continued on his way.

"I doubt it, but there's always hope," she whispered, then hurried toward home. Other than several passing wagons, which made her step back to avoid being covered in road dust, she had the roadway to herself while she mulled over whether or not to share the tale of poor Mr. Henderson's chicken problem with the others when she got home. She had decided against spreading this particular piece of gossip and was congratulating herself for being a good, charitable woman when she heard someone behind her call her name.

She stopped in her tracks.

When she turned around, being a good, charitable woman was the very last thought on her mind. She gritted her teeth together and greeted the man hurrying toward her. "Mr. Langhorne."

With one hand, he held his spectacles to his flushed face. With the other, he doffed his hat. "I . . . thought . . . that was you," he managed and paused to catch his breath when he finally caught up with her. After composing himself, he reclaimed the arrogance she had come to expect from him. "I need a moment of your time."

"As you can see, I'm rather preoccupied with finishing up my errands," she replied and shifted the bags in her hands. As much as she wanted to learn more about his interests in the Leonard properties and his connection with Andrew Leonard, she was not prepared to discuss either before she had more information of her own.

"There's a matter of utmost interest we need to discuss. Immediately," he countered, his hands balled into fists.

Caught in his gaze, her fear he might have learned about her predicament involving Hill House almost stole the very breath from her. Her mind scrambled to understand how Mr. Langhorne could have discovered that she did not hold legal title to Hill House.

Zachary Breckenwith might be difficult at times, but he was a man of honor whose ethics were above reproach. Instead, she simply had to assume Mr. Langhorne had somehow uncovered the truth, perhaps through his lawyers. Added to the fact that he had probably also learned that the parcel of land he wanted so desperately to buy from her had not, in fact, been sold as she had claimed, he was not going to be easily appeased. She realized almost at the same time that she had forgotten to tell Mother Garrett about the legal snafu involving that parcel of land.

Standing tall, she garnered her indignation and met his arrogance with determination to deal with this man on her own terms. "And you propose to discuss this 'matter of utmost importance' here? On Main Street?"

As if sent by angels to reinforce her question, a pair of wagons passed by, adding a rather dusty exclamation point to her question, if not a healthy layer of dust to her gown, which she saw as yet another barb.

Langhorne coughed and sputtered as he brushed at the dust on his frock coat before using a handkerchief to remove particles of dust from his spectacles. "Perhaps I might be so bold as to suggest I walk with you back to Hill House so we can discuss the matter more suitably in your office."

"You might," she ventured, fully aware he had not even offered to carry her bags. "Unfortunately, I have guests waiting for me. Might I suggest, in turn, we meet another time? Next Monday at ten o'clock would suit me best."

"Very well. Next Monday. At ten," he said curtly, then huffed away.

"That man needs two good lessons: one in etiquette and one in humility." She thought of a few more lessons he deserved to learn while she covered the last few hundred yards on Main Street before it curved west and she turned east to start up the lane to Hill House.

Oddly, she thought of Zachary Breckenwith and found herself wishing he were here in Candlewood, if only to have the peace of mind knowing she would not have to face Mr. Langhorne alone.

27

INSTEAD OF TRACKING IN ROAD DUST through the entire house, Emma used the back door and went directly into the kitchen. With one quick glance around the room, she immediately dismissed the plans she had for setting her bags on the kitchen table—not that there was much room anywhere else. If she did not know better, she would have thought Mother Garrett was preparing for an open-air market, but Emma had a good idea where all the foodstuffs had come from.

Three bushels of apples and several baskets of potatoes and turnips sat by the door to the root cellar waiting to be stored below. Twin bags of onions and carrots topped each end of the table with several smoked hams filling the valley between the vegetables.

She turned to the sink, saw that it was filled with cabbage, peppers, and green tomatoes, and rested her bags on the floor at her feet.

The sound of voices coming up from the root cellar drew her attention. One after another, Mother Garrett and Liesel emerged.

"You're back!" Mother Garrett noted. "If you'll wait just a

moment, I'll clear a place on the table for you," she promised and gave Liesel the task of removing the vegetables and storing them away in the root cellar.

Once the young woman left, Emma hoisted her bags one last time and set them on the table. "I see Andrew Leonard stopped by. Since I didn't see a wagon in the backyard, I take it he's left already?"

"How did you know he was the one who brought all this?"

Emma started unpacking her bags. "Simple. Aunt Frances told me her boys are very competitive and always out to best each other. I know what James brought for the larder, and I also know he went to Andrew to ask him to come here to try to resolve their squabble. When he did, I'm certain he told his brother about bringing the foodstuffs. I'm not as surprised by how much Andrew brought as I am by how quickly. I hope he had the decency to sit and visit with his mother for a spell."

Mother Garrett unpacked Emma's other bag. "That he did, although he didn't stay more than fifteen minutes." She paused and surveyed Emma's purchases, which were now spread out on the table. "All I asked you to bring back was a sugarloaf and some coffee. What's all this?"

Emma slid the sugarloaf and coffee toward her mother-in-law. "These are for you. The others are my surprises." She pointed to the rest. "The boxes of chocolates are for Opal and Garnet. The pincushion is for Aunt Frances to replace that old one of hers, and that's her licorice root, too. The penknife is for Reverend Glenn to replace the old one he's been using to whittle. And before you ask, Steven Cross said to say hello to you and thank you," she added and scooped up her correspondence, although, sadly, none of her letters was from her boys.

"Oh, I almost forgot. The daybooks are for Liesel and Ditty. I thought they might need something other than practicing their stitches with Aunt Frances to occupy their time, since they're not allowed to go visiting anymore." She stopped, scanned the items again, and smiled. "That's about it."

Mother Garrett narrowed her gaze and pointed to the licorice root again. "Who did you say that was for?"

"Aunt Frances. Why?"

"I thought that tin of licorice root over there was for her. You've got two tins of it, you know."

Emma feigned surprise. "I do?"

Mother Garrett set one small tin next to the other. "You do."

"Why, imagine that!" Emma managed before laughing. She pressed one of the tins into her mother-in-law's hands. "This one is yours. You know I wouldn't forget to buy you a surprise."

Mother Garrett slipped the tin into her apron pocket. "Thank you."

"You're welcome."

"I hope you like being surprised as much as you like surprising other people," Mother Garrett cautioned.

"Why?" Emma asked.

"I've got a few surprises for you. There's one waiting for you on the patio. Go take a peek. Just don't open the patio door until you know what you're doing," she warned.

Driven more by the gleam in Mother Garrett's eyes than curiosity, Emma left the kitchen and walked through the dining room to the patio door, with her mother-in-law at her heels. With Mother Garrett standing next to her, she peered through one of the glass panes in the door and gasped the instant she saw the chicken nesting on the brown fabric that had been left on one of the patio chairs. Unlike Mr. Henderson, however, she was not going to send for Sheriff North.

The irony of seeing her would-be riding skirt ending up just as ruined as Mr. Henderson's carriage did not inspire even a hiccup of humor. "What happened? Why did you wait to do something about this until I came home? Couldn't you do anything to get that chicken off my riding skirt and out of the patio? Like wave one of your frying pans at it to scare it off?"

"I cook *dead* chickens. I don't know anything about the creatures when they're alive, and that's the way I prefer it. I'm not going any closer to it than I am right now," Mother Garrett said. "Frances feels just awful about this. She only left the patio for a few minutes to come inside to get something to drink. Then Andrew arrived and they spent some time in the parlor talking. When she finally got back to the patio, the chicken was already sitting there."

"Why didn't she just shoo it away? She's lived on a farm all her life. She should be used to chickens."

"She tried, but that's one stubborn chicken. I imagine it would probably cook up tough, too."

Emma glanced at the high stone wall surrounding the patio and shook her head. "I don't think a chicken could fly over that wall—I'm not even sure they can fly at all. How did it get there?"

Mother Garrett tapped on the pane of glass in front of her. "The gate's been open, off and on, what with Opal and Garnet traipsing back and forth between the house and the gardens the last few days. See? The gate's open now. They potted up a few small rosebushes and took them to Diane Cross. I told them I didn't think you'd mind. I'm surprised you didn't see them while you were running errands."

"I suppose I was in one of the stores when they passed by on their way to Diane's. And I don't care about the roses, but what are we going to do about that . . . that chicken?"

Mother Garrett shrugged. "I've got a kitchen to set back to rights. I'm not going to do anything, but I'm sure you'll think of something."

"Me? What do I know about chickens? I've never lived on a farm." She paused, had an idea, and brightened. "Ditty! Ditty's family lives on a farm. Ditty should know what to do."

"She's not here. She left. That was my other surprise."

Emma's frustration doubled. She turned and faced her mother-in-law. "She's under punishment. She wasn't supposed to leave."

"Her father came to get her not all that long after you left. I guess you missed seeing him, too," she said.

"Both coming and going, apparently," Emma replied and wondered how she could keep missing so much in such a small town. "When I spoke with her father on Saturday, he seemed very agreeable to letting Ditty remain here to work."

Mother Garrett patted her arm. "Don't worry; he still is. He just needs her back home for a few days. Her mother burned her hand making soap and needs Ditty to help her with the little ones. He wasn't positive, but he thought he could have Ditty back here Sunday night."

Emma shook her head. "I can't imagine raising eight children, even with good health. I hope Ditty's mother recovers quickly. In the meantime, I suppose we can make do without Ditty for a few days. Unless we have guests arriving unexpectedly, it's only Opal and Garnet here until Friday; then I think we don't have anyone coming until Tuesday or Wednesday of next week. I'll have to check my notes in the office to be sure."

Emma's relief was immediate but short-lived the moment she spied the chicken out of the corner of her eye again. "That still leaves the problem of doing something about that chicken. I don't believe there's any hope of salvaging the riding skirt. I wonder if we just keep the gate open the chicken will just go away?"

"Frances thought it might. If not, she said chickens are easy to handle after twilight because they're sleepy. She could move it then. In the meantime, Reverend Glenn and Butter are going to confine themselves to the house."

Emma grinned. "Butter! Butter can chase that chicken away for us. Remember? Reverend Glenn said he thought Butter had seen one of the chickens in the woods and chased it off."

"I also remember it took that old dog a day or so to recover. You do what you think is best, but I want no part of it, especially if that dog dies because his heart gives out chasing that chicken."

"You're right," Emma agreed and gritted her teeth. There was no way she was going near that chicken, now or at twilight or ever, whether it was asleep or awake. "Where's Aunt Frances now?"

"She's up in the garret. I believe she's going through that trunk again to find something else to use for your riding skirt. Unless she already did. Then you'll find her in her room sewing."

Emma sighed. "It's awfully late in the day. No matter how hard she tries, she'll never be able to finish in time. We're leaving early tomorrow morning. I don't want her up all night on my account. I may just have to borrow a pair of trousers from Opal or Garnet."

"Or change your plans," Mother Garrett suggested and started back to the kitchen.

Emma checked the patio door to make sure it was secure and followed her mother-in-law. "Why would I want to change my plans?"

Mother Garrett picked up a ham from the table and passed in front of Emma to store it in the larder. "How long has it been since you rode a horse?"

Emma pouted. "A few years."

Laughing, Mother Garrett stored the ham away. "Must be quite a few, since I can't seem to recall that particular occasion."

"Warren was just a baby. You weren't living with us then."

Mother Garrett put her hands to hips. "And Warren is how old? Twenty-nine?"

"Not until next month."

"And after twenty-eight years, you suddenly decide you want to spend half the day riding about the countryside. And you don't see any sort of problem in that?"

"Mr. Adams has a gentle mount for me, and Opal and Garnet will be with me. I'm sure I'll be fine. I have a good mind. Once I've learned something, like how to ride a horse, I'm not apt to forget it."

Mother Garrett patted her shoulder. "That's true. You're a very bright woman. I'm sure you'll remember how to ride, just like I'm sure you'll remember this ride with Opal and Garnet as a special, special day, assuming you find something appropriate to wear," she crooned.

Emma had the distinct impression Mother Garrett was being just a tad patronizing and narrowed her gaze. "I think I'll go check on Aunt Frances now," she said and slipped from the room.

On her way upstairs, she prayed for four things. First, that the chicken who had claimed the patio would be off that same patio by morning. Second, that Aunt Frances would miraculously finish a riding skirt for her before bedtime. Third, that she might learn something on her ride that would help her to resolve the Leonard brothers' squabble should they need her help. And fourth, that she would return from her ride tomorrow with enough praises from Opal and Garnet about her riding ability to make Mother Garrett's words ring true.

And she had every faith her prayer would be answered.

28

E MMA WOKE UP EARLY Tuesday morning after a fitful sleep
and knelt at her bedside. Her prayer of gratitude for no
longer having the chicken on the patio was sincere, but the one
she offered for the riding skirt Aunt Frances had finished just
before Emma had gone to bed was halfhearted.

She got to her feet, stared at the dark purple sweater, matching
blouse, and the riding skirt Aunt Frances had made, and frowned.
In truth, she favored the blouse and sweater. To get the purple
color that deep, Mother Garrett had saved sugarloaf wrappers for a
good while. Emma smiled. Her mother-in-law's hands had been
stained purple for weeks, and she'd vowed never to use those
wrappers again.

The thought of wearing the striped silk brocade riding skirt—
even behind her closed bedroom door, let alone parading on
horseback down Main Street—made her shudder. "Even with
Opal and Garnet beside me, I'd draw fewer stares if I wore men's
trousers," she grumbled, fully aware that Zachary Breckenwith
would no doubt have more than a few words to say about the

gossip sure to follow. Dressing quickly, she re-braided her hair and pinned it atop her head. She grabbed the straw farmer's hat Opal had bought for her at the General Store, plopped it on, snatched a pair of leather gloves, and left her room.

She did not bother to check her appearance in the mirror. If she had, she might have changed her mind about not disappointing Aunt Frances, climbed back under the covers, and feigned illness to avoid being seen in this outrageous skirt, a tactic her lawyer would probably fully endorse.

Instead, she proceeded to go downstairs. When she entered the kitchen, she found Mother Garrett and Aunt Frances at the kitchen table and wished them a good morning but saw no sign of the picnic basket or the Mitchell sisters.

"They're waiting for you on the patio. Opal has one basket with breakfast inside, and Garnet has the basket with dinner," Mother Garrett offered, as if reading Emma's mind. "It's not too late. You can still change your mind about going riding."

"Not after all the work Aunt Frances did on my riding skirt. Thank you again, Aunt Frances. The skirt fits well and it really . . . swooshes when I walk," she replied, grateful to have two honest compliments to offer. In point of truth, she rather enjoyed the freedom of having no petticoats beneath the slim riding skirt, but she kept that notion to herself.

Aunt Frances beamed. "I'm so excited that you're pleased with it. You know, I'm almost glad that chicken ruined the brown fabric. You look so much prettier with a touch of lighter colors."

A touch? It was difficult for Emma to think of the garish, shimmering fabric that covered her from waist to toe as anything other than a huge nightmare that promptly stifled any urge to defy convention once in a while. A bizarre image of the guest who had worn a full costume made from this fabric formed in her mind's eye, and she quickly shuttered that memory. "I'm just glad the chicken is gone. I hope you secured the gate after carrying the chicken back down to the woods."

"It's secure. I checked it again before I went to bed," Mother Garrett insisted. "By now that chicken should be long gone, off looking for other chickens."

Aunt Frances nodded. "Most likely."

Relieved that one of her prayers had been answered, Emma said her farewells. When she reached the patio, she saw the two picnic baskets sitting on top of the back stone wall and the sisters standing next to them, gazing down the hillside.

They turned around as she approached, and the sunlight caught the pins they wore so Emma could easily tell them apart. Almost simultaneously, the sisters' eyes bulged, and Emma put a finger to her lips. "Not a word. Not one. Not a giggle, either," she warned in as loud a whisper as she dared.

Each sister clapped a hand to mouth and nodded, but that still could not stop the tears of laughter that escaped.

"I know, I know. . . . It's awful. But Aunt Frances worked very hard to make this for me, and we can't offend her."

Garnet was the first to break her silence. "You look like you're dressed to join a traveling circus or a theater troupe."

"All you need is some sort of silly cap," Opal whispered.

"In point of fact, one of my guests was part of a theater troupe, but she was leaving that life. This came from the costume she left behind. If I'm not mistaken, I believe there is a rather silly-looking bonnet still in the trunk in the garret. So . . ." She sobered. "Do you still want me to go riding with you?"

"Of course!"

"Absolutely!"

Convinced she was about to endure one of the most humbling

moments of her life, Emma let out a deep sigh. "The sooner we leave, the sooner I can be off Main Street and disappear into the woods."

Garnet grinned. "We're not using Main Street today."

"But the livery is at the south end of Main Street."

"True, but we're heading north today for a change, so Mr. Adams brought the horses here. They're tied up right behind the gazebo. See?" Opal pointed toward the woods. "If we ride single file at first, we can follow the path through the woods, cross the main roadway, and ride along the Candlewood Canal a ways before crossing over. If I'm not mistaken, it's only a mile or two. From there, we were hoping to . . ."

While Emma was relieved to avoid parading down Main Street, she found she could not really concentrate on Opal's words, for she was staring too hard at the gazebo. Shocked speechless, she pointed and eventually managed to give voice to her words. "That . . . what are those . . . purple stains on this side of the gazebo?"

Garnet took a look. "What a pity. That's probably from the mulberries. But don't worry. The season for them is done. There can't be much of them left."

"Most likely," Opal agreed.

"B-but you planted the mulberry trees behind the gazebo, not on the side. How could the mulberry stains be on this side, and what would smash the berries up against the gazebo like that?" Emma countered. "I hope this isn't some sort of prank."

Garnet redirected Emma's attention. "Look—on the gazebo steps. There's your culprit."

Emma took one look and stiffened as the renegade chicken maneuvered itself into the gazebo, up onto the benches, and finally along the railing edge on the side of the gazebo, where it set itself to roost. She ground her teeth together when the chicken's purple droppings hit the side of the gazebo.

Opal and Garnet both started giggling.

"That gazebo makes for the prettiest chicken coop. It's the mulberries, all right," Opal managed.

"Pigs and chickens just love them," her sister said. "I've heard some farmers even plant mulberry trees to feed their stock, although most of the trees are going to nurseries these days. The demand from farmers turning to the silk industry is really growing."

"That's because silkworms love mulberries, too," Opal explained.

"I don't know much about chickens and their habits," Garnet observed, "but I've also heard they make good pets. Maybe the chicken has adopted you instead of the other way around. It sure seems to like being here."

"Back home, Mrs. Billings had a pet chicken once. Don't you remember, Garnet?"

"Oh, that's right! She had the sweetest little chicken. It would eat right out of our hands. It followed her all around the yard, too. She even had a little shed built just for . . . What was that chicken's name?"

"No more talk about chickens—as pets or otherwise," Emma grumbled. "Yesterday I prayed for the chicken to leave the patio. This time, I'll be more specific and ask for the chicken to leave my property. I'm even going to add pigs to my prayers, just to be sure there's no misunderstanding should a wagonload of swine spill out onto Main Street and a renegade pig finds its way here for those mulberries."

She turned and grabbed the baskets. "Shall we go?" Emma asked, silently whispering her prayer, hoping the answer would be more akin to her liking than to His.

At the end of their outing, Emma rode back up the path through the woods behind Hill House wearing a grin that almost stretched from ear to ear.

After an hour or so astride, she had felt as comfortable and as confident as she had thought she would be. They had stopped for a bite of breakfast and dinner but otherwise traveled the rest of the day through woodlands and farmlands, some of which Emma had inherited. They were too busy chatting and laughing together to bother dismounting when resting their horses or pausing at creeks and streams for their horses to drink.

She set aside her disappointment that her prayer about learning something that might help her with the Leonards' squabble had gone unanswered, but Emma was almost giddy knowing she had proven Mother Garrett's patronizing words to be true. This had been a very, very special day she would long remember.

As planned, she reined up at the edge of the woods, dismounted, and handed her reins to Opal, who insisted on taking the horses back to the livery with Garnet.

Opal looked down at her and frowned. "As well as you did today, you're not as used to riding as we are, especially for so long. Are you sure you'll be able to get back to the house all right?"

Emma widened her grin. "I feel terrific. When you come back, you're both going to tell Mother Garrett how well I did, aren't you?"

Both sisters nodded.

"Good. I'll have plenty of fresh water ready in your rooms so you can wash up."

"Watch out for that chicken," Garnet teased before she and her sister turned around and led Emma's horse away.

Emma watched them until they reached the main roadway and turned south before she headed back to the house. She managed only a step or two before she realized she had been astride for so long, she did not quite have her equilibrium back. She held still for a moment, took a few tentative steps, and felt her back and leg muscles protest.

She dismissed the first few twinges as normal but worked the muscles in her hands and arms as she started walking slowly toward the house. She passed by the gazebo without sighting the chicken and made a mental note to speak with Aunt Frances again.

If Aunt Frances would agree to find the chicken again at dusk when it was sleepy, Emma would also ask her to solve the problem of that chicken once and for all. If not tomorrow, someday soon there would be chicken stew simmering on Mother Garrett's cookstove.

Tough or not, Emma was going to savor every single bite.

29

UNFORTUNATELY, MOTHER GARRETT had been right. Again.

Emma could not soon forget her day of riding with Opal and Garnet, even if she tried. Even two days later, every muscle, every bone in her body still ached. She was finally able to braid her hair on the first attempt today without too much pain. Bumping along in the buggy with the two sisters to see them off on the morning packet, however, was only slightly more bearable than the glint of amusement in Mother Garrett's eyes—a glint that showed no signs of disappearing in the near future.

Emma waited on the landing until the rest of the passengers boarded the packet boat. Once Opal and Garnet climbed up to the cabin roof, they started waving good-bye with their handkerchiefs from Aunt Frances. Emma instinctively responded with a hearty wave.

"We'll be back in the spring when the tulips bloom," Opal cried. "Tell Mr. Breckenwith we hope to see him then."

"And tell Reverend Glenn we've decided to give our crosses

to our parents and ask him to make two more for us," Garnet said as the packet boat moved away from the landing.

"I will," Emma promised. She carefully offered a final wave good-bye and struggled against the fear that when the Mitchell sisters returned in the spring, Emma might no longer be at Hill House. With a weary heart, she started the long, painful walk toward home, but by walking slowly and stretching her leg muscles very gently, she found the more leisurely pace almost enjoyable.

By midmorning, Candlewood was bustling with activity. One wagon after another, and occasionally a single rider, traveled up and down Main Street. Other wagons were still parked the length of Canal Street, waiting to carry away the merchandise and livestock arriving on freight barges or to deliver goods being shipped east to New York City via the Erie Canal.

She eased her way along the planked sidewalk and managed her way through the shoppers traveling in and out of stores and around the workmen beginning construction today on a clock that would stand in front of town hall.

On a whim she turned off Main Street onto Coulter Lane. With her meeting with Mr. Langhorne only days away, she stopped at Mr. Breckenwith's to see if he had returned from his trip. When Jeremy answered her knock, his cheeks flushed the moment he recognized her. Relieved to find that her lawyer had indeed returned, she followed Jeremy as he escorted her directly to his mentor's cluttered office before he promptly disappeared.

Zachary Breckenwith was seated behind his desk. When she entered the room, he stopped writing, looked up, and set his pen aside before rising to greet her. "I was just penning a note for Jeremy to take to Hill House asking you to stop by. Please, have a seat."

After she sat down, very gingerly, he followed suit. "I take it you enjoyed your ride the other day with the Misses Mitchell," he said with a very uncustomary twinkle in his eyes.

Her cheeks flushed warm. "And the news of my ride spread all the way to the county seat?"

He chuckled. "No. I came home by packet boat on Monday and spied the three of you. It's quite interesting how far one can see from the canal when standing on the cabin roof of a packet boat, especially when a rider is wearing something that catches the sun. The female travelers were quite intrigued and asked me if I knew the identity of the woman who was dressed in silk and went riding alone with not one but two male companions."

"And your reply?" Annoyed that she had been spotted and discussed by strangers, Emma was duly unsettled that he thought the incident was humorous and that he was responding to the whole situation as if he had set aside his role as her lawyer to become something . . . more?

He laughed at her question. "Client privilege. On all accounts. I trust the sisters enjoyed their stay?" he asked, reminding her that he found Opal and Garnet as delightful as she did.

"Completely. I just saw them off. They were disappointed you were out of town and said they hoped to see you on their next visit. I was on my way home when I thought I'd stop to see if you'd returned. May I assume you have the information I requested?" she asked, anxious to learn the content of Enoch Leonard's will before telling him about her upcoming meeting with Mr. Langhorne.

He nodded. While he rifled through his papers to find the will, she described the situation between the Leonard brothers as it now stood, grateful for the confidentiality he had mentioned a moment ago. "Unfortunately, since I asked you to get a copy of the will, James and Andrew still haven't resolved their differences."

"And Widow Leonard is still staying with you at Hill House?" he asked as he found the document he had been searching for.

"Yes."

He handed her the copy of the will and assumed a more serious demeanor as he slipped into his more formal and familiar role as her lawyer. "Unlike most people who wait until they're on their deathbeds, he had this will drawn up some time before his death. As I recall, that was in August of 1833. I'm leaving again tomorrow with Aunt Elizabeth for a visit with relatives in Bounty, and I thought I might even go on to New York City for a spell to see some old friends. I don't expect we'll return for a good month, at least. Since the will isn't very lengthy, if you have time, you might want to read it over here so I can answer any questions you might have. Unfortunately, I doubt you'll find anything in the will that might prove helpful to you."

Dismayed to learn he would be leaving before her meeting with Mr. Langhorne, Emma turned all of her attention to the will she held in her hand. She felt odd about reading it, despite the fact it was now a public document. She focused on her good intentions, started reading the will, but skipped over the beginning that attested to the man's sanity. By skimming over survey details, she was able to quickly verify that the present ownership of the land was in accordance with the dictates of the will.

The specific bequests to Aunt Frances, who had signed away her dower rights, were not unusual. She was permitted to keep her clothing and personal possessions, as well as "the bed linens, kitchen utensils, and a chair of her own choosing."

The part of the will that interested Emma the most was the section detailing the man's very precise wishes for the care of his wife after his demise:

I hereby direct my sons to be responsible for the happiness, welfare, and general well-being of their mother, said Frances Carter Leonard. For six months of every year of her widowhood, each son shall provide her with a separate, furnished room for sleeping, ten yards of fabric, seven spools of thread, one cord of wood, two tins of licorice root, and such foodstuffs as she deems desirable. Out of respect and with gratitude for her many years of faithful devotion and care, they shall likewise return the same tender affection she has given to them, that she might spend her final years living in comfort, peace, and harmony.

Struck by the obvious affection and concern he had for his wife, Emma was also moved that he had known his sons well enough to remind them, implicitly, to get along with each other. She struggled to find her voice. "He cared for his wife very deeply," she murmured.

"And provided for her accordingly," the lawyer noted. "Most men, however, are very precise in terms of assigning specific obligations to the grown children who are left to care for the surviving widow, assuming they don't wait until their last dying moments to dictate a will and have the time to give the matter some thought."

Troubled by the difficulties Aunt Frances was experiencing, Emma ran her fingertips across the document. "When it comes to caring for their widowed mothers, grown children should know what their obligations are," she offered, ever grateful she did not have to face a similar problem with her own sons. "They shouldn't need a will to tell them what they should or should not do."

"It's been my experience that with few exceptions, adult children generally honor all of their obligations to an aging parent, especially if it happens to be their mother."

"Perhaps," she said. Unfortunately, both James and Andrew were clearly following the letter of their father's will. The foodstuffs they had delivered to Hill House were proof of that. Aunt

Frances's final years, however, were proving to be neither peaceful nor harmonious, and she wondered if that might be something to be pursued legally so that James and Andrew had no alternative but to compromise and reconcile.

"What if they don't?" Emma asked. "What if the children do some things but not everything the will calls for them to do?"

He frowned. "If they don't, I daresay few widows have the wherewithal to force their children to abide by the terms of a will. I've never had such a case."

Startled by his words, she stilled her fingers and held the will firmly in her hand. "Never? Even if the will clearly states one thing and the grown children ignore it? Let me see . . ." She studied the document carefully. "Here. It says the two sons should make sure their mother spends her 'final years in comfort, peace, and harmony.' What if they don't?"

She did not wait for him to respond. "To my mind, by continuing their disagreement, James and Andrew are filling their mother's life with discord and disappointment. Her life is neither peaceful nor harmonious," she charged, giving voice to the private thoughts she had had only moments ago. "If it were, she never would have run off to Hill House."

He let out a deep breath. "While all that you say about Widow Leonard's situation may be true, as deplorable and disagreeable as it may be, the prospect of winning a lawsuit on that basis would be next to nil, in my opinion," he added. "Are you suggesting perhaps Widow Leonard is considering filing such a lawsuit? If so, let me caution you most sincerely, her suit will not prevail. You'll have to rely on some other method to get her sons to solve their disagreement, particularly in light of your own legal difficulties," he added without further comment.

Emma's heart sank. Despite her hopes, she respected and

trusted his opinion enough to face the harsh reality that the will would be of no help to her at all. She folded up the will and sighed. "No, I'm not suggesting a lawsuit. I'm just surprised. It seems to me that if a widow's children were not providing for her as they were required to do according to their father's will, she should find remedy under the law, if need be, and the law should respond favorably to her needs."

"I'm not suggesting she can't," he said. "For the sake of argument, let's put aside concerns about her happiness or her general well-being. Let's say her sons were not providing some of the items that were listed, the wood and the fabric, for example. The court would force them to do so, but that's assuming she'd even entertain the notion of a lawsuit in the first place. Most widows in that situation don't, and there are several reasons why they don't."

"Why? What reasons?" Emma asked.

He shrugged. "Shame, for one," he replied. "Most widows wouldn't want it known that their own children weren't providing for them, if the children were capable of doing so. Lawsuits are in the public domain, and there's no greater fodder for gossipmongers than a lawsuit of this nature."

She frowned. If Aunt Frances had been feisty enough to run away, Emma was fairly certain she would not have let the shame of a lawsuit stop her from filing it to force her sons to reconcile.

"Shame aside, why else wouldn't a widow pursue her rights under the law?" she asked, then realized the answer almost the moment she posed the question. "Funds, I suppose."

"Exactly. Depending on the people and the obligations involved, a lawsuit of that nature could be quite lengthy and very expensive, far beyond the means of widows like Widow Leonard."

"Very sad, but very true." Although Aunt Frances had no funds to pursue a lawsuit, Emma would have easily provided them.

Unfortunately, given Mr. Breckenwith's opinion that the lawsuit would not prevail, that mattered little.

She held up the will. "May I keep this?" she asked, although it probably had no value to her now at all.

"It's yours. In all truth, I wish I could have been more helpful," he admitted.

"No, you've been very helpful," she countered, impressed by both his knowledge and his eagerness to share it with her.

"May I ask if you've decided to proceed with the sale of that parcel of land to your mother-in-law or given any thought at all to pursuing other options, should the owner of Hill House decide not to sell it to you?"

"No, not yet. But soon. I just need to square away a few other matters first," Emma assured him. She hesitated, half tempted to tell him about her upcoming meeting with Mr. Langhorne and her suspicions that the man had learned about her not having legal title to Hill House. But ultimately she decided against it. Given the subtle shift in their relationship—which was all too tangible today—she was not prepared to deal with the prospect that he might postpone his trip for personal, rather than professional, reasons.

In all truth, she had struggled long and hard against the fact that there was nothing she could do to convince the owner of Hill House to sell the property to her. She had also struggled with her decision not to tell any of the others about the possibility she might lose Hill House, forcing all of them to leave. Whether or not that decision was right or fair also continued to trouble her.

If indeed she did lose Hill House, however, she had to cling to the fervent belief that His will for her and those she loved would unfold, all in His time, and all for His purpose.

Not hers.

And only if she learned how to truly submit her will to His.

30

TIME PASSED BY QUICKLY AT HILL HOUSE over the next several days, but not routinely or easily.

In less than a week, James and Andrew Leonard would arrive to air their differences. In precisely one hour, Mr. Langhorne would appear to keep his ten-o'clock appointment.

Emma was ill-prepared for both events, preoccupied by more pressing but mundane matters. Seated behind the desk in her office, she rested her elbows on the desktop and pressed her fingertips to her temples. If she had any hope of appearing calm and being competent during her meeting with Mr. Langhorne, she needed to clear her mind.

The renegade chicken was proving to be the winner in a frustrating but oddly comical game of hide-and-seek that made her plans for having this particular chicken for dinner seem unlikely, at least anytime soon. For the moment, she set that problem on a back burner.

The injury to Ditty's mother's hand was not healing as quickly as they had hoped, and the young woman's return to her job had been delayed indefinitely. Emma turned that concern over to prayer.

The arrival of two unexpected guests over the weekend had kept Emma working morning to night. Though still aching and sore from the extra work, she had reason to rejoice: the guests had left this morning after breakfast.

With her mind now free from those worries, she steepled her hands and rested her chin on her fingertips. Breathing slowly, she whispered no words of praise or made any requests; instead, she quietly welcomed the gentle peace of His presence and love into her spirit.

She opened her eyes when the grandfather clock struck the quarter hour and quickly surveyed the top of her desk. The guest register lay on the right side at the base of an oil lamp. On the left, where she normally kept a small vase of roses behind her box of writing supplies, a sampler no larger than the palm of her hand displayed a grand message: God is love.

Once she was satisfied there was no speck of dust anywhere and no smudge on the wooden desk, she smoothed the fresh paper on the blotter in front of her. She had no doubt Mr. Langhorne was coming to berate her for deliberately lying to him about selling the parcel of land he had been after. In turn, she would have to tell him again that she would not sell him that land. Not today. Not ever.

Assuming that he knew she did not hold legal title to Hill House, she suspected that his true purpose for coming here was to force her to do exactly that by using the knowledge of it as leverage. Giving in to blackmail of any kind, however, was abhorrent to her very nature.

She was also determined not to waste the little time she had before the man arrived on fear of what he might know or do today. Convinced her map held clues to Mr. Langhorne's purpose for investing in the surrounding area, which now involved at least Andrew Leonard, if not his brother, she retrieved the map from a side drawer and unfolded it. She spread the map out on her desk and made sure north was at the top so the map was oriented correctly in hopes she might discover his purpose for wanting the Leonard land, too.

Using a pencil from her writing box, she drew an outline around the Oliver property she had been told Mr. Langhorne had bought. Next, she outlined the land the Leonard brothers owned individually. The portion of the toll road and surrounding acreage they owned jointly she decided to mark with a series of crisscrosses. Using dotted lines, she marked the route she suspected a railroad would most likely follow by starting north at Bounty and moving south along the toll road through the Leonard land, then farther south to the end point of the toll road where the old toll collector's cabin, which the Cross family now owned, was located.

Finally, she outlined the parcel of land she owned on Hollaway Lane that Mr. Langhorne was no doubt coming to discuss again, even though it was too far north of the projected rail line to be of much use to him.

She leaned back, studied her work on the map again, and toyed with the pencil in her hand. Unfortunately, no matter how she tried, she could see no connection between the route she had drawn, Mr. Oliver's land that lay farther west beyond several smaller farms that bordered the Leonard land, and her land on Hollaway Lane. She had no idea whether or not Mr. Langhorne had purchased the smaller farms or not, and it was too late to pursue the matter now. In addition, she was puzzled that Mr. Langhorne had not bought the toll collector's cabin before the Cross family did, since the cabin was located in such a strategic location that would suit a depot for a railroad.

The grandfather clock struck the half hour.

The answers she had hoped to find on the map simply were not there. Despite all her efforts, she now had no more idea of what Mr. Langhorne intended to do with the land that he was buying than before she started drawing on the map. The only thing she had gained was the conviction that if and when the railroad did come, she knew precisely the route it would take.

Frustrated that she had wasted so much time and energy on the map, she folded it up, stored it away again, and sat quietly while waiting for Mr. Langhorne to arrive.

She counted the chimes as the clock struck the hour of ten and waited. At the quarter hour, she rose to stretch her arms and legs. At the half hour, she heard a commotion on the porch and rose to investigate. She scarcely got to her feet before the outer door flew open and Mr. Langhorne charged into her office, slamming the door behind him.

Rendered speechless, she watched him struggle to catch his breath. At the same time, he shoved several papers back into his coat pocket and fumbled with his spectacles to put them back on. Once he did, he glared at her. "In all truth, Widow Garrett, since you routinely expect callers and guests, I find it unimaginable that you wouldn't pen up your . . . your livestock, if that's how one defines a chicken, instead of allowing it to roost on your front porch! I've been trying for half an hour to get past that chicken and finally decided to charge my way, losing my hat and almost losing my papers in the process."

Her eyes widened, even more so when she spied the feather stuck to his sleeve, and she struggled not to smile. "I'm deeply sorry. I'll certainly replace your hat, but the chicken isn't mine at all. Apparently, it's one of the chickens that escaped when the wagon overturned on Main Street a few weeks back. We've had more than a few problems trying to rid ourselves of that pest."

"A good whack with a stick would suffice. Unfortunately, I couldn't locate one or you would be rid of your problem for good and have chicken for dinner as a bonus. That's how most of the shopkeepers solved the same problem. Don't bother yourself about the hat. I have others. You can toss this one into the trash pit."

Although she had nearly the same solution in mind to rid herself of the chicken, she felt oddly protective about the animal. "Please have a seat. May I offer you some refreshments?"

"Nothing, thank you." He sat down, wrinkled his nose when he saw the feather, and flicked it off, letting it fall to the floor. "What I've come to say won't take long."

She folded her hands together and lay them on top of her desk. While meeting his hardened gaze, she braced herself and took control of their conversation. "Before you begin, let me tell you that despite what I previously told you the last time we met here about selling the land on Hollaway Lane, the sale did not proceed, for a number of reasons I won't bother to detail. However, since then, I've had a change of heart. The land is not for sale, regardless of any offer you might be prepared to make."

His gaze grew cold. "I'm no longer interested in that land, at any price. As you suggested at our last meeting, I've chosen to more actively pursue a different venture—one I've been planning for some months now. My visit here today is for quite another purpose."

Her pulse quickened, but she held very still and kept a smile on her face, more determined than ever not to give him any inkling she even considered he might know she did not hold legal title to Hill House. Further, although she had a very good idea the railroad had something to do with the venture he claimed he had chosen to pursue, she did not want to broach the subject until she clearly understood it. "Frankly, I don't believe there's anything more for us to discuss," she insisted, prepared to hear the worst—his threat to take Hill House from her.

He squared his shoulders. "I disagree. Out of respect for your gender, I have come to tell you in person and in the privacy of your own office. Be forewarned, madam: Stay out of my business affairs. Should you continue to speak to either James or Andrew Leonard or anyone else about my business affairs, I shall file a lawsuit to stop you. Immediately."

He did not know. He did not know. He did not know!

Her heart pounded with relief that surged through her veins. He truly did not know she did not have title to Hill House!

Her relief was short-lived. "A lawsuit? On what basis?" she managed.

He offered her a sardonic smile. "On any basis my very expensive, very talented, and very experienced team of lawyers might suggest."

Her heart pounded in her ears. Even though he was unaware of the legal quagmire she was in, the absolute last thing she needed was a lawsuit. "There's no basis for a lawsuit against me. Whether or not I speak to someone with whom you're doing business or counsel someone for or against doing so is perfectly legal. It's not a matter for the courts. You can't sue me."

"Of course I can. I may not win the suit," he admitted, "but I can file it. In fact, I can instruct my lawyers to drag the lawsuit from one court to another, opening every one of your substantial holdings to the scrutiny of the courts, I might add. The process could take years, which would provide more than enough gossip about the esteemed Widow Garrett to keep gossipmongers' tongues wagging and to convince guests planning to come to Hill

House to choose a more suitable place to stay. I might also be tempted to file a lawsuit against your mother-in-law or perhaps Widow Leonard, as well," he added.

Horrified as well as outraged, Emma leaped to her feet to protest, but he held up his hand to silence her objections. "Don't bother to argue. You've been warned, which is what I came to do. I can show myself out . . . by the front door," he snapped and left by way of the connecting door to the library.

Trembling with fear and anger, she dropped back down into her seat and cradled her face in her hands. Though troubled by his intention to involve both Mother Garrett and Aunt Frances, she was completely demoralized by his threat to file a lawsuit against her. Once his lawyers filed a lawsuit and began investigating her affairs, they would invariably discover that she did not hold legal title to Hill House. In point of fact, she was rather surprised they had not discovered just that when he had presented his offer of a title to her only last month and could only assume his claim to know all of her affairs had been more bluff than substance.

Nevertheless, once he did learn the truth he could blackmail her into selling him the parcel of land he wanted in return for keeping silent about her not owning Hill House. Far worse, he might contact Mr. Meyers in Philadelphia in an effort to convince the legal owner to sell Hill House out from under her, giving Mr. Langhorne the right to evict her at will.

Additionally, because of his threat, she would not be able to tell Andrew and James Leonard that if they did settle their argument by selling any or all of their land to Mr. Langhorne, they could be giving up land that was going to explode in value in the coming years. If she did not tell them, she would always know she could have prevented the sale but did not do so.

Overwhelmed with despair, she wept uncontrollably until her

tears were spent, her body was exhausted, and her heart ached. With brutal honesty, she looked back over the past four years and admitted she had no one to blame but herself.

As much as she had believed that God had led her here to Hill House, she now understood that she had bought this property to escape her growing loneliness, surrounded at the General Store by memories that reminded her every moment of the husband she had lost and their three sons who had married and moved far away.

While her own selfish needs had prompted her to look at Hill House as an opportunity to change her life, it was pride in her ability to turn the abandoned property into a viable, thriving enterprise that had led her to ignore her lawyer's advice. Without having legal title to Hill House in her possession, not only had she sold the General Store but she had moved into Hill House and restored it, severing all ties to the past and possibly putting her future at risk.

It was also her pride that had kept her from seeking Zachary Breckenwith's advice before he left on his month-long trip . . . along with her suspicions that he had developed more than a professional interest in her.

She dried her tears and bowed her head. Buying Hill House had clearly been her will, not God's, and not an act of true faith. Humbly, she bowed her very soul before Him, asking for forgiveness, as well as His guidance now. "Thy will be done," she whispered, convinced that only with God's help would she be able to wait for His plan for her future to unfold . . . and then accept His plan, even if it meant leaving Hill House forever.

With her spirit refreshed, she focused on one problem she might be able to solve on her own: helping Aunt Frances. She rose, went to the window, and pulled back the curtain to glance back and forth along the side porch. The chicken was nowhere to

be seen, but she did spy Mr. Langhorne's hat and enough droppings to erase the fleeting thought she had had about protecting
that chicken.

She went out to the porch and tiptoed around the droppings
to retrieve the hat. When she picked it up and turned it over, she
found a paper wedged inside. It appeared to be some sort of correspondence, but it was badly smeared and stained, as if it had been
dropped into a mud puddle. Her eyes widened when she recalled
James Leonard's tale of tossing Mr. Langhorne out and the man
dropping both his spectacles and his hat in the mud.

She hesitated but decided any man who would threaten to sue
two elderly women like Mother Garrett and Aunt Frances did not
deserve privacy. "Besides, it's on my porch, and he told me to put
his hat in the trash pit, which means the letter is trash, as well,"
she rationalized.

She set the hat on the railing and attempted to make sense of
the few legible words the letter contained. The phrases "expected
to ship" and "in prime condition," along with a signature, "David
Barkley, Proprietor," indicated the correspondence was some sort
of reply to an order Mr. Langhorne had placed or was considering
placing.

"Maybe the man ordered a new pair of spectacles, ones that
won't keep falling off his face," she said and shoved the paper into
his hat. Since he had said not to bother returning the hat, she set
it upside down on one of the porch chairs. If there was any justice
at all, that chicken would decide the hat made for an attractive
nesting place—just once before the hat found its way to the trash
pit and that chicken wound up in Mother Garrett's soup pot.

31

ON FRIDAY MORNING, WITH ONLY A DAY left before James and Andrew Leonard were scheduled to appear, Emma was as exhausted as she was desperate.

She stood at the front door and watched the buggy carry away the three guests who had arrived unexpectedly on Tuesday. After closing the door, she went into the east parlor and collapsed on the sofa. The very idea of going upstairs to clean and change the bed linens in the three guest rooms kept her prone and lit the notion that since no new guests were expected for another week, she might simply close those rooms off, wait until Monday to tackle them, and pray no guests arrived unexpectedly in the meantime.

When she heard Mother Garrett and Aunt Frances coming down the center hallway, she did not bother to sit up. When they entered the parlor, dressed for an outing wearing their fall capes and their silly bonnets, she closed her eyes and prayed she was dreaming.

"Good, you're resting," Mother Garrett said. "Liesel's in the kitchen with enough work to keep her busy until she turns eighteen. We're off for a bit of shopping. Do you need anything from the General Store?"

Emma opened one eye. "No. Not unless you want to bring back some sort of net to catch that chicken. Are you sure you need to go shopping, or are you just using that as an excuse to take Aunt Frances around to meet someone else who might be a suitable match for Mr. Atkins?"

Mother Garrett sniffed. "In point of fact, we're planning to do a little of both."

"I'm hoping to meet Polly Shepherd today, so we're going to stop at the dressmaker's," Aunt Frances offered. "But I really do need to stop at the General Store. Between doing the mending and making handkerchiefs for all your guests, I've run low on thread already, and I wanted to pick out something special for Reverend Glenn while I'm there. He's been so very kind to me," she added and her cheeks turned pinkly. "But don't worry. If I forget to pay for anything, Mr. Atkins will simply put it on my account."

Emma opened the other eye. "You have an account at the General Store now?"

Mother Garrett nodded. "Just like I do. It was my idea. That's one way to avoid any misunderstandings."

"We want to make sure poor Sheriff North doesn't show up on your doorstep on our account again," Aunt Frances added.

"That's a fine idea," Emma admitted and sat up. "Just remember to see if there's any mail, if you would, Mother Garrett. I still haven't heard from the boys, and I'm hoping they might be able to come for a visit."

"Surely."

"And we'll bring you back a surprise, just like you did for us,"

Aunt Frances promised before the two of them left the parlor.

Emma listened to the two women as they chatted together on their way to the front door and across the porch. Aunt Frances seemed very content and almost happy these days, which Emma found confusing. With James and Andrew coming tomorrow, she expected Aunt Frances to be nervous, since the outcome of the meeting would determine whether or not she would be able to leave Hill House to live with her sons again.

Instead, Aunt Frances almost seemed more focused on staying here, even to the point of having opened an account at the General Store. Emma dismissed the idea as unlikely and assumed perhaps instead of confiding in her, the elderly widow had been talking with Mother Garrett or Reverend Glenn—both of whom must have been able to allay her fears about the future and indeed appeared to have become close friends. Judging by the blush on Aunt Frances's cheeks when she mentioned buying something for Reverend Glenn, Emma wondered if perhaps the friendship between her guests was blossoming into something more.

Emma sat for a spell, resting and thinking, then ventured outside to the shaded patio. She found Reverend Glenn whittling in front of the fire, which Liesel had started earlier that morning in the outdoor fireplace. Butter was sleeping alongside him on the stone floor, and the vise from Mr. Atkins was mounted on the arm of Reverend Glenn's chair.

She pulled a chair over and sat down beside him. "Would you mind some company or would I be interrupting?"

He set down his new penknife and smiled. "Sitting outside in front of a warm fire on a chilly day feels awfully good. I was praying you might join me. You know, I realized this morning when I was talking with Frances that I'd never made a cross for you. I was just starting on a new piece of candlewood to make one for you and thought you might like to watch."

She sighed and stared into the fire. "I'm glad someone's prayers are being answered."

He picked up his penknife and started working the wood again. "Prayers are always answered. Whether we like the answers or even recognize them is altogether another matter. Sounds like that may be the case for you. Which is it?"

"Lately, considering all the things I've prayed for, probably a little of both." She chuckled and shook her head. "The day that chicken ruined the riding skirt Aunt Frances was making for me, I prayed for that chicken to disappear from the patio. The next day, sure enough, the chicken was gone from the patio but had decided the gazebo made a handy chicken coop and now wants to roost occasionally on the porch railings, as well. I don't know why that chicken had to pick Hill House for its home any more than I understand why God had to take my prayer so literally. I suppose I should be grateful the chicken hasn't bothered any of the guests, except for Mr. Langhorne."

Reverend Glenn stopped his work. "You've had a great deal on your mind these past few weeks and extra work for yourself with Ditty gone home. Maybe the chicken is still here to remind you from time to time to have faith enough to trust Him."

She snorted at the idea the chicken served any purpose other than being an annoyance. "I'm trying. But where that chicken is concerned, I'm afraid I'm running out of both time and patience. On top of which, I have no idea how to help James and Andrew resolve their differences tomorrow if they don't resolve the situation themselves. I've prayed and I've prayed, but every time I think I'm close to finding a solution, I discover I'm further away than ever."

"Frances tells me I'm a good listener," he murmured, and his gaze softened with a tenderness that only reinforced the notion that he and Aunt Frances were becoming more than just friends.

Briefly, she confided in him and told him of her initial thoughts about the railroad, the details of Mr. Langhorne's visit, which undermined them, and the dilemma she now faced. She did not, however, tell him about possibly losing Hill House. "Even if I could think of something to do, I only have until tomorrow to do it, which means all my prayers to help Aunt Frances have gone unanswered."

"Maybe that's your answer," he suggested.

"What? To do nothing?"

He started rubbing his left arm. "Some time back after I suffered the stroke, when I was struggling living alone, do you remember coming to see me and asking me to come live here at Hill House?"

Disappointed he had changed the topic, she met his gaze and held it. "I do."

"After my stroke, I prayed and prayed, too, just like you've been doing. After all the years I'd spent calling others to follow the Word, I felt the Lord would answer my prayers to be healed, to be strong and healthy again. Instead, I stayed . . . like this. I was angry and hurt and confused." He dropped his gaze. "Then He sent you to me. If you'll recall, you had to come back several times to convince me I should come here to live at Hill House."

"Yes, I do," she admitted, moved by the minister's honesty and determined to continue to make a home for Reverend Glenn, wherever that might be.

"That's because at first, I didn't like the answer He'd sent. Not until I realized He'd sent you in answer to my other prayers— answers I found here when I trusted Him and had faith in Him. Caring friends. Companionship. Laughter. All the things I'd missed after losing my wife and prayed to find again. Even Butter here showed up at Hill House to help me," he whispered and reached down to pat the dog's head. "It took me some time to figure it all out. Fortunately, you didn't give up on me and neither did He."

He paused and looked at her again. "Don't give up on the Lord. Have faith and be open to His will, not yours. If there's something you're supposed to do or something you're supposed to know, you will."

Moved by his words, Emma bowed her head for a moment. When she searched her heart, she saw that same foolish pride staring back at her. "You're right," she admitted. "Solving this dilemma has become a matter of pride. I wanted to help Aunt Frances and not disappoint her, and now Mother Garrett and Aunt Frances are involved in ways I never anticipated," she whispered, deeply regretting the potential lawsuit Mr. Langhorne threatened to file.

She rose and pressed a kiss to the top of the elderly man's head. "Thank you. I'm not sure how to solve this dilemma or how to make up for not being stronger in my faith, but doing a little penance might be a way to start."

He chuckled. "Don't be too hard on yourself. What did you have in mind?"

"I'll start with cleaning out the clutter I've stashed away on the first floor. After that, we'll see," she teased and returned to the house with her troubled heart and mind a little lighter.

———

After two hours of nonstop cleaning, Emma had cleared every bit of clutter from the first floor, but the clutter that once had been hidden in drawers or cupboards was now stacked in piles in the center hallway near the front door. An assortment of broken vases and chipped or cracked china were now ready for the trash pit, which is where she should have put them in the first place. Two piles held dated newspapers, journals, and magazines to be used over the winter when kindling was scarce. Wiping her hands on her apron, she remembered she had forgotten the papers stored in the sideboard and retrieved them, then returned to the center hallway and bent down to add them to one of the piles.

Reluctant to see the expensive magazines go to ashes, she decided to sit down on the floor to sort through the piles and donate what she could to the lending library Mrs. Cooper had started in her home just last fall.

The process was tedious, in part because she would stop to skim an article in one of the magazines or newspapers that caught her eye, especially if it concerned canals or railroads. After nearly an hour, she stopped herself. At this rate, it would take her a year to sort through everything. She started working more quickly and promised herself not to let any more articles distract her.

Her good intentions lasted less than five minutes when she spied an article in one newspaper about the silk industry. Feeling stiff from sitting on the floor for so long, she picked up the newspaper and stood up to stretch her legs and back. She realized how quickly she had forgotten her promise and bent down to put the newspaper back into the discard pile.

At the very same moment, the front door swung open and Ditty rushed inside, colliding with Emma, who dropped the newspaper. She caught herself from falling by grabbing for the wall but knocked over the piles of papers on the floor in the process.

"Oh, I'm so sorry," the young woman gushed. "Please tell me I haven't hurt you."

Emma sighed and shook her head at the mess on the floor.

"No, I'm fine. I thought you weren't coming back for a while yet."

"My mother's feeling much better, so my father brought me back earlier than I expected. I can work the weekend to make up for all the time I've missed, too."

"We'd better start here," Emma suggested. "Go hang up your cape and bonnet and fetch Liesel to help me, too. Maybe if you're here with me, I won't be tempted to read everything that seems interesting."

Once Ditty was gone, Emma picked up the newspaper she had dropped. She caught a glimpse of a name in the article on the silk industry that had grabbed her attention, thought it seemed familiar, and skimmed the article to find the name again. "David Barkley," she whispered and recognized it as the same name on the correspondence she had found in Mr. Langhorne's hat.

Intrigued, she carefully read the entire newspaper article that discussed an 1828 report from the Secretary of the Treasury on the silk industry, which included information supplied by a Mr. David Barkley from Connecticut. The more she read, the faster her heart began to race and the broader her smile became.

She pressed the paper to her heart as she walked back to the hallway. "Of course! My first impression of Mr. Langhorne was right after all. It's not the future prospect of a railroad that interests him. He's not that wise of an investor. He's much more interested in the present. I'd be willing to guess his new venture is in the silk industry and he needs land to plant mulberry trees to raise silkworms. I'm not sure how that will help James and Andrew, but somehow it might. In any event, Mr. Langhorne has lots of other property he could buy instead of theirs, although he won't be able to control the toll road."

She bowed her head. "Thank you, Lord. Thank you for leading me to that newspaper. Thank you for bringing Ditty home to knock some sense into me. And thank you for Reverend Glenn, too. I trust you. I have faith in you. Please show me what I should do to help the Leonards," she prayed.

When the front door swung open again, Emma instinctively stepped back, prepared for almost anything now that Ditty was home.

Instead of Ditty, however, Mother Garrett entered the house, with Aunt Frances hurrying close behind. "You won't believe who's here."

"It's the best surprise we could have gotten for you, although in truth, they were already in the front yard when we got home. Look!" Aunt Frances insisted and stepped aside to let Opal and Garnet into the house.

Both sisters were wearing their flannel shirts and trousers.

Opal grinned. "We hope you don't mind, but we only got as far as Bounty when we had to leave the packet boat. There's a leak in the canal up there so they have to drain it to repair it, which means we'd be stuck there for a few weeks."

"We could have traveled by coach to go around that section of the canal. But there were so many passengers doing the same thing, we were there for days and still waiting to secure passage by coach," Garnet explained.

"And you won't believe who we met while we were waiting!" Opal cried gleefully.

"Zachary Breckenwith," Garnet replied without giving Emma a chance to guess. "We even had dinner with him and his aunt."

"That was before we rented a pair of horses to ride around the area to help pass the time. Then, on the spur of the moment, we decided to ride back here hoping you'd have room for us for another week or two. We found another shortcut, too, so you wouldn't hear from anyone that we were coming."

Emma hugged them both. "I'm so glad you came! Of course there's room."

An idea suddenly touched Emma's heart and quickly turned her frustration into hope. When she glanced around at all four women in the hallway with her, the true answer to her prayers now became very clear. Just as joining their voices together gave greater power to prayer, combining their efforts would surely lead to a solution to her dilemma about whether or not to tell James and Andrew about the prospect of a railroad.

"I need your help. All of your help," she began, but before she had a chance to explain why, all four women volunteered and followed her to her office, anxious to discover how they might be of assistance.

32

". . . ACCORDING TO YOUR WILL. AMEN."

Once they concluded their mutual prayer for guidance, all four women who had gathered with Emma around her desk looked to her for an explanation of how they could help her.

Quickly, just as she had done with Reverend Glenn, she explained the situation, omitting only her legal problems about not owning Hill House. This time, however, she took her time, detailing her first encounter with Mr. Langhorne and ending with her last.

She folded up the map she had used during her briefing and set it aside. "Here's my dilemma," she concluded. "Whether I'm right or wrong in believing that the railroad will be part of Candlewood's future, I still feel obligated to share what I've learned with both James and Andrew before they meet with each other here tomorrow."

"Which you can't do," Opal noted, "without risking a lawsuit from Mr. Langhorne that would involve both Mother Garrett and Aunt Frances. Have you discussed this with Mr. Breckenwith?"

"No, he'd already left before I met with Mr. Langhorne and he made his threat. I'm afraid I have to handle this without his advice," Emma replied, having second thoughts about not asking him for his advice when they had met to discuss Enoch Leonard's will.

Opal sighed. "I'm not sure how much he'd be able to help anyway."

Emma nodded. As much as she might want his advice now, if not his support, as her lawyer he would simply remind her yet again not to get involved in the Leonards' troubles any more than she already had done. She suspected, however, that if he set his role as her lawyer aside, he might approve of their plan.

Garnet shrugged. "Let's get back to the problem, shall we? Even if you don't warn James and Andrew, if it turns out they refuse to sell Mr. Langhorne the land, you think he'll still blame you for influencing their decision, so the risk is the same. And he'll own property, which unbeknownst to him might become even more valuable than he thinks it is now. Is that right?"

"Exactly," Emma replied. "I can't be certain, but since Andrew obviously told Mr. Langhorne of my role in helping to resolve the problem between himself and his brother, I suspect he may have also told him about our meeting tomorrow, as well."

"We don't have much time, then," Mother Garrett noted.

Emma looked to Aunt Frances for guidance. "Whatever we do, your sons have the most to lose or gain financially, but I'm more concerned about the trouble that has divided them as brothers and sent you here to Hill House. What do you think would happen if I did go to Andrew and tell him what I know? Or would it be better to speak with James first?"

Aunt Frances sighed. "Telling James first only proves him right and makes him the clear winner in their feud. If you tell Andrew first, he's likely to change his mind about selling, but that wouldn't sit well with him because James will have been proven right about not selling out. Their tug-of-war will only continue."

Mother Garrett looked at everyone and frowned. "There's another dilemma. Now we have two."

Emma's heart sank. Joining efforts had not solved her dilemma but doubled it.

"Maybe not," Garnet murmured. "Let's see that map again."

"I'd like to see it, too," Opal added.

Once Emma unfolded the map and laid it on the desktop again, the sisters both studied the map for several moments. When they finished, they began to smile at each other. "I see only one course of action," Opal offered.

Garnet nodded. "So do I."

Emma's heart skipped a beat. "What? What do you see?"

"Don't rush them," Mother Garrett cautioned.

"No, I think I'm ready," Garnet countered and looked directly at Emma. "First, you must tell Andrew what you've learned. True, James will be proven right about not selling out to Mr. Langhorne, which means he wins, just as Aunt Frances said."

"But since Andrew is the one who uncovers the future potential for profit, he wins, as well," Opal continued. "Do you agree, Aunt Frances?"

The elderly widow smiled. "Yes, I do. I hadn't looked at it that way."

Emma was heartened but still troubled. "Just in case you've all forgotten about how far it is to Andrew's home, let me remind you: There's no way I could ride out to see him and return home before dark, which means I'd be forced to spend the night."

"You could stay in my room," Aunt Frances offered.

"And I would, thank you," Emma replied and looked around

at the others. "Even if I did tell Andrew and returned to Hill House in the morning so I could be here for the meeting, there's still the threat of the lawsuit to consider. Even though Mr. Langhorne wouldn't prevail in the courts, the process would be lengthy and expensive, not to mention the gossip that would result."

"But that's only a problem if he believes you're the one responsible for Andrew changing his mind," Garnet argued. "You'll have to make sure he doesn't."

Emma rolled her eyes. "To do that, I'd probably have to be with Mr. Langhorne tomorrow while James and Andrew are here at Hill House, which is where I'm supposed to be, too. I'm afraid we're right back where we started, simply because I can't be in two places at once."

Garnet looked at her sister for a moment, smiled, removed her pin from her collar, and set it on top of the map. "No, you can't, but we can."

Opal removed her pin, as well, and laid it next to her sister's. "Yes, we can, which means you won't have to tell Andrew, and Mr. Langhorne won't even think to bother with a lawsuit against anyone. Now let's start from there."

For the next hour and all through dinner, the five women hashed out a number of possible scenarios. By dessert, they had settled on one and relegated different responsibilities to one another to assure its success.

When they had finished, Aunt Frances looked around the dining room table. "I've lived all my life on a farm with the closest neighbor miles away. Until I came to Hill House, I never knew what it was to have friends, truly good friends. Thank you for helping me and my sons. I just knew you'd all think of something to do to help."

Emma swallowed hard. Although the plan they had settled upon had a good chance of succeeding, there was an equal possibility of failure. Aunt Frances's faith in all of them now was as strong as her faith in God had been during her stay at Hill House, a lesson Emma would not soon forget. She rose from the table, resigned to the limited role she would play. "There's not much time. We should get started."

The others rose, too, and scattered off into different directions. Aunt Frances took both sisters to the garret to rifle through the trunk of left-behinds to find the costumes one of the two sisters would need. Mother Garrett headed to the kitchen to make up a parcel of foodstuffs for Mr. Atkins at the General Store.

Liesel and Ditty were cleaning up the dishes from dinner before leaving to deliver the notes Emma would write for the livery and the hotel. She did not like involving the two young women any more than she was happy about rescinding their punishment, but she realized how anxious they were to earn back the trust they had squandered and to help their aunt-by-affection.

Emma walked to her office to write her notes first. Then she was off to the trash pit to find Mr. Langhorne's hat. She could only hope and pray the hat would be somewhere close to the top and not buried too far beneath other items tossed away. Otherwise, she would need a good bath before she went anywhere.

33

A S PLANNED, OPAL LEFT ALMOST immediately after dinner to ride out to Andrew Leonard's farm using back roads to avoid being seen, just as the sisters had done when they had ridden back to Hill House to make sure their arrival would be a surprise.

Armed with Emma's map and a note from Aunt Frances, her role was to explain Emma's thoughts about the railroad to him, as well as to inform him of Mr. Langhorne's threatened lawsuit. If anyone could talk Andrew out of a temper, Opal or her sister could. She would spend the night in Aunt Frances's room and return the following day with him.

While Liesel and Ditty were off delivering Emma's notes, and Mother Garrett changed into another gown, Emma worked in the kitchen on Mr. Langhorne's hat to restore it to some semblance of its former appearance. Removing the stains left behind by the chicken droppings proved irksome, but paled when she considered she had found not one but six or seven chickens roosting together near the trash pit. She had not told anyone yet about her discovery or her plans to resolve it.

She was wondering how poor Garnet was faring, when Aunt Frances poked her head into the kitchen. "She's ready. Come see. It's almost time for her to leave."

Emma set the hat down and followed Aunt Frances to the east parlor, with her skirts rustling as she walked.

Aunt Frances looked back over her shoulder and smiled. "You were right. You do swoosh as you walk. Don't go too quickly, though, or you'll tear open those temporary stitches holding the split in the skirts closed."

Emma forced a smile. If parading on horseback down Main Street wearing these skirts had not appealed to her before, walking down Main Street wearing them now appealed to her even less. For once, she was even glad her sons did not live nearby so they would not see her, but at this moment, she cared little if the legal owner of Hill House eventually heard of the tale. Keeping Hill House meant nothing when compared to helping Aunt Frances and her sons to resolve their differences. "I'll try," she said, but the moment she stepped into the parlor and saw Garnet, she rushed forward to get a closer look.

Emma cupped her hand to her mouth. The transformation was miraculous. Wide-eyed, she stared at the woman standing in front of her. The dove-gray damask gown and matching gloves and bonnet made her look as elegant as the woman who had left them behind. If the many ribbons decorating the thinly veiled bonnet did not draw one's attention to the bonnet itself, rather than her features, then the overpowering perfume she wore would force people to turn away to avoid the odor.

"Garnet? Is that really you?" she managed, nearly choking on the smell of the perfume.

"No, thank heavens. Garnet Mitchell wouldn't be caught dead or alive dressed like this. Everybody knows that." She bobbed her head as if mentally changing identities. "Allow me to introduce myself. My name is Wilhelmina Stokes. Widow Stokes, if you will, late of Albany and about to register at the Emerson Hotel," she said in a cultured voice.

Emma lifted up the veil to lock her gaze with Garnet's. When beautiful, long-lashed blue eyes stared back at her, she frowned and dropped the veil back into place. "As ugly as it is to you, don't take that bonnet off. You'll be recognized for certain."

"I'll be fine. People see what they want to see. No one will be the wiser," Garnet insisted before sliding quickly back into her role when the front doorbell rang. "Now, if you'll excuse me, I believe my carriage has arrived. Don't bother to see me out. Perhaps if you had a more properly run boardinghouse without livestock overrunning it, I wouldn't be forced to leave wearing this hideous bonnet." With a haughty shake of her head, she paraded to the hallway and out the front door.

Aunt Frances chuckled. "Mr. Langhorne has no idea what he's up against, does he?"

"Let's hope not," Emma replied. "Are you sure you're up to another walk into town?"

"I wouldn't miss this for all the world. I just need a moment to get my reticule and a sweater."

"I'll get mine, fetch Mother Garrett, and meet you back here," Emma suggested and tried not to hurry on her way.

Within ten minutes, the three of them were headed down the lane. They turned at the end down Main Street and walked along the roadway past the homes gathered at the north end. They did pass Liesel and Ditty, who were on their way back to Hill House after delivering Emma's notes, which gave Emma some relief from worry.

Once they reached the planked sidewalk in front of the shops and businesses, they crossed from one side to the other, frequently retracing their steps. At the confectionery, Emma told an unfortunate tale about Widow Stokes's departure from Hill House while she selected the largest box of chocolates they carried. After penning a note to Widow Stokes, she paid extra to see the chocolates and her note would be delivered immediately to the woman at the hotel. At the millinery, Emma repeated the same tale and left more than enough so that Widow Stokes could pick out a suitable replacement for the bonnet that had fallen victim to the same renegade chicken that had cost Mr. Langhorne his hat.

As they had all hoped, by the time the three women had stopped in at several other stores, as well as the bank, gossip about Emma's garish skirts, if not the tale she had been telling, preceded them as they neared the General Store.

Mother Garrett leaned close to Emma and whispered, "If Mr. Langhorne doesn't hear that you spent the better part of this afternoon in town trying to make amends to Widow Stokes, and not at Andrew Leonard's, then he'd have to be deaf."

Aunt Frances grinned. "Let's hope the poor, irate Widow Stokes made enough noise when she registered at the hotel so it isn't the first time he heard the tale."

"Whether he was there or not, I'm sure the smell of her perfume she left behind will prompt him to inquire about the awful odor," Emma quipped.

"I could tell you how I made it," Mother Garrett offered.

"I don't think I want to know, but I wouldn't worry about him finding out what we're doing. I truly believe Mr. Langhorne lives at the hotel precisely because he hopes to gather up all the gossip he can. He'll know what allegedly happened," Emma said as they arrived at the General Store.

She led them inside, garnering more than a few surprised looks from the women shopping, and they walked directly to the counter.

To his credit, Mr. Atkins accepted Mother Garrett's offering, but he did not comment on Emma's attire when he turned his attention to her. His smile stretched from ear to ear as he handed her three letters. "These all came with this morning's post."

Her hands trembled the moment she recognized the different handwriting and pressed the letters from her sons to her heart. "They're from Warren and Benjamin and Mark," she exclaimed, earning broad smiles from both Mother Garrett and Aunt Frances.

Although she was anxious to read the letters, she was resigned to reading them later and stored them in her reticule. "I'll read them when we get home," she explained.

"Nonsense," Mother Garrett insisted. "I'm as anxious as you are to know if and when my grandsons are coming for a visit."

"We don't mind waiting. Read them now," Aunt Frances urged.

Mr. Atkins cleared his throat. "I believe I have an order to pack. I'll be right back," he said and quickly disappeared behind the curtain and into the hallway that led to the back room.

With no further prompting, Emma removed her gloves, laid them on the counter, and retrieved the letters from her reticule. She skimmed each letter, first Warren's, then Benjamin's, and finally Mark's. By the time she finished, her eyes were brimming with tears of joy. "They're coming! They're all coming in April for my birthday! We'll all be together again, just like I dreamed we'd be!" she gushed, too overjoyed to worry about whether or not she would still be at Hill House in April. Wherever she was living, they would all be together again, and that's all that really mattered.

Beaming, Mother Garrett swiped at her own tears and hugged Emma. Hard. Aunt Frances added hugs of her own before Emma stored the letters safely back in her reticule.

Mr. Atkins returned, still wearing a smile. "Good news?"

"The boys are all bringing their families home for a visit. In April."

"I'm anxious to meet them. Oh, and before I forget, I got the note you sent earlier. We're about ready to deliver the supplies you ordered."

"Actually, I'd like a few more." She handed him the list she had made after returning from the trash pit.

His eyes widened. "If I didn't know better, I'd think you might be building some sort of pen at Hill House."

"I do believe we are, assuming we can convince either Steven or his brother to help us."

Mother Garrett gasped. "A pen? Whatever for?"

Emma grinned. "I'll tell you all about it on the way home."

34

T HEIR PLAN WOULD SUCCEED OR FAIL, according to His will.

The next morning, promptly at nine-thirty, a full half hour before the Leonard brothers were to meet at Hill House, Emma arrived at the Emerson Hotel. Dressed in a deep crimson cashmere gown that complimented her trim figure, she was rested and confident that they had all done what they could, and far more than she could have hoped.

She had no idea how Opal had fared at Andrew's home or whether or not he had gone to see his brother instead of waiting until their meeting today. She had no idea how successful Garnet had been when she had registered at the hotel yesterday, either. Emma was not even sure Mr. Langhorne would be waiting for her in the hotel dining room as she had requested in the note she had asked Liesel to deliver to him. She was certain, however, that the Lord was watching over all of them this day.

She squared her shoulders. "Be not afraid," she whispered before entering the hotel and following the scent of Widow

Stokes's odorous perfume to the dining room. A number of guests were gathered about, eating breakfast or ordering it.

Her heart sank. Mr. Langhorne was not among them.

Her heart beat faster.

Zachary Breckenwith was sitting at a table to her right.

He returned her shocked look with a smile that was more friendly than professional, but he made no attempt to speak to her. However unexpected his presence might be, she was both re-assured and comforted to have him close by during the final moments of their plan, even though he had no idea of the drama unfolding before him.

Widow Stokes, on the other hand, had taken a table in the very center of the room. She was sitting alone, which was troubling for two reasons. First, she and Andrew were supposed to arrive at the dining room together. Second, they weren't supposed to arrive until later, after James and Andrew had their meeting at Hill House.

Walter Emerson, the proprietor, quickly approached and garnered her full attention. "Widow Garrett. How good to see you again. I'm as surprised to see you here as I am pleased."

"Unfortunately, it doesn't appear I'll be staying. I was supposed to meet—"

"Mr. Langhorne. Yes, I know. He sent word down that he's been delayed for a few moments but asked if you'd mind waiting for him. I have his usual table set aside so you can talk privately," he suggested, escorting her to a table in the far corner and helping her into a seat facing the wall.

She had no sooner set the fully cleaned hat on the table when Mr. Langhorne appeared and slipped into the chair opposite her, giving him full view of the dining room at her back. "I apologize. I'm usually very punctual," he offered, glanced at the hat on the table, and frowned. "I thought I told you to put that in the trash pit."

"As you can see, there was no damage done at all, and I thought the least I could do was to return it to you and offer you a good meal, considering the inconvenience you've suffered. It seemed a pity to discard a perfectly good hat."

He took the hat from the table, set it on the seat of a side chair, and smiled. "Unfortunately, the same cannot be said for Widow Stokes's bonnet. I hope it wasn't too uncomfortable for you to come here to the hotel, especially since she seems to be having breakfast here now, as well."

Emma blushed, more from the realization that part of their plan was working than from the embarrassment she hoped he would assume was the source of her discomfort. "Obviously you've heard about what happened."

"In truth, I thought you'd have rid yourself of that chicken by now. Our breakfast notwithstanding—which was a very kind gesture on your part—that chicken is proving very costly, given the price of chocolates and new bonnets."

Her blush deepened. "Indeed, it has, but I do believe we're very close to resolving the problem."

The waiter finally appeared and interrupted their conversation. Once they had placed their orders, Mr. Langhorne directed the conversation right back to Widow Stokes. "I understand Widow Stokes has come to Candlewood hoping to make a few investments with the very sizable inheritance she received from her late husband."

"Which reminds me of my other purpose for wanting to meet with you today," Emma said. "I've given our last meeting a great deal of thought, and I wanted to reassure you, in person, that I have no intention of speaking to either James or Andrew about your business dealings with them. Whatever they decide to do will be entirely up to them."

Instead of responding, Mr. Langhorne stared past her. When she ventured a discreet look over her shoulder and saw Andrew Leonard sit down with Widow Stokes, her heart skipped a beat. At least he was here.

"Mr. Langhorne?" she asked, hoping to distract him from staring at the other table.

He flinched and met her gaze again. "Yes, you . . . you were saying?"

"I was going to say that I hoped we could set aside the problems we've had between us."

"Yes, yes, of course," he managed before breakfast arrived. While the waiter set the plates onto the table, Mr. Langhorne had the opportunity to observe what was happening.

All Emma could do was stare at the wall and hope and pray Andrew and James had met last night or earlier today and ended their feud. Given Andrew's arrival here now, she suspected they might have done that, but she could not be sure.

Until Andrew arrived at their table only seconds after the waiter left and greeted them both.

Exhaustion etched his features, and he looked as if he had not slept all night. When he spoke to greet them, his voice was firm but raspy.

"Both of you probably have business to discuss. I should leave," Emma said and started to rise.

Wearing a smug smile, Mr. Langhorne urged her back into her seat. "Please don't. You may as well hear the news firsthand. I trust you do have news?" he asked Andrew without rising or inviting the man to sit down.

"I'm hoping to save you a trip all the way out to see me, which may be the only good news I have for you," Andrew said. "I spoke with my brother again at great length only last night. We've both decided against selling the land at this time, which is what I just told Widow Stokes, despite the fact that her offer was substantially more generous than your own."

Mr. Langhorne bolted to his feet, and his face turned scarlet. "I made my offer months ago, and I've waited all this time for you to convince your brother to sell. If this is an effort on your part to spike the price of my offer, it won't work. Do you take me for a fool? I know that woman only arrived in Candlewood yesterday."

Andrew clenched and unclenched his fists, but his gaze was rock steady. "Widow Stokes came to Candlewood precisely to speak to me. Once you made your offer, did it not occur to you that I might also seek out other buyers? Or that I might consider once I sold the land to you or anyone else, my brother could be forced to sell out if the new owner refused him passage on the toll road?"

Mr. Langhorne's spectacles slid down the length of his nose, and he shoved them back abruptly. "What about the business you wanted to open here in town? Are you really going to let your brother force you to abandon that idea, as well?"

Andrew let out a long breath, as if further exhausted by Mr. Langhorne's questions. "Right now, restoring peace in my family is far more important than anything else I might want to do. This, I might add, is what I told Widow Stokes just now and what I intend to explain to my mother when I leave here and go to Hill House. I can always open a business later. For now, my brother and I are going to combine our farms and work together for a change. It's what I want. It's what my brother wants. And I believe it's what will please my mother the most."

He paused and looked directly at Emma. "James is meeting me

at Hill House later this morning, just as we planned to do, but I have a few errands to attend to first. Would you care to join us? I'm not sure which one of us my mother will be going home with, but I'm sure she'd like to say good-bye to you before she does."

Overwhelmed, Emma swallowed the lump in her throat. "Mr. Langhorne and I were just about to have breakfast. Perhaps it might be better if—"

"I've lost my appetite," Mr. Langhorne snapped, grabbed his hat from the chair, and stormed from the room.

Andrew watched the man storm from the dining room, looked back at Emma, and grinned. "It appears the plan has worked perfectly! I'll see you back at Hill House as soon as I've finished my errands," he promised and promptly left her sitting at the table all alone, stunned by their apparent success.

Seconds later Zachary Breckenwith eased himself into Mr. Langhorne's empty seat, smiled, and pointed to the breakfast platter in front of her. "It'd be a shame to waste good food. You haven't had much time to eat. Why don't I fill you in on a few details while you eat, and then I'll take you back to Hill House?"

Emma clutched the edge of the table. "W-what details? What are you doing here?"

His smile broadened. "Helping, I hope. At least, that was the plan. I came here this morning simply to be near in case you needed help. I didn't want you to face Langhorne alone," he added.

"You knew about the plan? How? The last we spoke, you were going to be away for at least a month. Opal and Garnet said they'd dined with you and your aunt in Bounty, but that was before we'd even thought of this plan."

"All true," he admitted. "With the canal being repaired, I decided to ride back to Candlewood instead of sitting around

Bounty waiting to continue on to New York City. I met Miss
Garnet on the toll road on my way back when she was on her way
to Andrew's late yesterday. She told me what you had all planned
and recruited my help with this part of that little scheme of yours.
I hope you don't mind."

She swallowed hard. "As my lawyer, I'm surprised you'd want
to be involved in a scheme of any kind."

"I'm not here as your lawyer," he said softly.

When his eyes locked with hers, Emma's heart skipped a beat
and she smiled. "I'm glad," she whispered. Feeling a bit awkward
and unsure of herself, she turned her attention back to more
reliable concerns and drew in a deep breath. "Do you know where
Andrew went now? I'm not sure what errands needed to be done,
but I should think he would want to go directly to Hill House to
see his mother and tell her the good news that her sons have
resolved their troubles with each other."

"James is there now, so I'm sure she already knows. At least,
that was the plan."

"I thought they wanted to tell her together."

"I believe they changed the plan a bit. That's all right, isn't it?"

She laughed nervously. "I suppose it is, as long as everyone is
happy, except for Mr. Langhorne, of course." She peeked over her
shoulder and saw that Widow Stokes had left the dining room.
"It's a shame Garnet has to stay here until tomorrow, just for
appearances like we planned. I know she'd like to say good-bye to
Aunt Frances before she leaves."

He grinned. "That wasn't Miss Garnet in the dining room.
That was Miss Opal. They switched places early this morning.
Don't ask me why. That's what they wanted to do."

Emma leaned closer and lowered her voice to a whisper. "I
never can tell them apart without their pins, let alone being all

gowned up, but I do know that what one sister does, the other one has to do, too. But Garnet—I mean Opal—can't leave now and go back to Hill House! Mr. Langhorne will find out, and then everything we've all done will come undone. She has to stay until tomorrow."

"Miss Garnet isn't leaving," he countered. "Widow Stokes is leaving. Poor woman. She's so distraught about losing out on buying the Leonards' property, I believe she's packing to leave town as we speak. I'd plan on seeing Miss Garnet for dinner. Your mother-in-law apparently invited everyone to stay for dinner to give Widow Leonard time to decide whether she'd like to go home with James or Andrew. When I stopped at Hill House earlier, while you were still getting ready to leave for your meeting at the hotel, she invited me to join you for dinner, as well."

Mr. Breckenwith smiled and pushed his chair back from the table. "Since you don't seem to have an appetite, shall we go? On our walk back to Hill House, I'd like to hear more about this railroad you think is coming to Candlewood."

———

The walk back to Hill House was short and conversation steady, and Emma's heart was filled with both joy and sadness. Though her mind was distracted both by Zachary Breckenwith's presence and his support, her heart was troubled by the dilemma facing her now.

Having the Leonard brothers resolve their differences would no doubt ease their mother's heartache, for which Emma offered a host of thankful prayers. At the same time, however, she was saddened by the prospect of saying good-bye to Aunt Frances, a woman who had taught her the power of faith and a woman who had truly become a member of her Hill House family.

Emma's dilemma intensified through the tearful reunion that began once they arrived back at Hill House, where Aunt Frances's entire family had gathered with those from Hill House for the joyous occasion. Through dinner, as they all told and retold the details of the plan as it had unfolded and evolved into a new plan that had included Zachary Breckenwith, Emma's heart grew heavier.

When dessert was finished and the table cleared, Aunt Frances rose from her chair and glanced around the table.

Emma battled tears of joy and sadness. The moment had finally arrived for Aunt Frances to announce her decision, and the time to say farewell was near.

"I love you all," Aunt Frances began. "Every one of you is a blessing to me, which makes it impossible for me to choose between you. I think I'd like to go home to spend a few days with Andrew and Nora first, then do the same with James and Sarah so I can enjoy being a grandmother again."

She paused and looked directly at Emma. "After that, I was hoping I'd be welcome here at Hill House until the season ends in November so I can spend time with my new family here. I'll spend the winter with James and Andrew, but I'd like to come back to Hill House each spring for the season again. If you'll have me, Emma dear."

Stunned, all Emma could do was nod. Her heart was beating so fast she thought it would burst. Her throat tightened with emotion, but her tears fell freely now. Her spirit trembled with His very goodness, His wisdom, and His love for them all, and she looked forward now to the time when His plan for her would unfold, according to His will.

Epilogue

THE BARE TREES AND CHILLIER WINDS of early November forecast the annual closing of the Candlewood Canal in a matter of weeks and the end of the hectic tourist season.

From where Emma stood on the patio with a warm cape wrapped around her, she looked beyond the freshly painted gazebo to the new pen she had had built for the chickens in front of the mulberry trees. Inside the pen, near the hen house, the renegade chicken—now named Faith—remained dominant, controlling the flock Emma had discovered at the trash pit. Faith reigned by acting like the rooster Emma refused to get out of concern her guests might object to waking early to the crowing.

The very air that whipped at her cape and cooled her cheeks promised that winter would soon come and life at Hill House would change dramatically, especially as she waited for the owner of Hill House to arrive. The flock of chickens she was watching now would be moved closer to the house. The number of guests would dwindle to the precious few who would be forced by necessity to brave the elements and travel by coach. Aunt Frances would be returning home to live with her sons until spring, and Reverend Glenn and Butter would have to save their walks down to the gazebo until the arrival of fairer weather.

She slid her hand into the pocket of her cape and fingered her keepsakes until she felt the smooth piece of silk she had cut from the riding skirt Aunt Frances had made for her, and smiled.

There was so much to be thankful for and so much to look

forward to this winter, as well. With fewer guests, there would be more time to sit and read or sit in front of a fire on the patio, perhaps with Zachary Breckenwith. After his aunt Elizabeth decided to move to Bounty to live with a cousin, he had purchased her home, and his decision to make Candlewood his home permanently was yet another development in their evolving relationship.

Emma would also have more time to spend with Mother Garrett and Reverend Glenn, as well as with Liesel and Ditty, who were already planning the samplers they would make using the fancier stitches Aunt Frances had been teaching them. Come spring, her children and grandchildren would come home for her birthday in April, making it a special day indeed.

The amazing gifts that surrounded her filled her with a deep sense of awe. Although her future here at Hill House remained uncertain, she was now content to let Him lead her to even greater wonders in the days ahead and trusted that there would be a hearth in Candlewood to call her own.

Emma bowed her head and her heart to the One who filled every day of her life with love and hope, the One who offered her so many opportunities to renew her faith in Him each and every day, and to the One who would reveal His will for her, all in His time, if only she held tight to her faith.

AUTHOR'S NOTE

THE OPENING OF THE ERIE CANAL in 1825 triggered an exciting era of canal building that quickly spread throughout our young nation, especially in New York State. Inland waterways carried settlers west, linked rural areas to eastern markets, and created incredible commercial wealth for entrepreneurs and investors alike.

In their heyday, the canals virtually transformed small towns like the fictional Candlewood and changed the everyday rhythms of life for the people who lived there. Opportunities seemed boundless until after the Civil War, when the railroad emerged as a more cost-effective form of transportation.

Although the New York Canal System, which included the Erie Canal, continued to operate, many lateral canals were ultimately abandoned and fell into disrepair. Today, however, the packet boats, freight barges, and drivers urging mules along the canals' towpaths have been replaced by pleasure boats, cyclists, hikers, and fishermen, who are enjoying the canals as recreation centers that reflect the glories of our historical past.

For more information on canals throughout the country and for opportunities to enjoy some of the outdoor adventures they offer, please visit an informative Web site, *www.canals.com/northam.htm,* or the official Web site of the New York Canal System, *www.canals.state.ny.us/.*

Be the first *to know*

Want to be the first to know
what's new from
your favorite authors?

Want to know all about
exciting new writers?

Sign up for BethanyHouse newsletters at
www.bethanynewsletters.com
and you'll get regular updates via e-mail.
You can sign up for as many authors or
categories as you want so you get only
the information you really want.

Sign up today

Discover a New Novelist

Kim Vogel Sawyer's new novel is reminiscent of the story-telling of Janette Oke and the charm of the characters created by Beverly Lewis.

After losing her family to illness, Summer Steadman suddenly finds herself in a small and very close Mennonite community on the Kansas prairie. With her own will to live nearly gone and the suspicious locals unwilling to help an outsider, will they overcome their reluctance and suspicions to help each other?

A novel full of hope, *Waiting for Summer's Return* shows the triumph of faith and love over fear.